What's Left of Me

Hannah Bird

Editor: Lea Ann Schafer

Cover Design: Y'all, That Graphic

Formatter: Miranda Grissom

Published in the United States.

NOTE FROM THE AUTHOR:

This book contains discussions about domestic violence and remembered moments of abuse. This content may be triggering to some and should be read with caution.

Also by Hannah Bird

Loveless Series:

The End and Then (Book 1)

What's Left of Me

Dedication

To Avery, who has never given a soft, white damn whom she touches.

And to Jennalee, and every other woman who has found the strength to walk away. You are all heroes to me, but more importantly, you are heroes to yourselves.

Chapter One

A plume of smoke blurs my vision as the acrid scent of cigarettes stings my nostrils. My two less-than-dedicated line cooks and the tagalong dishwasher are relaxing against the brick wall to my right, unaware that they're being observed. I place one hand on my hip and make a disapproving *cluck* with my tongue, causing three pairs of eyes to spread wide in embarrassment as the heads they're attached to whip around to find out who has caught them.

"Santi has three tickets on the order wheel. It'd be a lot easier to fulfill them if he had anyone in there cooking," I say.

A chorus of, "Yes, Boss," and, "Sorry, Jefa," rises up on the last tendril of smoke as Eric and Mateo put out the cigarettes under their restaurant-grade non-slip shoes. They trudge past me while Marcelin takes one last drag and then does the same.

"My apologies, miss," he mutters in a thick Haitian accent, ducking his head as he follows the other two inside. I pour a splash of water from my insulated bottle over the flickering butts to make sure no sparks remain. When I'm satisfied, I return to the kitchen, pulling the door shut behind me and arming the alarm.

"You guys gotta be careful; you could start a fire," I say. They keep their heads low while taking turns scrubbing their hands in the sink basin before returning to their workstations. Santi winks at me as he doles out tasks, grateful I don't mind being the hard-ass so he doesn't have to be.

I push through the saloon doors as the sounds of the party reach me. It seems like the whole town is here, which probably still wouldn't be enough people to fill the bar considering Loveless's population after the summer tourists leave is laughable. It just goes to show how many people are rooting for Chase and Eden and want to celebrate their engagement.

My best friend saunters out of the crowd like Moses parting the Red Sea, holding an empty copper cup in the air and shaking it, the melting ice cubes singing the siren call of someone needing a refill. I reach for the mug, but Eden dances past me with a smirk, clinking it against the already made whiskey sour Maddie is garnishing for Chase's mother.

"Ed*en*," Maddie whines. "If I make a mess, it'll be your fault."

She tucks a bar napkin under the sweating glass and passes it to Laura before gathering the ingredients for the Honeybee Mule I created specifically for Eden's engagement party. Eden just rolls her eyes at Maddie, pinching her elbow affectionately.

"If I recall correctly, you once caused me to take a power shower with a beer keg." Eden tries to give Maddie a hard stare but ends up wiggling her eyebrows to soften the blow. "Seems like I'm overdue for some revenge."

"That one was also your fault," Maddie reminds her. She scrunches her nose at the memory, the diamond stud nestled there winking in the low light of the bar.

"Touché," Eden replies. "I'm sorry. I wanted to give Zo a chance to stop working for just a second and actually enjoy the party she worked so hard to put together."

"Zoey never stops working," Gary chimes in, his grumbly voice cutting through the noise of the crowd. "But I don't have to tell you that."

Eden smiles, taking the refilled copper mug from Maddie's outstretched hand and sidling up to me, her free arm looping through mine. "But we love her for that."

"That we do," Gary agrees, stroking his white beard, which looks more like a puffy cloud with every inch it grows. He drops his empty glass over the bar, refilling it with Sprite from the soda gun Maddie passes to him. Only she could be working as a bartender and somehow still have the patrons pour their own drinks.

She waltzes to the other end of the counter where Eden's brother-in-law, Jarrett, has his arm outstretched to get her attention. I haven't seen him in several years, with how busy his patients keep him. Gray is beginning to creep up his hairline, turning his temples more salt than pepper, though it makes him look distinguished rather than aged. He ducks his head to calmly request another beer for himself and a margarita for Ella, who's no doubt locked in an emotional discussion somewhere with Rose. He catches my eye, and I nod at him with a smile, my thousandth time thanking him for taking the weekend off to be here for Eden.

"Seriously, Zo," Eden says, her voice low as her eyebrows pull together. "I can never thank you enough for doing all this."

Her emerald eyes shimmer with a fresh set of happy tears threatening to spill over, and I swallow back the lump rising in my throat. I pat her hand where it rests against my bicep, feeling the rough edges of a diamond ring scraping against my palm. The gratitude I feel for her happiness after so much undeserved pain is almost enough to drown in.

Instead I clear my throat, and she shakes her head with a laugh, looking skyward to encourage the tears to return to their holding cells. "Anything for you," I say.

She smirks as her gaze flickers over my shoulder, and I turn to see Aaron and Chase approaching. With chilly fall nights making their way into the valley, Aaron's dressed in a cream-colored Henley that he's left unbuttoned. It hugs the contours of his body, each ridge of lean muscle pressing against the fabric. His dark jeans sit low on his hips, and I know if he turned around, I'd see them conform to an ass that looks like it was sculpted from marble. A cocky grin tugs at his lips when he catches me checking him out, and I pull my gaze from his to leave him wanting more.

Not that that's ever a problem with Aaron. He always wants more. More than I'm capable of giving.

As if she can read my mind, Eden leans in and whispers conspiratorially, "It'll be your turn soon enough."

My head snaps around so fast it almost gives me whiplash. She's smiling even wider, and I know for her she's just offered me the best outcome she could imagine. But it's not in the cards for me, and I don't know how to tell her I'll have to fold without showing my entire hand.

"I keep telling Aaron to lock her down before she wises up," Chase adds. He cuts behind me and tucks his head between ours, planting a friendly kiss on my cheek before locking his lips with Eden's. It's so much unadulterated love that I have to step away for fear it might burn me up from being too close.

A smile tugs at Aaron's tantalizingly full lips, but he doesn't correct his friend. It's one of my favorite things about him. He knows it's not him that's holding us back from that step, yet he takes the blame anyway, shielding me from having to produce an explanation for everyone when I haven't even found a way to give one to him.

"Can I get a Coors Light?" Chase asks. Eden grins as she takes a sip of her drink, the alcohol flushing her lily-white skin a rosy hue.

Maddie nods a quick acknowledgment before muttering, "Can't wait for Zander to be back."

"You've got about a month left," Eden says.

Chase nips at her earlobe, making her laugh. She leans into his side so easily, unaware that for every inch he moves, she mirrors him, and he does the same to her. It's an invisible string tied between them, one that tugs the other in the direction they are going without a second thought. I let myself envy it for just a moment before patching that wall back up.

Aaron slides an arm around my waist, pressing a kiss against the pulse point at the base of my neck and sending the rhythm skyrocketing. His breath disturbs the tangle of blonde curls escaping from my clip, bringing with it the familiar scent of whiskey and ginger ale. How many nights have I poured him that very drink and then licked it from his lips in the dark parking lot behind the bar, away from prying eyes?

The pleasure of that thought is so rich, so velvety soft in my mind, that when Aaron pinches the space just below my ribs and a memory like a sharp knife cuts through the moment, the juxtaposition is shocking. I go perfectly still, waiting for him to admonish me for the weight I've gained. I prepare myself to go on defense. *I've been working so much lately. It'll come off so easily, I promise.*

But it's not Aaron in my memory nor his harsh words invading my mind, and just as quickly as I found myself a decade in the past, I come back to the present. I look up to meet his concerned gaze, his eyes two pools of jade green so beautiful that just looking at them feels like slipping into a cool lagoon. His playful pinch was meant to elicit a laugh or a squirm or a shriek like most women would react with, not the rigid spine and clammy skin he now feels underneath his touch. A wrinkle forms between his scrunched-up eyebrows. I smooth the crease out with my finger, shaking my head as I pull away from the embrace. I couldn't explain it even if I tried, so I don't.

"Okay, enough relaxing for me." *If you could call this relaxing.* "Back to work."

I tug the gold *Engaged* banner from the last remaining hook where it was secured, letting it flutter to the ground in front of the barstools. While I'm up here, I check the leaves of my golden pothos plant running wild across the wooden beam over the counter. The leaves are lush and healthy, as though it thrives on meaningless gossip and bad attempts at flirting, both of which abound in a bar.

"Kitchen is back in order," Santi grumbles as he crosses beneath my ladder. "Guys are all gone home. They're a mess."

"I know, but aren't you glad we have them? We'd never have survived a night like tonight with just you and me cooking," I reply.

Santi blows a shrill whistle out, wiping imaginary sweat from his brow. "Things were definitely less busy when Gary was running the place."

"That's what good marketing will do for you," I say, wiping my hands off on my sweater. "You keep making the magic and I'll sell it."

He smiles up at me and tugs on the leg of my flared jeans.

"Good night, Zoey," he says. "And you, Aaron."

"Night, Santi," Aaron calls from the other side of the room where he is meticulously disassembling a rather impressive balloon arch by cutting a small hole in the base of each balloon to let the air slowly leak out.

"Why don't you just pop those?" Santi asks, shaking a pair of headphones in his hand like dice.

Aaron glances up at me, and I press my lips together to fight back the smile trying to form. "Zoey hates the sound."

I mouth, *Thank you*, to him over Santi's shoulder as I finally plant my feet firmly on the ground, fold up my stepladder, and gather the rumpled banner.

Santi scoffs, looking from Aaron to me and back. "You got it bad, man." He shakes his head and turns to leave, waving a hand over his head in a final farewell.

"Don't I know it," Aaron replies, more to me than to Santi, who is already closing the door behind him. He holds my gaze, a dare in his eyes that I shy away from even as it causes goose bumps to stand at attention on my forearms. I'm grateful for the long sleeves covering the evidence.

I busy myself with disposing of the remaining decorations while he slits the throat of the last gold balloon. When they've all been reduced to a depressing puddle of latex, he heaps them into the waiting garbage bag and brings it over to its rightful place next to mine.

"I've been thinking," he says, reaching for the clip at the back of my head and releasing what little of my mane has managed to stay clenched in its teeth. He tangles his hands in the swath of curls, massaging my scalp. My eyelids flutter closed as a moan climbs up my throat.

"About what?" I hum, wrapping my hands around his waist and tugging him closer. I slip a hand under his shirt, searching for the comfort of his scorching-hot skin and tightly coiled muscles.

"About what Eden said."

My hands freeze in place, nails inadvertently digging into his skin a little too hard, but he doesn't say a word. He ceases his massage, but my hair remains tangled in his fingers, cradling my head a breath away from his face. I open my eyes and we lock gazes. We are in a standoff, neither of us one to back down from a challenge.

"Aaron, I told you—"

"I know, I know. 'We're nothing serious.'" He cocks his head, a sad smile distorting his otherwise perfect face. "The problem is, you've been saying that for a year and a half. That timeline alone would suggest otherwise."

"It's what we agreed on." I step backward. He releases his hold, letting his hands fall but capturing one of mine on its retreat from his waist. "This is what we both wanted, remember? No strings."

"That was before, Zoey." He looks down at our joined hands, his dark skin in direct contrast to my pale knuckles. "I think I've proven to you how I feel, but in case I haven't made it clear enough, I'd marry you tomorrow if you'd let me."

I fight the urge to run away, forcing myself to study the familiar planes of his face. His smooth jaw free of stubble, his perfect nose and downturned eyes. Gone is the carefree guy who wanted nothing more than to sneak around with me and flirt under the noses of everyone else. He's been replaced by a man as serious as the relationship he's asking me for. The one I can't give him.

I can't take the desperate hope in his expression. I lean forward, pressing my forehead against his collarbone. I listen to his familiar heartbeat, quickened as it is when we summit a mountain, or when I sink my teeth into his shoulder as he buries himself inside of me.

"I just don't want the same things." My voice becomes a whisper. "I don't know that I ever will."

He scoffs, stepping away from me completely, leaving me so suddenly cold I cross my arms to insulate myself. "Bullshit, Zo. I see the way you look at me. I feel the way you respond to my touch. I know I'm not alone in this."

His anger flips some switch inside me, hot flames of indignance lapping at the tendrils of sadness. I bristle, glaring at him with what I hope is an intimidating amount of rage despite the five-foot-tall, blonde-haired, blue-eyed package it's being delivered in.

"I have never been anything but honest with you," I say through gritted teeth. "About where I stand and what I want. If you misread anything, that's on you. I am who I am, and you can take it or leave it."

"Zo, please—"

"No." I have to say these next words clearly so he will understand their weight. I can't let him have any false hope, because I've had it before and it's soul crushing. "No talk of forever. No commitments. I'm not ready. I don't know if I'll ever be ready. And if you insist on demanding a final answer, that answer will be no."

I can't stand here one moment longer; my skin feels like it is too tight for my body and any second I'm going to break free of it. I grab the garbage bags and march toward the back door, leaving Aaron standing there with the muscle in his jaw twitching, hands flexing and unflexing in a rhythm all their own. What he doesn't know is that he's clenching around the remnants of my heart, which I've torn to shreds and left tucked into his fists.

Chapter Two

I've gotten a cumulative hour of sleep between all the tossing and turning by the time the aggressive vibration of my phone sends me crawling across my king-size bed, over the mountain range of throw pillows, to my bedside table. It's been a week of radio silence from Aaron, and I tell myself I'm not hoping this middle-of-the-night surprise is from him but seeing Maddie's name on the screen sends a pang of disappointment deep in my gut that screams *liar*.

"Hello?" I answer groggily. Somehow getting just a little sleep is worse than none at all, and it has made my bones feel heavy.

"Hey, Zo, sorry to bother you," Maddie says. Her usually indifferent tone hitches in a way that wakes me up completely. "I had to call the police, and they said to call you."

I jump out of bed, fumbling along the wall in the dark for the light switch that is somehow not exactly where I thought I left it. "Oh my God, are you okay? What happened?"

"Yeah," she replies, her voice warbling. "I told Santi to go on ahead while I was closing up because I was waiting for Camille to get dropped off by some friends, but when we walked to my car, all the tires were slashed."

I release a pent-up breath from its prison cell in my lungs. Relief that she—and selfishly, my bar—are not hurt rushes through me.

"I'm on my way, Maddie. Be there in ten."

I end the call as I slide on a pair of joggers and zip a jacket over Aaron's ratty Loveless Middle School T-shirt that I definitely didn't put on because I miss him. My feet nestle into a blush-colored pair of fuzzy slippers, and I slip out into the cool night.

The flashing lights of a sheriff's cruiser create an offensive glare against a backdrop of dense darkness when I pull into the lot behind the bar. Maddie has her hoodie sleeves pulled over her knuckles and clutched close to her face, a puff of hot breath floating up between her fists. Camille stares at her with a pinched face, her disheveled bob tucked behind heavily pierced ears.

I shift my car into park and shut down the engine. After opening the door, I wrap my arms tight around my middle in an attempt to keep the crisp air out. Even the mild breeze created by walking toward them causes me to shiver. The officer has his back to me as he scribbles something in his notepad while shining a small flashlight on each tire of Maddie's van. In the streak of light, I see an angry, jagged scar of shredded rubber.

"Are you all right, Maddie?" I sidle up to her. She rolls her eyes toward me and purses her lips, but beneath the agitated exterior I see a glimmer of fear.

"I'm fine, just annoyed," she says. Camille grimaces but doesn't comment.

I give Maddie a hard stare, trying to see through the indifferent facade. Last month she dyed her hair a deep red color that leaves her pale face looking especially gaunt under the circumstances. There's a sheen to her dark eyes that tugs at my heart, and I wrap my arms around her thin shoulders, pulling her stiff frame against me.

Despite her bristly attitude, I'm going to miss Maddie when she graduates in the spring. She and Camille bought the van six months ago to turn it into a home they could travel in, Maddie working the remote finance job she's been offered upon completion of her degree, and Camille painting the various landscapes they pass through. Seeing vandalism on the vehicle they've poured so much money into is heartbreaking, though I send up a silent thanks to whoever is listening that it was just the tires that were damaged.

The officer turns at the sound of our voices, and even in the harsh staccato of blue and red lights I can tell that he is handsome, albeit unfamiliar. In a town this small, running the best place to get a drink downtown, I like to think I know everyone. His purposefully tousled brunette waves appear to be the source of the overwhelming scent of hair cream swirling around us. The strobe illuminates a sharp jawline that dead-ends in a formidable chin holding up a thin pair of lips and a charmingly crooked nose. He drags a long, lazy look from my pink slippers up my body, pausing longer than I'd like on my breasts before coming to rest on my less-than-impressed face.

His cocky grin slips, but only a little.

"Ma'am, you must be the owner," he says in a distinctly Southern drawl. It's not the twang of my home state of Alabama but the lilting rhythm of a man who grew up near the Gulf. Mississippi? Louisiana, perhaps? "I'm Officer Llewellyn, but you can call me Kit."

He extends his hand for me to shake. I unravel one arm from around Maddie and accept. I'm not sure if it's an overactive imagination brought on by sleep deprivation or if he's truly lingering, but after three foggy breaths and a pass of his thumb over my knuckles, I jerk away, smoothing a stray curl back behind my ear to ease the suddenness of the movement. If it's possible, the glint in his eyes shines even brighter. I can't tell what color they are in the dark, only that they are not light blue like mine nor a refreshing jade like Aaron's.

"Officer," I say, taking neither of his suggested monikers. "What the hell happened?"

Those thin lips stretch into a smirk that just barely reveals the perfectly straight set of pearly teeth he possesses. Something about his aura of both indifference and intrigue tries to draw me in, reminding me of the beautiful, aloof men I used to pursue like it was my job. The type of man Aaron was until he wasn't. Until he was more.

"Some jackass slashed all four tires," he says. I have to fight the urge to say, *Obviously.* He ducks his head when his own words reach his ears. "Pardon my language, ladies."

"We can handle it," I reply, a little more spice in my tone than I intend. I've been away from the South for so long I forgot the way the men handle women with kid gloves, as if a little foul language will overwhelm our delicate brains.

One manicured eyebrow perks up, but he doesn't comment otherwise. He studies the small notepad in his palm and then glances back up at Maddie. "Miss Parker, do you know anyone who might be angry at you? A customer you cut off after too many drinks? Vengeful ex-boyfriend?"

Camille scoffs just as Maddie steps fully away from me, looping an arm around Camille's waist and pressing a firm kiss against her cheek, both to soothe her visible discomfort and to prove a point to the dense officer.

"An ex-girlfriend, maybe?" he corrects himself. I'm not sure if it's just a trick of the red lights flashing from his cruiser, but I think I might see a hint of a flush creeping up his stubbled neck.

Just then another deputy pulls up alongside my car without any lights flashing. Tomas steps out of the second cruiser, smiling at us before his gaze falls on the van.

"Llewellyn, I've got it from here," he says. Kit flounders for a moment before regaining the confident exterior he had when I arrived. "Ladies, I see you've met the rookie."

"It would appear so," I reply pointedly. Kit tosses me a withering stare but bites back any rebuttal.

"Zoey, you got any security cameras out here?" Tomas asks,

pointing at the brick wall of the building lined with wrought-iron staircases to the apartments above. Eden and Chase are out of town for the weekend, taking Penny camping somewhere before it gets too cold at night, but I'm shocked that Gary hasn't woken up from all the commotion.

"No, I don't." It honestly hadn't even crossed my mind until just now that it was something I might need. I know everyone in this town; I'm the one who keeps them drunk and fed. And besides, I decided long ago not to live my life in fear. Never again.

"And I don't suppose you have any idea who might've done something like this, Maddie?"

She shakes her head this time, much more willing to comply with Tomas than Officer Foot-in-Mouth. Tomas scratches at his dark head of buzzed hair before dragging a hand down a tanned face wrinkled from hours spent in the sun at the shore of a lake, likely sat right alongside Gary while they down a few beers and wait for the fish to come to them.

"You got their statements?" he asks, turning to Kit. Kit nods, and it gives me a small sliver of satisfaction to see him submit like this. He stands at attention like a soldier might, and I wonder briefly what his story is before I remind myself that I don't care.

"All right, girls, it's late. Why don't I give you two a ride home, and I'll look into possible witnesses in the morning."

Camille pipes up finally, a slight tremble evident in her smoky voice. "The van is our home."

Tomas and Kit wear a twin set of puzzled gazes before the senior officer rounds the bumper and points to the side door. "May I?"

Camille nods and he opens it, revealing a cozy and eclectic space crafted with custom storage cabinets that make up a kitchenette with a small sink and microwave combo. I know from their reveal of the project last month that when Tomas sticks his head inside, he'll see a full-size bed tucked against the back of the van with a drop-down desk Camille built herself mounted to the ceiling.

String lights complete the look, giving the space a soft glow that can't be seen through the covered windows.

"Well, damn," Tomas says at the same time Kit mutters, "That's incredible." Tomas adds a shrill whistle of agreement.

"You two can stay with me," I say. "I still haven't rented out the studio apartment since Eden moved in with Chase."

Maddie looks wary, eyeing their home and all its contents.

"Just until the tires are fixed, Mads. It'll only be a couple of days," Camille assures her.

"Yes, ma'am, we'll have it towed to the shop for you, and I'll bet they have new tires on bright and early Monday morning," Kit says.

"Whatever," Maddie replies, pressing her lips together. Camille takes what compliance she can get and begins shuffling toward my car, dragging a listless Maddie alongside her. She smooths a delicate hand over her girlfriend's garnet hair, following its path down to the middle of her back. Maddie leans into the comfort of her touch.

"Tomas, do you think we'll find out who did this?" I turn to the same man I pour a gallon's worth of beer for every Thursday night during happy hour.

He chews at the inside of his cheek, measuring his words before delivering them. "Honestly? Without cameras or motive, it's unlikely. Could be some random punk-ass teenagers or a case of mistaken identity—"

"Who else in town drives a van like this?" I ask, locking my hand on my hip.

He shakes his head with a laugh while Kit's eyebrows rise in the background. "Exactly. But we'll keep an eye out for any similar events and hopefully catch them that way."

"That sucks." Looking back at my car, the girls' two shadowy figures are barely visible through my back-seat windows. I draw my bottom lip against my teeth, wishing I could do more.

"It does," Tomas agrees. "But hey, let's just be grateful no one was hurt."

He claps a hand against my shoulder blade, jostling me. I laugh and release my lip.

"Get home. It's only getting colder out, and I can tell you what color your toes are painted, which means that is not proper footwear," he says gruffly. Kit flips his notebook closed and tucks it into a pocket, staring down at my feet at the same time I do, where we both observe my red toenails peeking out from my slippers.

"Point made. I'll be calling to follow up with you on Monday."

"I'd expect nothing less," Tomas replies. He grins at me before locking a firm hand on the sensitive muscle between Kit's shoulder and neck. "Thanks for helping the rookie get his feet wet."

"My pleasure." I don't miss the flare of heat in Kit's eyes as he allows himself a final once-over of my body. I can't imagine he's seeing much. I'm in sweatpants and a hoodie, for Christ's sake.

"The pleasure's all mine." The words practically slither off his tongue.

"Whoa there, boy, better rein that in," Tomas cautions. He winks at me over his shoulder before steering Kit away. "That one's taken. And I happen to like that Moore kid."

The words sting more than they should, leaving me unable to respond. I spin on my heel and trudge back to the warmth of my car and beyond that my too-big bed, devoid of the man I desperately want to be there despite pushing him as far away from it as possible.

Chapter Three

The familiar sensation of cool, damp earth between my fingers coupled with the rich scent of fresh soil is usually the perfect distraction from my racing thoughts. Today, though, despite the black crescent moons forming under my nails after nearly an hour spent planting pansies, any reprieve escapes me.

I sit back on my heels, wiping the bulk of the dirt onto my jeans. Waking up at the crack of dawn after only a few hours of sleep might have sucked, but the results of my early morning visit to the nursery—following a mildly pathetic stop by Aaron's house to deposit a peace offering—are impressive to behold. On each side of my front porch steps, I've added a rainbow of the fall-loving flowers in every shade from luscious indigo to a startling white. It makes me smile at least, even if it doesn't quiet the running commentary in my brain. Between stressing about Maddie's tires to wondering what Aaron is doing, the chatter is enough to drive me mad.

I roll the half-empty bag of gardening soil shut and tuck it under my arm before scooping up my hand trowel and the stack of plastic pots that the flowers came in. I assume Maddie and Camille are still sleeping since I haven't seen any signs of life coming from the apartment while I've been working. The rattling of the garage door will definitely put an end to that and I'm not trying to be rude, so I attempt to maneuver the plethora of supplies into one hand in order to free one up for opening the side door.

"Want some help with that?" a familiar voice calls. I turn too quickly, and suddenly my carefully tucked bag of gardening soil drops to the ground, a puff of black powder spraying both mine and Aaron's feet.

The huff of frustration that follows is entirely involuntary, but he winces and I immediately regret it. If his unexpected arrival hadn't shocked me silent, I would explain that I'm not upset about his presence, rather the amount of dirt now filling my socks. As it stands, all I can do is stare at him and let the relief of his proximity wash over me.

His white teeth flash as he bites at his full bottom lip. "Does it help if I tell you I brought compost?"

I choke on the laugh that bursts forth, earning a smile from Aaron. "Figured I'd bring you a restock since a certain anonymous donor dropped off a fresh batch of eggshells and coffee grounds on my front porch sometime early this morning," he says, a knowing look flashing in his eyes. "You wouldn't happen to know anything about that, would you?"

Dirt scatters across his soft skin when I swat him. I glance theatrically in every direction. "Keep your voice down; you'll have the whole neighborhood thinking I don't know how to stand my ground."

The edges of his lips curl upward, lifting a little of the weight off my heart. It's a full-blown shit-eating grin now. "Sure, Zo, I'll keep pretending you're not a complete softie when it comes to me."

He steps past me to open the door, and I see a five-gallon bucket sitting on the driveway behind him filled to the brim with the biodegradable, nutrient-rich contents from his compost pile, something no other thirty-one-year-old I know possesses.

I choose to ignore his last comment—and its accuracy—and go for the easier topic. "You know the way to my heart is broken-down food scraps and horse manure."

"Yes, for most women, some jewelry and chocolate. For mine?" He winks at me. "Horse shit."

I step into the darkness and drop the plastic pots onto my workbench along with the small trowel. Light illuminates the cluttered space with the clipped *click* of a switch. Aaron deposits the bucket beside my bench and then retrieves the bag of soil from where I dropped it.

"What can I say? Simple tastes." My voice sounds calmer than I feel; nervous energy bubbles just beneath my skin like a freshly opened soda can.

I remove my wide-brimmed hat and hang it from a hook on the wall. Aaron's arms are crossed over his chest, and despite the cooler weather he's wearing a short-sleeved shirt that shows off the rippling muscle he works hard for in his early morning gym sessions. Which I'm guessing is where he's just come from based on the damp fabric clinging to every contour. He smirks, but there's a sadness to it. His eyes are guarded. It's all a reminder that things are not normal, and it's entirely my fault.

"I haven't heard from you all week." The sole of my shoe scuffs when I kick it against the concrete, joining my muttered words in their attempt to break the awkward silence that has settled, thick, between us. I grab my shears and dig at the reservoirs of dirt under my nails, keeping my hands busy so he won't see them tremble.

"I know." He studies my hands rather than my face. "I just needed some time to think about what you said."

"And what'd you come up with?"

He finally glances back up at me, his eyes calculating. I've seen the expression before, though not usually aimed at me. He's viewing this as one of the experiments he does with his students. Form a hypothesis, gather data, draw conclusions. Like maybe if he just asks the right question, he can find the solution he wants.

But I'm not a crystal that he can grow with a little borax, hot water, and food coloring. It's more complex than that, and he doesn't know all the variables at play.

"That I'm sorry." His voice interrupts my spiraling thoughts, stopping them in their tracks. In the wake of my shock, I drop the shears onto the counter with a little less grace than I intend. "For pushing, for not listening when you tell me what you want. For thinking I can change you, or even that I *should*. It's not fair to you."

He steps closer to me, and even though he's sweaty and I smell like dirt, I fold into the familiar comfort of his embrace with an exhaled breath, comprised of relief.

"I'm sorry, too." I whisper it into his chest so he won't see the color rising on my cheeks. "You're not unreasonable for wanting what you do, and you didn't deserve for me to act like you were. It's just that..." My voice falters, and I realize that I'm tiptoeing along the edge of a vast chasm of truth that I can't allow myself to fall into, so I retreat. It's what I'm best at. "Things are just so good the way they are. Why would we want to mess that up?"

He tucks his chin against the crown of my head, his voice rumbling in my ear with his rebuttal. "I don't think marrying you would mess anything up," he grumbles. "But it doesn't matter if it's not what *you* want."

I lean back so I can look at his face, his palms against my lower back keeping me close even as I pull away. There's no way to explain that none of this has anything to do with what I want; rather it has everything to do with what I can never let myself have. For a moment the fear is fresh in my memory and I swear I can feel the vise of Topher's hand around my throat. "You don't want a wife like me anyway."

"What is that supposed to mean?"

I meant the chastisement as a joke to lighten the mood, but the dark flash across his face has me scrambling, and all I'm coming up with are my truths. "Aaron, you and I both know I'm not wife material. I work too much; I'm mean and I'm loud. I'm good for casual sex only, of which I've had far too much."

Not that there's any such thing as too much casual sex, nor does having it make anyone less valuable. After all, sex without commitment is fun. It's safe. It's easy to leave. It's when feelings get involved that things get complicated. Case in point: *us*.

Which is why I have to say it, even if I don't believe it.

He cocks his head to the side and rolls his eyes, settling them on me with a hard stare that straightens my spine.

"Zo, I don't care who you've been with before. It's your body and your life. And you're not mean, nor have I ever cared that you're loud. My hearing is shit anyway."

I stare at his lips, those perfect pillows that I know feel like silk when I press mine against them. I trail my gaze across his high cheekbones and down the slope of his curved jaw. Any of it is easier than looking him in the eye when he tells me everything I want to hear but can't let myself believe.

Especially when I'm holding back the one truth that matters most: I can't let this be more than casual, because the last time I fell in love, it nearly killed me. And I swore it would never happen again.

"Zoey, we can do this on your terms. At your pace. But you can't talk about yourself like that, like us being more is something you don't deserve, or I'm going to have to prove you wrong."

I feel it instantly, the splintering in my heart. A fracture in the scar tissue, a break I'm familiar with. Before it can get out of hand and go beyond what is repairable, I close what negligible distance remains between our lips. What I initiate, he quickly takes control of, covering my mouth with his and diving deeper. His tongue brushes against mine, awakening a heat low in my stomach that replaces any remnants of trepidation.

He steps backward, pulling me with him as he goes. He deftly navigates the maze of terra-cotta planters and wire ladders for climbing vines, moving around discarded rain boots and a spilled bag of seed packets until we arrive at his desired destination: the small standing shower I had installed out here after one too many mud stains became permanent on my last living room rug.

He reaches behind the curtain, turning the nozzle till water begins screaming through the pipes. A graze of teeth across my bottom lip accompanies his fingers undoing the zipper on my pants. I drag his shirt over his head, catching a glimpse of his hazy stare before my own disrobing blocks my vision. After what feels like an eternity spent undressing, he drags me with him into the hot stream, shutting the curtain behind us like we're two teens about to make out in a photo booth at the mall.

Only this is so much better.

A prickle of chest hair scrapes against my nipples, causing a moan to escape my lips. He takes that opportunity to slip his tongue back into my mouth while a hand ventures between the curve of my thighs. Between the water and his touch and his kisses, I'm drowning in the best way possible.

One finger and then a second push into me and I cry out. It's only been a week, but my body has missed him. Craved him. More than my body. *Me.*

"I love the way you sound when I touch you," he growls against my neck. Teeth tug at my earlobe, trail down my throat, nip at my collarbone. It's too much and it's not enough.

"I know something you love even more," I whisper.

That gets his attention. Those soothing pools in his eyes have turned to hot springs, his gaze leveling with mine and not faltering even as I slowly kneel before him. The stream of water hits his back, casting droplets off in every direction until a halo forms around his body. I take him into my throat, watching with satisfaction as a shudder runs down his spine.

"*Fuck*, Zoey."

I love the way he says my name, especially when he's inside my mouth. While I draw him to the edge, my nails dig into his ass and pull him closer. His fingers twist in my dripping wet curls, holding me away from him so he can come back from the brink.

"I'm not finishing without you."

With that, he pulls me up to him, covering my mouth with his once more. We aren't even kissing, not really. Just breathing each other's air. He lifts me, gripping my ample hips tightly so that I can wrap my legs around his waist. When he finally enters me, I can't control the volume at which his name pours out of my lungs and into his.

With every thrust my pulse beats faster, trying to match his rhythm. The steam of the shower swirls around us, and it's perfect, this heat and this steady tempo and the way I feel him against every nerve ending in my body. I cannot breathe and I don't miss the oxygen. Suddenly everything that was coming together explodes within me and I'm crying out his name again with what little air remains in my lungs.

It's the sound of his name on my lips that is his undoing. I feel him stiffen against me and then come apart, every muscle in his body trembling beneath my touch. He settles me back onto my unsteady feet, legs wobbling like they belong to a newborn deer, but he doesn't let go. His forehead finds purchase in the curve of my neck, and I feel his lips move against my skin as he speaks.

"God, I've missed you."

I giggle, nipping at the top of his ear. "Let's fight again so we can make up."

He pulls me tighter against him, lifting his gaze to mine. It's more serious than I expected, and it steals my laughter away. "I love you, Zo."

"I love..." I choke on the word, clearing my throat before finishing my sentence. "How cool you are."

The disappointment is gone from his face almost as quickly as it appears, replaced by a grin at my signature response. He presses one final quick kiss to my lips before he turns to face the stream and grabs soap from the metal rack suction-cupped to the wall.

"Time to get you clean, Zo. You smell like horse shit."

I laugh even though I don't mean it. His words, and my inability to return them, are heavy stones in my gut. A reminder of what I'm letting him give to me, knowing I'll never be able to return it.

Chapter Four

"I've really got to stop eating these. If I keep it up, you'll have to stuff me into the wedding dress," Eden says, swallowing another bite of the rich and fluffy cinnamon roll drenched in caramelized pecans. "It's so much worse now that I live with Chase two doors down. They're too accessible!"

I chuckle, sucking the remnants of sticky caramel off my thumb. Rose keeps the whole town supplied with enough of her treats to tip the scale of American obesity rates in an unfavorable direction. The only resident unaffected seems to be Penny, who is currently running herself ragged in my backyard hunting down a butterfly. Despite her size, she's still very much a puppy, with her gangly limbs and sorely lacking coordination.

"Do you guys think you'll stay in that apartment long term?" I watch as Penny finally gives up and flops into a hole she's dug, her copper fur glowing in the autumnal sunshine. From my vantage point in the kitchen, I can see at least two matching craters scattered throughout the small, fenced-in yard. I'd be mad at her if she didn't look so damn happy, sprawled on her back and panting like she's just run a marathon.

Eden follows my gaze, a soft smile tugging at her lips, their surface still littered with pecan crumbs. She brushes them away with a napkin, her nudie-pink lipstick coming off with the debris. "At least until after the wedding. It's tempting to stay forever because he owns it free and clear, but Penny needs a yard and I need to be able to separate my work and home life."

"I definitely get that," I groan. I'll never understand how Gary and his wife lived above the bar all those years. Owning a business demands so much of me as it stands; I need to keep some things separate. Like where I *sleep*, for instance.

I turn back to the plethora of fabric swatches and notebooks scattered across my kitchen island. There's a Pinterest mood board loaded on Eden's laptop. She scrolls absent-mindedly through images of place settings, bridesmaid dresses in various shades of blue and gold, and venues overlooking mountain ranges and vineyards. Everything is pristine and light, just like her.

"You know I love you, right?" I grab a swatch of powder-blue fabric with a floral print embossed on it. My lip curls involuntarily when I rub a thumb over the gauzy material. "I'd do a lot of things to make you happy. But if you ask me to wear the same print as my grandmother's curtains circa the 1960s, I *will* revolt."

"Aw, come on!" She snatches the swatch from my hand. "You'd look so pretty in this! Think of how it would bring out the blue in your eyes." Her lower lip forms a pout to accentuate the thick fan of eyelashes she's batting in my direction. When my hard stare doesn't falter, she turns and tosses it into the garbage can at the edge of the island with an exaggerated sigh of defeat. "Got it, no florals."

"I'll be carrying a bouquet; I don't need to wear one, too."

"Fair."

She thumbs through the pages of one of her notebooks, finding a list that presumably contained floral bridesmaid dresses because she promptly draws a thick line of ink through it. She brings the pen to her mouth, giving her something to chew on as she scans the remaining contents of the list.

"Do you think this blue is okay for an August wedding? Or is it too wintery?" Her auburn brows pull together and she worries the pen cap even harder. She's staring at an image of a table decorated simply with an ivory cloth and a band of golden chargers encircling various shapes of vases and candleholders. Within the vases lie sparse bundles of blue thistle and eucalyptus, acting as a backdrop to a single cluster of periwinkle hydrangeas in every arrangement. The candles are the color of forget-me-nots, standing tall and proud in the calming sea of blue.

"I think it's perfect," I assure her, patting her fidgeting hand. "And not just because it would make my eyes pop."

All that earns me is a huff of laughter, but she sets down the pen, which feels like a small victory. As much of a planner as she is, organizing an event like this plays to every strength she has while also agitating a few of her weaknesses. Namely, her perfectionism.

She slaps the laptop shut with more force than necessary and rubs the wrinkle between her eyebrows smooth. "Okay, enough of that for today. I'm getting a headache."

"Don't have to tell me twice!" I gather our empty plates and bring them to the sink, scrubbing the caramel off before it hardens. "Do you want more coffee? I can start a second pot."

"Have I told you lately how much I love you?" she croons, tilting her head back to look at me, which causes her hair to unravel from the loose bun that was previously imprisoning it.

"Yes, about twenty minutes ago when I told you I'd take finding a DJ and caterer off your plate," I say with a wink. "But it never hurts to be reminded."

I place two scoops of 8th & Main's medium roast into a paper liner before setting the ancient coffeepot to brew. Once the telltale gurgling begins, I retrieve our already twice-filled mugs from the counter and prep them with the preferred amounts of sugar and creamer for each. When I'm satisfied that her cup contains at least twice as much as mine, I settle in to wait.

"Have you heard anything from Tomas about Maddie's van?" Eden asks, thumbing a satin swatch.

"He called yesterday." My phone rang first thing in the morning. Smart man knew that if he didn't call me right away, I'd be blowing him up as soon as I was conscious. "Said it's as he suspected. No witnesses, no cameras, no evidence. Probably just some punk-ass teenagers."

"Why would anyone do that?" She looks horrified. "Even as teenagers we were never cruel."

"You're right; we were just stupid." She rolls her eyes at me but can't stay irritated for long because the coffee is done, and a steaming cup of blonde liquid is on its way to her. "You know I'm kidding. I have no clue why anyone would think that was a funny prank. But they were able to get the tires replaced this morning, and the girls are back in, so all is well."

She sighs. "I guess so."

I straddle the barstool next to her, taking a sip of fresh coffee that singes my taste buds. Penny trots through the open sliding glass door, her tongue lolling out of her mouth and leaving a trail of slobber in her wake. She goes straight to Eden, resting her chin on her owner's lap in a plea for pets. Eden buries a hand in the irresistible fluff behind her ears, granting the request.

"So how are things with Aaron?" she asks. Penny's eyes pop open at the sound of her third favorite person's name, trailing behind her owners but somehow beating me out, which only pisses me off a little bit. "You two seemed a bit tense at the party."

"Oh, we made up." I flick my hand in the air flippantly.

"I have no doubt you guys *made up*," Eden replies, one eyebrow perched high on her forehead. "But did you actually fix the issue?"

"Eden, you know there's nothing a little steamy sex in the garage shower can't make right." I run a salacious tongue over my lips.

Her eyes go wide at the same time she pretends to stick a finger down her throat and gag. "Was this before or after Maddie and Camille left the apartment?"

"Before, but we were quiet. For the most part."

"Ugh, Zo!" she groans, shaking her head. "You're forgetting I shared a wall with you in our college apartment. You're *never* quiet."

"I am when my mouth is busy." I grin wickedly, knowing how uncomfortable this kind of conversation makes her, yet I'm unable to resist poking the bear.

"There's a mental image I didn't need," she says, grimacing. "You two keep fucking like rabbits, we're going to end up with some bunnies running around soon enough."

"Relax, I'm on birth control." I dismiss her concerns with a wave of my hand, both for her benefit and mine. The idea of getting knocked up makes me more nauseous than morning sickness ever could. "If anyone's getting pregnant, it's you."

"If you recall the aforementioned wedding dress I have to fit into, you'll bite your tongue."

She says the words gruffly, but I don't miss the softening around her eyes. She might not want them right now, but I can see how she interacts with Cleo, how she watches Chase play peek-a-boo with the toddler by hiding his face behind one of Rose's giant cookies and popping out to a chorus of giggles. Children are on the horizon for her, albeit not the immediate one.

"But seriously," she says, her sober tone reeling the conversation back in. "You're sure you two are good? He seemed to be making himself pretty scarce this week."

"Yeah, I think we're fine now."

She's watching me intently, measuring the things I'm not saying more than the ones I am. Which is fair because I'm not saying much. But the problem is her X-ray vision and its ability to dig beneath the surface, to find the skeletons in my closet that I don't want exhumed.

"You know, I haven't seen you this serious about anyone since Topher."

It's an innocent observation, but it strikes through me like a lightning bolt. Just the sound of his name, even after all these years, still fills me with white-hot anger that I can barely contain. It's not her fault she's triggered it. After all, I never told her the truth about what happened with me and Topher. To her, he's some long-forgotten high school boyfriend. My first heartbreak, sure, but not someone that should still affect me the way he does.

But the pain runs so much deeper than that. For probably the millionth time, I'm tempted to divulge my secrets. To let her in. If I were to tell anyone, it would be Eden. But saying it out loud means admitting I was weak enough to let it happen to me, and I can't stand it. Can't bear to think about how stupid I was, how naive.

It's why I can't let my heart get ahead of my brain. Because being in love means being trapped, and I will not be held captive again.

"It's not that serious," I mutter.

She cackles, a little too harshly in my opinion. "Yeah, *sure*."

I glare at her, and she presses her lips together, holding up both hands in surrender. It's one of the things I usually love most about my best friend, her ability to push without it feeling like pressure. I kick myself for snapping at her. I'm just so tired of everyone thinking they know more about what's happening between me and Aaron than I do. It's why I usually don't let things get this public. Once it's out in the world for everyone to see, they all think they have a right to an opinion.

"I'm sorry, Zo. I won't mention it again." Her emerald eyes soften. "Just know I'm here if you want to talk."

"I know that." I'm not used to being the one in this position. Usually it's me dragging information out of her. Being on this end of things has me rattled, and I feel guilty for taking it out on her. "I'll wear the floral gown if you want."

Her head rolls back, a guffaw flying out of her lungs and startling Penny. She grips her stomach, her whole body shaking with laughter. It releases the tension in my spine, and I find myself laughing with her. Penny paces back and forth between us, lapping at our hands. She doesn't know what's going on, only that she wants to be included.

"I'm not going to make you look like a tablecloth," she manages to say on a sucked-in breath between chuckles. "Though I appreciate your willingness to make a fool of yourself on my behalf."

"Anything for you." I grab her hand and hold it tight. We lock eyes and her lips press tightly together. A knowing look passes between us, riding on the current of a lifelong friendship and a depth of understanding that surpasses any words we could speak aloud.

"Likewise," she replies. And I know in my bones she means it.

Chapter Five

"Aaron?"

"In here!" The bright timbre of his voice piggybacks on the scent of Asian cuisine wafting out of his kitchen. I drop my purse over the back of his overstuffed sofa, careful to check that Bagel isn't sitting there. When I find the spot empty, my gaze scans the rest of the cushions and the recliner on the opposite wall. Two watchful orbs glow in the low light of his living room, reflecting back the nature documentary flashing across the muted television.

Bagel is at least thirteen years old and as many pounds overweight. He's the color of cream cheese with speckles of orange smattered here and there, like smoked salmon slivers on a New York style bagel, which is what Aaron was eating for breakfast while we explored NYC last winter when he decided on a whim that he had to adopt a cat. For the rest of the weekend, in between introducing me to all his favorite sights and suffering through his hundredth showing of *Wicked* just to make my dream come true, he scoured the humane society website, looking for the perfect addition to his bachelor pad.

When Bagel popped up on their website the Monday we

returned, looking like that familiar, plump snack, Aaron was sold. The cat's name was George, which Aaron promptly changed, and he wanted nothing to do with either of us. Still doesn't. If Penny's preference is Aaron over me, Bagel's is no one over everyone.

His indifferent gaze tracks me as I cross the room, and he finally chirps an acknowledgment— or a threat, it's unclear— just before I cross the threshold into the kitchen.

"What are you cooking?" I gingerly discard the awkward weight of my wine bag onto the ceramic tile countertops I keep offering to help him replace. He insists he likes the charm of all the original fixtures in the ranch-style home built in the early 1980s. I suspect he just doesn't want to find out how much better than him I am at home remodeling.

I step up behind him, wrap my arms around his waist, and tuck them under his thin cotton shirt. It's partially to protect my skin from whatever he's frying in the frothing pot of oil on his stove, and partially because I'm just craving the contact.

He uses chopsticks to grab a piece from beneath the bubbling amber surface and dabs it against a paper towel set to the side before rolling it through what looks like a thick barbecue sauce. He blows on the nugget softly, winking at me over his shoulder. When he's satisfied that it won't burn me, he slips the delicious creation into my waiting mouth, pressing a kiss to my temple as I chew.

"Korean barbecue–style cauliflower," he explains.

"That's cawifwower?" My words are muffled by the still-hot vegetable in my mouth.

"Mhm." He nods, amusement sparking in his eyes. "I thought we could make tacos."

He points with the chopsticks at the selection of accoutrements arranged on the opposite counter of his galley-style kitchen. Crisped-up tortillas are stacked next to a bowl of pickled cabbage and a small ramekin of creamy sauce that I don't question.

"Korean barbecue...cauliflower...tacos?" I say it slowly to add up all the seemingly unrelated pieces in my head. I love to try new things. After all, I'd run a terrible restaurant if I didn't. Plus, my stomach is growling for another bite, so clearly he's on to something.

He watches the pieces fall into place in real time, grinning when he sees me fully come on board.

"Just nobody tell my abuela I put cauliflower in a taco," he warns, suddenly looking grim. "She'd come back from the dead just to keel over again."

I cross my heart, chuckling. "No vegetable tacos in Puerto Rico?"

"If there were, she wasn't eating them," he muses. He turns back to the sizzling liquid and uses a spider to fish out the remaining nuggets. "She died of complications from type 2 diabetes."

I grimace even though he has his back to me. "Sorry about that."

"I miss her, definitely." He shrugs. "But she came over from the island to get better medical care, bringing my mother with her. If she hadn't, my mom wouldn't have met my dad, and I wouldn't have been here to meet you."

"Still, that's a little grim."

He finishes tossing the cauliflower in the sauce before spooning it out onto a plate and adding it to the dinner assembly line. I grab one of his homemade tortillas and begin the work of putting together my taco.

"I'm just saying, the bad thing was going to happen anyway, because sooner or later bad things happen to all of us. I'm just grateful something good came out of that one, for once."

I hum my passive agreement, stepping into the breakfast nook and setting my plate down at his small dining table. The truth is, I don't know if I believe it. That all the things that happen to us are preorchestrated before our time and will happen to us one way or another. If that's true, then I have to accept that Topher was always going to happen to me. And if I can't blame myself, who can I blame? Fate isn't nearly as satisfying to hold a grudge against, that elusive bastard.

Aaron settles into the seat next to me just as Bagel skirts around the corner of the doorway. He slinks into the seat at the head of the table opposite us, the farthest spot away that he can occupy while still being included. Aaron and I share a knowing glance. The cat, it seems, might like us after all.

"Oops, forgot the wine!" I mumble over a mouthwatering bite. I fetch the bottle from his kitchen along with two glasses, and fumble through his junk drawer looking for a wine opener. When I come up empty, I move to the silverware drawer, but still no luck. By the time I've scoured every nook and cranny of his kitchen, Aaron realizes that something's amiss and launches a search party of one.

"What are you looking for?" He steps into the kitchen, surveying the scene.

"Wine opener." I hold the bottle up by the neck and blow a flyaway out of my face. He follows in my footsteps, checking all the usual locations and coming up just as empty.

He's staring hard into the junk drawer, as if he can manifest it, when I watch a realization dawn on him. He looks over at me, rubbing a hand against his close-cut curls. "I think I left it at your house."

As soon as he says it, the mental image pops into my head. His simple metal corkscrew sat atop my kitchen counter next to the coffee maker, the one he brought over when my electric wine aerator broke two weeks ago.

My bottom lip puffs into a pout. "Welp, no wine for us."

"Nonsense," he says, rummaging in the junk drawer until he finds what he's looking for, which he holds up for me to examine. It's a random screw and a screwdriver, but he's showing it off proudly like it's the solution to all our problems.

"Are we hanging up a painting or...?"

He huffs at me, reaching for the bottle of wine. "Just give it here."

I surrender the bottle, more out of curiosity than actual belief that he'll accomplish whatever he intends to. I watch as he drives the screw down into the cork until a little less than an inch remains between the cork and the head. Then he opens the cabinet under his sink and pulls out the portable toolkit he keeps there. Retrieving his hammer, he slides the forked edge under the screw and tugs.

"It's going to break," I warn.

"It's not going to break," he replies.

It breaks.

He glances at me sheepishly. "Fifty percent of the time, it works."

I laugh, grabbing the bottle from him and peering in at the other half of the cork still lodged in the neck. "Fuck it." I shove a finger down the bottle's throat, poking the cork into its belly.

When we return to the dining table with two glasses of red wine littered with bits of cork, we catch Bagel with one paw outstretched, poised above Aaron's half-eaten taco. When he sees us, he freezes, as if his stillness will render him invisible. Only Aaron's firm warning of, "Don't even think about it," startles him from his pose and sends him scrambling off the table.

"Aw, you crushed his dreams," I say, putting on a mock pout. Aaron laughs in response, but not before I see a flash of something else pass over his face. I tell myself I'm being overly sensitive, that I imagined the slight clenching of his jaw and the flare of heat in his eyes. But no amount of self-reassurance fixes the souring in my gut.

Suddenly I'm very much aware of how domesticated this whole scene is. Making dinner together, chastising the cat, jailbreaking a bottle of wine. A thick film coats my throat, and I struggle to swallow it down. It's lovely, the natural give-and-take. The easy way we orbit around each other as we accomplish such menial tasks. I'd be happy to accept it for what it is if I didn't know it meant so much more to Aaron.

"Anyway." He clears his throat. It's enough to shake me from the spiraling thoughts, but the discomfort still lingers in my stomach. "Some friends of mine from college are renting a lake house next weekend just outside of Denver."

"That's nice," I mumble, still a bit distracted.

"They invited us," he adds. This gets my attention. I let my gaze return to his face, relieved to find it void of whatever darkness passed over it just now. "I know it's last minute, but it's only for a weekend. Eden could cover for you, and I thought it'd be nice since we haven't been on a trip in a while."

"Definitely." There's excitement in my voice now. It'll be more than nice; it's exactly what we need. An echo of how we were at the beginning, constantly running off on some adventure whether it was an outdoor concert two cities over or a cheap airfare for me used in conjunction with the flight benefits he gets from his dad to explore some random destination for a couple days. If anything can remind him how good we are when we're just two people enjoying their time together, without any ties that bind us so tight we can barely breathe, this is it.

His smile turns up a thousand watts, a sheen from the barbecue sauce making his lips look honey glazed. I'm overwhelmed with the urge to lick them clean. Something I can do all weekend, bundled up in a cozy lakeside cottage with a fire roaring in the stone hearth. It's perfect. More than perfect.

He sees the shift in my eyes, and his jaw is ticking again, but this time it isn't disappointment or anger or whatever that was from before. It's hunger. He gathers both our plates and drops them in the sink, hooking an arm under my legs as I try to rise from the table. He hoists me up and marches past an unimpressed Bagel down the long hallway to his bedroom, ready to devour me.

Chapter Six

"You've got to place the order by eleven, or else it won't be delivered until Monday."

It's probably the tenth time I've said as much, but wanting to give Maddie more responsibility is one thing. Actually letting go and trusting that she will rise to the occasion, at the risk of my business's success, is another.

"I know, I know," she groans. Her lips are practically shellacked with a magenta gloss that smudges against her teeth when she bites at the golden hoop embedded in her lower lip. It's her tell, the only evidence that she too is nervous about the responsibility I'm giving her. I realize that doubting her out loud is only making her doubt herself, and that's the last thing I want to do.

"You've got this," I reassure her, trying to wipe the apprehension from my tone. "You've done it a million times; it's nothing new."

Granted, all those times involved either myself or Santi reminding her constantly and at least five troubleshooting questions before the food order was ready to submit, but I don't mention that.

Her brown doe eyes widen at me, a little tendril of anxious hope creeping through her otherwise stoic expression. "You're right, I'll be fine."

She says it more to reassure herself than to converse with me. With that decided, she gets up from the desk chair and tightens her apron back around her waist, returning to her station. She gathers an armful of limes and a fresh jar of cherries from the fridge beneath the counter so she can prep her garnishes for the evening. I wait until her back is to me before leaning over and pressing the submit button she forgot to, holding back an exasperated sigh.

Just then, Santi pushes through the saloon doors, heading to the bathroom for his regularly scheduled appointment. He catches my eye, peeking around Maddie's back with a pointed expression. I can see him gauging my slumped shoulders and the hand poised on my hip. He glances at her and then back to me, nodding to assure me he's got it.

I love you, I mouth to him.

One corner of his mouth twitches into a faint grin. He loops his chef's coat through the hook mounted on the wall next to the double doors and makes his way to the back of the restaurant, where his throne awaits.

Knowing that's my cue for my other least favorite task, I exit the office and shut its heavy oak door behind me. Maddie doesn't glance up as I pass behind her; she's too focused on slicing the limes into perfectly sized wedges for the inevitable hoard of margaritas she'll have to prepare tonight. Ladies' night never fails to leave all of us sticky with tequila residue and a fine layer of rock salt on every surface as far as the eye can see.

Just as I expected, when I make my way into the kitchen, all stations have already been abandoned. Like clockwork, Santi has left his flock, and they've all wandered off into the wilderness. The back door is propped open, alarm turned off, and I can smell the cigarette smoke before I turn the corner.

What I don't expect to see is Eden, arms crossed and spine rigid, going over the script I've nearly mastered at this point.

"Look, I get that you guys need smoke breaks, but you can't all abandon the kitchen at once just because Santi's left the room for two seconds."

Marcelin looks to the two ringleaders for direction, beads of sweat forming on his brow. Eric simply grimaces and drops the cigarette, grinding it into the ground with his boot. He's the begrudging leader of their motley crew, and while sometimes he irritates me no end, he will also be the first to take one for the team.

"I can wait; you two stay," he tosses over his shoulder. His bright orange hair flashes in the midday sun as he passes Eden and finally realizes I'm standing in the doorway. "Sorry about that."

He says it to both of us, offering an apologetic smile to me when I step aside and let him pass.

"I was done anyway," Mateo adds. He's Santi's nephew, and the familial resemblance is uncanny, right down to their matching buzz cuts and widow's peaks. He smiles shyly at Eden and me before following Eric inside, the scent of his Curve cologne overwhelming my senses as soon as he's within a couple feet of me.

Marcelin watches the two of them, not wanting to be left out of their easy camaraderie. He drops the cigarette reluctantly and kicks at the last of the embers until they flicker to a silent death.

"Marcelin, you're older than them. You could set a good example if you quit." Eden's voice is gentle with a signature compassion I envy. Sometimes it feels like even the kindest things I say come out harshly, while her tone is just naturally comforting. Even when she's cutting off a drunk patron at the bar or correcting one of the guys for their attendance, she does so with a grace that eludes me. "Smoking is terrible for your health."

He stands up straighter under the spotlight of her scrutiny and shares a rare smile, his bright teeth flashing against the backdrop of his ebony skin. His face is weathered more from stress than age, having immigrated here after a massive earthquake destroyed his home in Southwestern Haiti. I know from experience what it's like to be new here, untethered to the community.

Adding to that the devastation he left behind, I can't imagine how he must be feeling. His tendency to follow behind Eric and Mateo makes all the more sense, fueled by a determination to seek some kind of bond.

"You're right, miss," he says, nodding. "I'll do my best."

"That's all I ask." She pinches his shoulder affectionately. He abandons his post against the brick wall, leaving just an empty stack of crates where the three of them were lounging.

She turns to follow him inside, finally noticing me with a start. A hand flies up to her heart as she stumbles backward. "Jesus, Zo, it's not nice to sneak up on people."

"Sorry about that," I say, laughing. "I was just watching the master at work."

She rolls her eyes, stacking up the crates so she can bring them inside. "I don't know what you're talking about."

"You just have a way with people," I commend her. "Sure, they do what I ask them to *because I asked them to*, but they do it for you because they want to make you proud."

The praise brings a rosiness to her cheeks. She waves a hand as if she can bat my words right out of the air. "I don't know what you're talking about. We'd all follow you anywhere. Though if you're going to lead us into battle, I need at least a week's notice to get my armor to the dry cleaners."

It fills my chest with a bubbling laughter, a lightness that bursts against the stress of preparing for my absence and lifts all that weight right off my shoulders. She regards me more carefully, recognition flashing in her eyes. She sets the crates back down, separating them into two stacks and sitting on one. She pats the other, beckoning me to join her.

"Aren't we setting a bad example by hanging out here when we just got on to them for the same thing?" Even as I say it, I take the seat next to her, the hard honeycomb of plastic digging into my backside through my linen pants.

"Nonsense, it's a management meeting," she scoffs. "We just forgot to invite Santi."

"He's a bit preoccupied at the moment," I add, and a shared peal of laughter breaks out between us. When it finally subsides, she settles back against the hard brick wall, staring out at the parking lot rather than at me. It relieves a little of the pressure, and I'm tempted to squeal like a teakettle from the release.

"Zo, you know you're allowed to take breaks. We've all got your back. Santi, Maddie, me. Even those guys in there would step up to the plate to take care of this place." Her gaze turns skyward, projecting her voice in a way that directs my attention to the metal landing above us like a pointed finger. "And if all other lines of defense fail, you know Gary's not going to let anything happen to the bar. He'd be out of a place to live!"

She says it a little too loud, and from what I imagine is an open kitchen window I hear Gary's gravelly voice call down, "Damn straight!"

"I know," I concede, the words coming out in a sigh of breath.

"I know you know." She kicks at a discarded cigarette butt. "So what's really going on? You've been away tons of times and it's never stressed you out this badly."

She's looking at me now, and the pressure is building again. I flop my head back against the brick, albeit a little too roughly, which sends stars spinning across my vision. Excellent. Give myself a concussion and maybe that'll solve my overthinking.

"I don't know, honestly," I say. "Aaron and I have been on dozens of trips like this before. This one just feels different for some reason. Like there's more expectation."

A grumble sounds at the back of her throat, her way of acknowledging me without interrupting. I wish she would, though, just to save me from having to do all this self-reflection.

"It's like ever since you guys got engaged, he's got it on his brain that we have to be next."

After a lengthy pause, she realizes I'm not going to elaborate without a little prompting, so she pipes up to nudge me along. "Was it not a topic of conversation before?"

I think back over the course of our relationship. Last summer had been a seemingly endless blur of radiant heat and lighthearted fun, like plucking a tuft of cotton candy from its cone and feeling it melt on your tongue. As the leaves changed and winter set in, we were still sneaking off whenever we could, talking about our most nonsensical dreams and thoroughly embarrassing pasts over the course of a plethora of late-night rendezvous and short trips during his breaks from teaching over random school holidays.

But as the world grew warm again, something shifted, not just between us but within me. I felt that dangerous string dangling between us, growing thicker and more taut by the day. Even though I knew the stronger it got, the harder it would be to sever, I ignored it. Because once acknowledged, I had to do something about it, and for the first time in forever I wasn't sure that I wanted to.

There were whispers, sure. Late at night as we lay breathless in bed, he would paint the picture of a future that involved both of us, together. I'd pretend to be asleep but couldn't deny the glowing feeling in my skin as I imagined the life he depicted. In the silence of those evenings, long after his words had trailed off, I'd allow myself to want it, if only for a moment.

"Barely," I say at last, running away from the memories. "But it multiplied tenfold after the engagement."

I let myself peek over at her, finding her almond-shaped eyes crinkled at the edges, framing her face with a hint of sorrow rather than amusement. She gathers her long, straight hair into a bundle and tucks it to the opposite side, leaving me with a clear view of her pity.

"Why is that such a bad thing?" She's genuinely trying to understand. I don't know how to explain without spilling my guts, and this is neither the time nor the place. I don't know when or where ever will be, but at my bar in broad daylight within earshot of a nosy Gary certainly isn't it.

I pick at my cuticles, desperate to avoid the question. But I'm trapped in the spotlight of the sun and her observant gaze, so I know I have to give her at least a nugget of the truth, even if I can't explain the complete backstory.

"Look, I'm so happy that things have worked out for you and Chase. He is an incredible man and everything you deserve, and I'm so glad I can trust him to take care of you, because I'd murder him if not. And I'm thrilled for my parents, that it has worked out for them, and for Santi and his wife and for Gary and Wendy, for as long as they had together.

"And it's beautiful. When it works, it really, truly is. But what about when it doesn't? What about for your mom? Not once but *twice*? For every bit that it is beautiful when it works, it is absolutely *horrifying* when it doesn't. I just don't know that I'm willing to risk it, you know?"

There are pools of tears threatening to spill out of her eyes, and I immediately regret everything I've said that is responsible for their presence. Just because she's come to terms with what happened to her doesn't mean she wants to be reminded of it, and I suddenly feel even lower than dirt for being the one to do so.

"I'm sorry I said that. God, I'm sorry, Eden. I had no right."

"It's okay," she says, her voice faint but firm. She reaches for my hand and holds on to it, even when I know she must want to recoil from how clammy it is against her warm palm. "You have every right to feel the way that you feel. It's not like I haven't had those same fears. I think we'd be crazy not to, after having front-row seats to something so awful."

I watch as a quiet tear escapes the corner of her eye and snakes its way down to her quivering lip, all the while feeling its twin roll over my cheekbone. "If love could make your mom stay with a man like that, what other awful things could love convince someone to accept?"

I ask the question even as I know the answer. Even as the memory fills my brain, clouding my vision with tears until it's all I can see.

"Who the fuck are you talking to?" he asks, the words coming out of his twisted mouth on a snarl of spit and teeth.

"It's just Eden. She asked if I could come over tonight." I hate myself for feeling the need to explain, but I know it'll only make things worse if I don't.

"Bullshit," Topher snaps, ripping the phone out of my hand and hurling it at the wall. I wince as it makes a dent in the drywall that his grandmother will inevitably ignore, just like the other miscellaneous pockmarks left by his angry punches and one from an accidental collision with my head.

"I swear. It's her birthday party this weekend, and she wanted help picking out an outfit." My voice trembles in a way I despise.

His eyes are black, more like a bird of prey than a human as they rake over me. I can practically feel their abrasion on my skin, like two razor blades scraping every surface they touch.

"And what are you going to wear?" There's a hint of sickening lust threading with the anger, a warped echo of the desire he once exhibited whenever he touched me. Every once in a while it's still there, mostly when he hasn't made it into his grandfather's liquor cabinet yet. It's in those moments, when I catch a brief glimpse of the person I fell in love with, that I convince myself he doesn't mean any of the bad things he says or does to me. That I convince myself to stay.

"I don't know," I hedge. It's what I have to do when I don't know what the right answer is, when I'm unsure what will set him off instead of setting me free.

"Bullshit," he repeats, lumbering toward me. He only has a few

inches on me in height, but he makes up for it in muscle and anger, both built with hours in the gym and an unhealthy dose of steroids. As if there is a healthy dose, I mentally chastise myself. "You and I both know you're going to wear some slutty outfit you're too fat to wear because you think it'll make the guys want inside of your pants. But why would they? No one is going to want you but me, not once they know what a whore you are. Why even bother, Zoey?"

He's towering over me now. I'm surrounded by him. Tucked into the corner of his bedroom, I'm standing on a pile of discarded gym clothes that smell like they are rotting with dried sweat. He grabs my side hard between his fingers, digging his nails into the extra weight I carry there.

"You're mine, and you'll be showing what's mine to no one," he growls, the sweat mixing with his hot, scotch-scented breath and nearly making me retch. "Say it, bitch."

"I'm yours," I mumble, the words strangled in my throat by fear.

"Say it like you mean it." There's a threat in his voice, one I know he will make good on.

"I'm yours," I repeat, stronger this time even though I don't feel strong. I feel incredibly weak, trapped against the man I thought I knew. An oily lock of his shaggy black hair falls into his eyes, and I push it away on instinct, my hands gentle against the wall of his hatred.

The corners of his eyes soften, and there's a flicker of something in their murky depths. Not affection, but a cold iteration of it. The closest he's capable of feeling.

"That's my girl," he whispers, and I nod because I don't know how to be anything else.

Chapter Seven

The world is a vibrant swirl of oranges and reds and yellows as we snake back and forth down into a valley between the mountains, gravel crunching under our tires when Aaron turns at the bequest of the GPS onto a driveway tucked under a canopy of color-changing trees. The dense forest of birch and towering pine falls away from the road to reveal a cottage so perfectly formed from the materials at hand it almost blends into the edge of the woods where it rests.

The sprawling front porch sits perpendicular to a lakefront, where I can just see the water lazily lapping at the shore. An L-shaped dock juts out into the lake, sporting a wooden bench at its farthest point similar to the other docks I can see in the distance, serving larger and more expensive vacation homes for people who've never heard of the word *budget*.

Neon kayaks lean against racks, tucked away for the winter season that approaches quicker than my Southern bones would like. I tuck the open edges of my flannel tighter around my midsection, enjoying this season of in-between, right before everything changes.

"We have arrived!" Aaron shifts into park and kills the engine.

The last of whatever nervous energy was still plaguing my body drifts away on the ebbing surface of the lake when I step out of the car and take a sharp inhale of air. My lungs prickle as they expand, both grateful for the fresh breeze and suspicious of the crisp temperature.

"When will your friends be here?" I ask. The trunk slams down, revealing Aaron with my years-old leopard print Victoria's Secret bag tucked under one arm and his Patagonia duffel under the other.

He tucks his keys into his pocket and leads the way toward the front steps. "They live just outside of Denver and get off at five, so I imagine they'll get here sometime after food o'clock but before wine-thirty."

"More fire-roasted weenies for us, then." I hold up the bagful of buns clutched in my right hand.

"The best kind of weenies," he tosses over his shoulder.

"*Mmm*, I don't know," I hum, tugging at his belt loop while he tries to figure out the hide-a-key code beside the door. "I can think of a better kind."

"If you think you're being sexy by referring to my dick as a weenie," he warns, pushing through the door at last and flashing a stern look in my direction, "think again."

I giggle, following him into the cottage. We find ourselves in a living room filled with overstuffed couches and a coffee table stacked high with ancient board games whose cardboard boxes are peeling apart at the edges. The smell of fresh air swirls with the musk of old books, the source of the latter being a wall of shelves lined with paperbacks sporting wrinkled spines from years of readers scanning their pages. There's a fireplace to our right that has been modernized to allow us to see through its hearth into the sunroom that faces the lake on the other side of weathered French doors.

"I love it," I whisper, crossing the room and dropping the

groceries onto the Formica countertops dividing the living space from the kitchen. Aaron returns from depositing our bags in a room somewhere down the hallway lined with cheesy Hobby Lobby wall art touting that *Heaven Is a Little Closer at the Lake.* He leans against the pale blue shiplap walls and crosses his arms over his chest.

"I thought you might."

I grin, closing the space between us and throwing my arms around his neck, which gains me a *humph* as I slam into his chest. He drops his arms from their guarded position and locks them around my waist, holding me against him. I press a featherlight kiss to his chin, close enough to his lips to leave him wishful but not satisfied.

When he ducks his head low to take what he's wanting, I pull away an inch or two so I can catch his gaze and begin batting my eyelashes in the flutteriest way I can muster.

"Can we build a fire?" I ask sweetly.

He groans, swiping his lips across mine before I have a chance to dodge him. "Sure, I'll do that while you get out whatever's irritating your eyes."

"You're *so* funny."

He walks past me to swing open a French door and step onto the screened-in sunroom, leaving me rolling my eyes. I follow him out, catching sight of the empty firewood rack at the same time he does. His lip curls up as we both turn to examine the grassy expanse between here and the water's edge, and find a shed tucked against the tree line with a pallet of uncut logs stacked against its side.

"All right, Lumberjack Aaron, it's your time to shine," I say, patting him on the butt.

He glares at me, lip remaining curled.

"C'mon, can't roast weenies with no fire."

"Better not be the only weenies getting attention tonight," he groans, grabbing the ax beside the screen door before stepping out into the yard blanketed in fallen leaves.

"So we *are* calling it a weenie then?" I tease. All it earns me is a middle finger tossed over his shoulder as he continues walking away.

It doesn't take long before he sheds his plaid button-down and I'm forced to watch a shirtless Aaron swing the ax repeatedly against the logs, splintering them into manageable sections for the fireplace. Well, *forced* isn't the right word. It's a privilege, really, with the way his chestnut skin ripples over the well-defined back muscles aimed in my direction. By the time he has a sizable pile created, he locks the ax into the top of the base log with a hard swing and turns to face me, swiping a gloved hand over his brow in response to my appreciative whistle.

It elicits an easy chuckle from him, that smile he gives away so freely spreading across his face. He gathers up as much as he can carry and brings it back across the yard, shirt thrown over his shoulder haphazardly.

"Did you enjoy the show?" He grins when he steps through the screen door, the weather-beaten floorboards groaning under his footsteps.

"Oh yes. Do you do repeat performances? I'd like to buy season tickets."

He attempts to fix his face into a disapproving frown, but he's betrayed by the glimmer of amusement dancing in his eyes. He tosses a few pieces into the fireplace and sets them alight. The sky has blurred into a mixture of purples and hazy whites, twilight settling into the valley around us. It reflects off the surface of the water, creating a mirrored glow only broken up by the dense line of trees encircling the lake. The crackle of flame licking at firewood joins the melody of lapping water and the few remaining crickets that still sing into the cooling night, reluctant to admit that summer is long over.

Aaron sits next to me on the rug in front of the hearth, tugging my feet into his lap. He grabs one of my boots and then the other, tugging both free before rubbing long, hard strokes with his thumb up the center of my arch, where he knows I ache after days spent on my feet at Nomads. A groan crawls out of my throat in response, not even waiting for permission to exit. He smiles at the noise, the flickering firelight dancing over his glistening skin. I trail an absent-minded finger over the surface, leaving a path of sparks that I know we both sense.

"You look delicious," I murmur, catching him by surprise. His thumb pauses in its path, his whole hand flexing around my foot in response to my words.

"I'm covered in sweat," he warns, locking his heavy-lidded eyes on mine. Our backs are resting against the furniture we're meant to be sitting on, and he leans in toward me so close I can smell his unique scent, like all the spices in my favorite rum. One hand leaves my foot, traveling up my leg and gripping the inside of my thigh in a squeeze just tight enough to draw a gasp from my lips.

"I don't mind." The words are breathier than I intend. His hand moves farther into the apex of my legs, the thin fabric of my leggings no match for the scorching heat of his touch.

"Is that so?" His voice is honeyed and thick with that familiar hunger, so much so I can almost taste a hint of its saccharine sweetness on my tongue. "I might taste a little salty."

I lick my lips involuntarily. His eyes track the movement, their color in the light more like an emerald reflecting the sun. "I'd like to find out."

A hum forms in the back of his throat, the hand that was mere inches away from where I need it most suddenly abandoning its station, leaving me feeling cold and desperate. He doesn't keep me waiting for long, though, because soon both his hands are gripping my waistband, tugging the spandex over the curve of my ass and down, down, down until he frees me of the leggings completely.

"I think," he begins, settling himself on his belly between my legs, "I'd rather have a taste of you."

His breath brushes against the sensitive skin between my legs, a hint of what is to come. My heart is in my throat as I watch him, his playful gaze teasing me while a hooked finger tugs the edge of my thong to the side. I can see the hunger I feel for him reflected back in his jeweled eyes when he licks his lips at the sight of me.

"Well," I say, breathless, "if you insist."

It's all the encouragement he needs. His mouth presses against my core and pulls a whimper from me instantly. He grips my hip with one hand and holds the thong out of his way with the other, his tongue swirling around that bundle of nerves until my vision begins to blur at the edges. I don't dare take my eyes off him, watching his lips move against mine as he sucks and delves deeper, his tongue flicking exactly the way I like.

When he senses I can't take much more, he buries two fingers inside me, curling them up and stroking until the fire in me burns hotter than any flame in the hearth.

"Fuck, you're going to make me come," I cry out. The edge of his mouth curves upward. It's the closest he can get to a satisfied smile while grazing his teeth over the most sensitive place on my body which sends me careening over the edge of climax.

It takes a moment for my breaths to stop coming in ragged, desperate gasps. Once they settle, the familiar sound of tires crunching over gravel has my head shooting up from where it rests against the floor.

I find Aaron staring back at me with amused alarm in his gaze. He rises to his feet and grabs his shirt from where it rests on the back of the armchair.

"That must be Dani and Jeremiah," he says, retrieving my leggings from where he tossed them across the room and dropping them onto my thighs in a puddle. "You get dressed; I'll distract them."

He wiggles his eyebrows at me, earning a laugh before he disappears into the living room just as I hear the front door swing open and two voices filter through the house to my ears. I quickly yank my pants back on and attempt to smooth my hair where it has turned to a rat's nest at the back from my dramatic writhing. I catch a glimpse of my reflection in the tiny circular mirrors making up bubbles on yet another nautical-themed piece of art hanging on the wall. My cheeks are flushed and hair unruly, a black smudge of mascara blurred under my eyes. I do my best to wipe it away with my thumb, giving myself unintentional winged eyeliner in the process. *Good enough.*

When I step into the living room, Aaron's embracing a beautiful Black girl with long, intricate braids and a tattoo of roses climbing up her forearm to disappear beneath her cropped jean jacket. Behind them is a bear of a man looking much like Aaron did two hours ago when we arrived, arms piled high with two floral duffel bags and one backpack so full it looks like the globe of a turtle shell on his back.

"Zo, this is Dani," Aaron says with a knowing smile, winking at me over her shoulder. "And this is her husband, Jeremiah."

"Nice to meet you both!" I offer, pushing the door closed behind me to keep out some of the chilled air. The fire has turned the living room to the temperature of a warm hug, causing a relieved shiver to course through my body. "We were just enjoying the sunset from the screened porch."

Aaron takes the floral bags from Jeremiah and leads him down the hallway to deposit them in the other room, all the while trying to muffle a snickering we all can definitely hear. I smile awkwardly at Dani, taking in her high-waisted black jeans and neatly tucked graphic tee as she sheds the jacket and hooks it by the door. The tattoo travels up her entire arm, blooming into a full bouquet against her dark skin.

When she turns back to face me, I'm overwhelmed with this

strange sensation of recognition, like we might've met before. She crosses the room before I can place her, wrapping her arms and the scent of flowers around me in an instant.

"So nice to finally meet you! I've heard so much about you," she says, her voice smooth like silk.

"You have?" I ask, surprised. Until proposing this trip, Aaron had never mentioned a friend from college named Jeremiah, nor his wife standing here before me. Up close, I can see that she has a beautiful pair of jade-green eyes, the likes of which I've only seen once before.

"Oh absolutely, Aaron never shuts up about you," she gushes, squeezing my bicep lightly. A nagging alarm bell is going off in the back of my brain, and ignoring it is getting harder the longer I look at her. The slope of her jaw seems so familiar, her lithe and muscular frame a more petite version of the one I know so well. I tell myself I must be wrong. *There's no way, right?*

"What are you two chatting about?" Aaron returns to the room as if floating in on a breeze. His words start off lighthearted but end in a hitch my ears detect immediately. I'd almost think he sounds nervous if I didn't know any better. I study him carefully, watching the way the muscle in his jaw tightens as he grinds his molars together. Is it because we were almost caught with our pants down? Well, with *my* pants down.

"I was just telling Zo how my big brother is head over heels in love with her," Dani quips.

A stillness settles in the air, but it is vibrating with an energy so intense you'd think lightning had struck the room. Aaron presses his lips tightly together, a hard stare locking on a point behind me that I assume is Dani's matching green gaze.

"You mean figurative big brother, right? Like one of those co-ed fraternities or whatever?"

Aaron squeezes his eyes shut, pinching the space between his eyebrows for good measure.

"Um, no," Dani answers, causing me to whip my head around and face her. Her face is mottled with confusion as she glances back and forth between us. I rack my brain for the memory escaping me. For all those late-night, whispered conversations about our families that I kept at arm's length. Aaron *has* mentioned his sister before, but I don't remember her name being Dani. It was something like—

"I'm Daniela Moore, Aaron's little sister."

Chapter Eight

"I thought you said Jeremiah was a friend from college," I say, voice clipped.

Aaron's ears have taken on the dark tinge of a blush when I turn back to him, one hand raised up and clasped in a fist as if he was trying to capture Dani's words before they could reach my ears. The sharp talons of panic begin slicing at the lining of my stomach, more bird of prey than butterfly.

"Oh, I am!" Jeremiah pipes up. He's leaning over the kitchen counter, head bobbing between the three of us like it's the most interesting tennis match he's ever watched. The look he shoots Dani tells me he just now realized we're supposed to be playing teams. "Dani and I met when I came home with Aaron on break one time to go snowboarding."

I must have a look on my face because he gestures to the broad expanse of his body and adds, "I may look like a bear, but I move with the grace of a fucking gazelle."

Dani huffs a laugh at the same time Aaron grumbles, "I still haven't forgiven you for hooking up with my sister."

"Dude, we're *married*."

"Still." Aaron shrugs. "Everyone knows that friend's sisters are off-limits."

Jeremiah just shakes his head and returns to the chips and dip he has spread out before him, seeming to decide he likes his role as a spectator better than being a participant.

"I also went to the same college as them, just a couple years later," Dani adds, sounding slightly hurt. "Why didn't you tell her she was meeting your sister?"

The frenzied flock of nerves has moved to my lungs, and I'm afraid if I speak I'll cough up a tar-black feather, but I try to offer her my sincerest look of kindness so she knows I'm not angry, just surprised. Taken off guard. *Terrified.*

"I thought I did," Aaron hedges, shrugging and zeroing in on a point on the ceiling so as to avoid the daggers I'm staring his way. "Must have slipped my mind."

Dani scoffs and marches past me to stand beside her brother, that same floral scent from her hug wafting on the breeze left by her passage. Lilies and jasmine and honeysuckle, all things light and summery. I suck it in like laughing gas at the dentist, hoping it will make me loopy enough to calm the hell down.

She locks her manicured hands on either side of Aaron's squared shoulders, their resemblance even more evident now that I'm searching for it. His skin is two tones lighter, but their face shape and eyes are hauntingly similar. I've always thought Aaron was too beautiful for words, but seeing his features in female form is even more striking.

"Please forgive my brother. As intelligent as he may be, he is also prone to spectacular displays of idiocy." She digs those stiletto acrylics straight through the fabric of his flannel and into his skin. He winces only slightly, finally meeting my hard stare and offering an apologetic grimace.

Jeremiah follows his gaze, and suddenly all three of them are looking at me expectantly. I try to tamp down the anxiety climbing up my throat, but my efforts work less like a hydraulic press and more like a potato masher, silly strings of stress shooting out in every direction.

I haven't met anyone's family since Topher. It was an executive decision made on behalf of my sanity, because long after I'd learned not to miss Topher's strong hands and infectious laugh and tone-deaf harmony to Nickelback tracks, I still longed to sit across from his grandmother at their white oak kitchen table and listen to her gossip about the elderly folks at the Baptist church in town.

If loving someone makes it difficult to leave them, loving their family makes it nearly impossible.

This doesn't have to be a big deal, I tell myself firmly.

My clenched fists are flexing around the hem of my shirt, reminding me of the way my mother squeezes the bulb of her blood pressure cuff. I'm hoping the repetitive motion will steady my focus and dull the thrum of my heartbeat. I've let an awkward amount of time pass. Jeremiah and Dani are glancing at one another, trying to figure out if their brother's an idiot or his girlfriend's just crazy. Aaron's frowning at me because he knows it's the former, and I'm not about to let them think it's the latter, so I release the pent-up air in my chest and plaster a smile across my face that I desperately hope reads as friendly.

"It's no big deal," I manage to say, hoping that repeating the phrase will convince my brain of its validity. "Just surprised, is all. We were about to roast some weenies; do you want any?"

"So, how'd you end up in a town like Loveless?" Dani asks, her delicate fingers shielding her mouth so she can speak and chew simultaneously without being rude. "That town's so small I swear the neighbors can hear your thoughts. I got out as soon as our parents moved away."

"Yeah, what is there, like, one stoplight?" Jeremiah chuckles, a glob of ketchup caught in his scruff. Dani reaches over and wipes it away with her thumb, poking the tip of his nose in a quick follow-up show of affection that comes so naturally I doubt she'll remember she's done it ten minutes from now.

"Hey now," Aaron says firmly, giving me a chance to swallow my food. "The town of Loveless doesn't believe in stoplights. We have stop *signs*, and they're a suggestion."

"Is that why Tomas is so fond of you?" I pinch him in the ribs. He raises his hands in a profession of innocence, shrugging as if to say, *What can you do?*

"I was on a cross-country road trip after college." I direct my comment across the coffee table, where our paper plates are stacked on board games used as makeshift place mats, to Dani. "I stopped there overnight because it was late when I finally made it through the national park. Got a drink at Gary's, where we ended up chatting until well after closing about his experience running the bar and my dream of owning one someday. The next morning I stopped in at Rose's coffee shop to get a little caffeine before hitting the road. She'd just opened up and was still in the process of renovating."

I pass a napkin to Aaron when I notice the relish from his hot dog about to spill over. Sure enough, it covers his chin. "I affirmed her decision to run batten board along the wall of tables and helped her pick out a color, and before I knew it we were talking about our childhoods and my stomach was growling for lunch. I stayed that whole day, figuring it wouldn't hurt. When I eventually finished my trip in California, I couldn't stop thinking about Loveless and Gary's bar. So I came back."

Dani's staring at the hand I left resting on Aaron's knee after handing him the napkin, her knowing expression causing a shiver to run down my spine. I pull my hand back, using it to gather my paper plate instead and snatching Jeremiah's up as soon as he lifts what looks like it could've been two more bites of a hot dog but will have to be one large mouthful since I've taken his plate. I flee to the kitchen, tossing them into the trash and grabbing the uncorked bottle of wine on the counter. I finish it off into a fresh wineglass before returning to the living room.

"...was thinking we could go tomorrow!" Dani's expression is filled with enthusiasm when I step back into earshot. Jeremiah is still trying to chew the massive bite of weenie, his jaw looking slightly unhinged. Aaron is smiling as he watches me approach.

"Go where?" I ask.

"There's a horseback riding place nearby. It's only fifteen minutes or so back up the mountain the way we came in. They do guided tours down to and around the lake. I thought it could be a fun group activity."

Her eyes are wide as she waits for me to jump in with any excitement of my own, but suddenly all the breath I had in me has disappeared. Instead I'm left with a memory of searing pain in my ribs so strong it feels like the injury happened five seconds ago instead of eleven years.

"No thank you," I say quietly, tucking the lopsided throw pillow from the couch against my side for comfort.

Aaron nudges me playfully. "C'mon, it'd be fun!"

Dani's studying me closely, picking up on some energy that's clearly flying under Aaron's radar. I look away from her gaze, picking at the pilling fabric of the couch. "I don't want to go horseback riding."

He lays his head over on my shoulder, peering up at me with fluttering eyelashes reminiscent of the ones I used earlier to sucker him into chopping firewood for an hour. His usual charm doesn't reach me though; I'm too far gone.

"It's okay if you don't know how," he teases. "I can teach you, Zo."

"I didn't say I don't know how." The words come out harsher than I intend. I only wanted to back him off the subject. He startles, sitting up straight as the fog of amusement clears his eyes and he finally sees the message I'm trying to convey. "I said I don't want to."

"I'm with her," Jeremiah adds on the huff of an exhale, having swallowed his massive bite at last.

"Just the two of us could go," Dani says, quickly redirecting from whatever standoff Aaron and I are having. "If it's okay with you and Jer, of course. I just don't get a lot of bonding time with my big brother these days."

Aaron throws her an exasperated look, but I can see in her eyes how badly she wants to spend time with him. It's the same expression I used to aim at my older cousins, begging to be included.

I shift my weight in my seat, leaning into the arm of the couch. "That's fine with me; I'm happy to hang around here and read."

"A long, uninterrupted nap? Sign me up!" Jeremiah adds.

"Then it's decided." Dani's face transforms into a wide grin. Aaron sighs but the corners of his mouth twitch and I know he's equally excited to spend time with his baby sister. Watching the way he looks at her, with a swirl of pride and annoyance and affection, causes a pang in my heart. It's the same expression he gets when he talks about the antics of his students. The same one I know he'll wear one day when he has children of his own.

Yikes. Not a road my mind needs to go down.

"Well, I'm exhausted." Still clutching the pillow to the phantom pain in my ribs, I stand and step over Aaron's legs, heading toward the cheesy, nautical hallway that will lead me away from this room and its uncomfortable feelings and memories. "I'm going to bed. Night, everyone."

"Good night!" Dani and Jeremiah call in unison. I don't look back to see what Aaron does, but I hear his familiar footsteps on the creaking floorboards padding after me just as I slip into the door at the end of the hall where my leopard-print bag lies in the middle of the canopy bed.

The door closes behind us with a soft *click*, wrapping us in a cocoon of unspoken frustration and, beneath it, the barely there embers of burning desire from before.

I keep my back to him while I gather my toiletries and head for the adjoining bathroom, stripping out of my clothes in front of the mirror. He steps into the doorway, leaning against its frame and dragging a long gaze up my naked body, lingering in all the right places before landing on my less than enthused face.

He startles. "What?"

"*What?*" I mock, yanking an oversize sweater onto my body, which causes him to pout ever so slightly. "What the hell, Aaron? You weren't going to warn me I was meeting your *sister?*"

"If I had, you wouldn't have come, and you needed a vacation." His tone is matter-of-fact, arms crossed over his chest in defiance of my indignance.

"That's not true." My chin juts out even as it trembles.

He doesn't honor that with a response, just a stare made of stone. I hold it for as long as I'm able before I crack.

"Okay, it is, but that's what's so shitty about it, Aaron. You knew I wasn't ready for this, and you didn't even give me a choice in the matter!"

I squeeze the toothpaste out onto my toothbrush and douse it with water, angrily scrubbing at my teeth despite my dentist's insistence that I brush with a gentler hand lest I need gum surgery in a few years. She's one to talk. I see her ordering the most sugar-laden cocktails imaginable from Eden every Friday after work. Those can't possibly be good for her teeth.

"Look, I know I fucked up!" he whisper-shouts. "I'm sorry, Zoey, I am. But it's only because I knew how weird you'd be about it, and if you could get past the fact that we're related for two seconds, you'd realize that she's actually a really cool person that I thought you'd enjoy hanging out with."

I glare at him as I spit the toothpaste-and-blood-swirled spit out into the sink. Okay, maybe Dr. Wozniak has a point about the harsh scrubbing. *But still.*

He stares back at me unabashedly, eyes wide and full of an emotion I don't have a name for, or more likely that I wish I didn't. I can see how hard this is on him, how much of himself he is holding back at all times just so he doesn't overwhelm me. I know how important his family is to him, how many times he's invited me along on dinners with his father when he has a layover in Denver or to go on a weekend trip to their home in Arizona to meet his mother. I've seen the disappointment in the wrinkle that forms between his brow every time I make up a reason not to.

For a moment my facade slips slightly, all the reasons for its presence disappearing from my mind as I watch this beautiful man try to keep closed the floodgates of his longing for me. I reach for him, tracing my pale, trembling hands down the distressed canyons of his face. He's right, after all. Dani is exactly the kind of person I'd want to hang out with, I know that from one dinner spent watching her debate the benefits of pesticides in farming with her brother on the same breath that she used to finish the joke Jeremiah was repeating from the most recent stand-up comedy show they attended.

"I'm sorry." My voice cracks under the weight of all the walls I've put up to protect myself. "You're right."

"What was that?" His lip quivers with the hint of a smile. It's one of my favorite things about him. Where Topher held so tightly to his anger all the time, Aaron can't keep even mild frustration grasped for very long between his fists. It slips out of his hands with all the grace of a damp bar of soap in the shower.

"You heard me."

"I know." He crooks an arm around my shoulders and drags me to him, his other hand slipping under my sweater and over the bare expanse of my ass, causing warmth to pool in my belly. "I just don't get to be right that often, so I want to soak up the feeling."

"Don't get used to it." My breath mingles with his now that our lips are mere inches apart.

"Mmm, maybe I will," he hums. "I kind of like it."

I nip at his lower lip, drawing a husky laugh from him in return. He pulls back from me, his eyebrows furrowing and gaze trained on some nondescript point on the wall as though he is deep in thought.

"What are you thinking about?"

"Oh nothing," he trills, mischief dancing across his face. "Just trying to remember what we were doing before we were so rudely interrupted."

The memory draws a blush not of embarrassment but scorching desire, one he recognizes the moment it forms. He looks so confident when he sees it, so unbearably cocky, that I can't let getting what I want distract me from the perfect opportunity to humble him.

"I don't know," I muse, slowly dragging my fingers over the contours of his abdomen, lower and lower, until I'm able to grab on to his desire and hold it firmly in my palm. "Something about roasting your weenie."

Chapter Nine

I've re-read the same page of a blush-inducing romance book at least five times when I'm finally rescued by the sound of a shutting door. It's not the book's fault, really. It's perfectly riveting. The problem is that my mind is just as shrouded with clouds as the peaks of the mountains I can see in the distance through the windows, and none of the words on the page before me are getting through that fog.

I slam the book shut with as much force as the paperback will allow, glaring at the enamored couple on its cover with a misplaced frustration at their seemingly effortless road to happiness. Even the conflicts in romance books aren't really *conflicts*. They're speed bumps, meant to slow down but never stop.

That's just not reality. At least not mine. My speed bumps are military-grade security perimeters even I'm not sure how to circumvent.

Jeremiah stumbles out of the mouth of the hallway, rubbing his eyes to get rid of the remnants of the three-hour nap he just took, according to the clock on the microwave. I feel every minute of the time that has passed in my back when I rise from the oversize chair perched in front of the fireplace, a dull throb radiating from the base of my spine upward as I stretch.

An involuntary groan escapes me, causing Jeremiah to move his eyes lazily in my direction from where they were studying the contents of the fridge.

"Same," he mutters, a yawn punctuating the word. When it finishes, he smacks his lips once before continuing his search. I can see the imprint of the sheets in the bronze skin of his face, the depth of the wrinkles indicating it was a very good nap. "I swear, we're too young for sitting wrong to throw out our backs, but here we are."

I grunt my agreement while depositing the novel back in its rightful place on the crowded shelf, resigning myself to the fact that I will not be finding out how Fabio and Fabiette's story ends.

"Do you know what time they'll be back?" Jeremiah asks, more to the fridge than to me. I decide to answer anyway, glancing at my watch even though I just checked the time.

"Dani said the ride was about two and a half hours round trip, so I'd imagine they'll be home anytime now."

"Good, I'm starving." He rubs his belly to drive the message home.

Mine gurgles in response. "What are we having?"

He starts grabbing ingredients out of the fridge that must've come from the grocery run he and Dani did this morning while Aaron and I slept in. A jar of red sauce and a block of cheese are all my stomach needs to see for the grumbling to intensify.

"I'm making parmesan chicken." He adds a package of chicken breasts to the counter before searching the cabinets for the tools necessary for preparing the meal. My eyebrows shoot up in surprise, which I quickly correct before he turns around.

"You cook?" I try not to sound incredulous. The raw chicken breasts land on the wooden cutting board with a wet *slap*. He quickly butterflies each one and hammers them into submission with a precision that screams experience.

"*Do I cook?*" he mocks in a voice that's much higher than I would attribute to myself. "Aaron never told you? I kept his ass alive in college with my chef skills."

He sets up a dredging station while the oil he filled a cast-iron skillet with begins to bubble on the stove top. I watch as he expertly coats the chicken filets first in beaten eggs and then in the flour mixture, then repeats. A double dredge.

My man.

"What was Aaron like when you two first met?"

I take a seat at one of the barstools in front of the counter just as what can only be described as a cackle shakes Jeremiah's broad shoulders. "He was wild."

I suspected as much, which was why I asked in the first place. I lean onto my elbows and wait for him to elaborate, practically giddy at the idea of digging up dirt I can tease Aaron with later. When Jeremiah senses that he's being watched, he peeks up at me from under his eyelashes and shakes his head in exasperation at some memory he's recalling.

"His parents moved out to Arizona just before freshman year. They let Dani move in with her grandma so she could finish up high school in Loveless, but it meant Aaron had pretty much no supervision through college, at least those first two years before Dani joined us on campus."

"Yeah, I'd say having your baby sister as a witness would put a bit of a damper on things."

He smiles at the mention of his wife, obviously smitten. "It wasn't so bad. But he definitely had to rein it in on the drinking and the smoking and the girls—"

He catches himself, looking up at me from the thermometer he's using to temp the chicken with a panicked expression. "My bad."

I shrug, brushing a hand through the air. "I know he had a life before I was part of it; doesn't bother me."

There's only a minor tug of jealousy, nothing I can't ignore.

Hell, I had a life before him, too. It's part of why I felt so comfortable right from the start. He didn't care what I'd done or who I'd been with, never even asked. Not like every other man before him who thought he had some right to be the first and the last and the only. As if I were damaged goods otherwise.

He throws an appreciative smile over his shoulder at me, using tongs to remove a golden-brown breast from the oil. "I like that. Dani's the same way. When you're with the person you're meant to be with, everyone before is insignificant."

I want to correct him, to say that Aaron and I aren't the same as him and Dani. That we aren't meant to be; that it's possible I'm not *meant* to be with anyone. But I don't. And I don't have time to question my restraint, because the front door swings open behind me, bringing with it the chaotic energy I've come to recognize as Aaron's presence.

"Ooh, something smells good!" he exclaims, that familiar million-watt smile right at home on his face.

Dani shuts the door behind them both, laughing as she shrugs off her coat. "We decided to make Jer's signature chicken parmesan tonight."

"And by we, she means me," Jeremiah corrects, clicking his tongs at her. She winks in return before mounting the stool beside me, smelling like flowers and horses. It's a decidedly less appealing combo than her usual scent, but I don't mention it.

Aaron takes the remaining stool, and we sit side by side by side, eagerly awaiting our dinner like a set of hungry children. Jeremiah finishes plating it all up on a bed of pasta and tops the dish off with a fancy cheese grater he had to have packed in his bag because there's no way it was just waiting for him in the old cabinets of this cottage.

"Bone apple teeth," he says with a bow.

"What did you say?" I ask.

"It's French for *enjoy*," Aaron adds sarcastically, clearly in on the joke. Dani just shakes her head and carves out a bite, closing her eyes in pure bliss when it hits her tongue.

"Fuck, I've missed your cooking!" Aaron tosses his head back and does a little jig as he chews. Jeremiah laughs and then zeroes in on me, watching expectantly as I lift the bite to my mouth. My eyes go wide when the flavors introduce themselves to my taste buds.

"Oh *wow*, that is unreal," I moan around my bite. He lets out a triumphant yelp and high-fives Dani and Aaron.

"We've impressed the restaurateur!" he says, making me laugh. "Better than Olive Garden, yeah?"

"I don't know if that's the standard you should be holding yourself to." I pause for a sip of wine. "But since you asked, yes. Definitely better than Olive Garden."

"What's better than Olive Garden?" an unfamiliar voice calls from behind us just as the sound of the door creaking open reaches my ears.

"Dad?" Dani squeals, lurching around and practically launching out of her seat.

"Dad?" Aaron and Jeremiah repeat, sounding slightly more confused.

Dad?

That one is my internal monologue.

By the time I'm able to force myself to turn and face our new visitor, Aaron has joined in on a very energetic group hug two steps inside the entrance that Jeremiah charges across the room to complete. In the fray, I catch sight of their father. He's lean and muscular just like his children, looking distinguished in a pilot's uniform.

"How are you here?" Dani asks, finally unhanding the jovial man.

He laughs, squeezing her face between his palms. "Someone has no sense of privacy and posted her exact location on her Instagram account. Which is very unsafe, by the way."

She rolls her eyes as he releases her cheeks. "Since when do you have an Instagram?"

"A while ago! Your old man is hip. I'm cool." He says it in a way that is decidedly *uncool*. "The fact that you don't follow your own father says a lot about how much you love me, though. I'll remember that at Christmas."

She makes a *pffft* sound and walks back to her dinner, making eye contact with me for the first time since her father's arrival. She must recognize the sheer terror written across my face because she mouths, *I'm sorry,* as she approaches with a pained expression.

"How long is your layover?" I hear a hint of terseness in Aaron's voice that has nothing to do with how he feels about seeing his dad and everything to do with how *I feel* about seeing his dad.

"Just overnight. Hit my hours for the day a little earlier due to a weather delay, so when I saw Daniela's post, I thought I'd surprise my kiddos."

Jeremiah's eyebrows furrow. "I didn't make enough chicken."

"Don't worry about it; I already had dinner." Their father drops his overnight bag onto the reading chair and surveys the room with his hands on his hips, finally landing on my stock-still frame. "Well, you must be Zoey! You're even prettier than Aaron described you!"

He's coming my way with his arms outstretched, and the realization dawns on me that he's going to hug me at the same moment it hits Aaron, who slaps a hand against his face so he won't have to watch the horror scene unfold.

I don't have time to react because his dad's arms are already around me. He smells like Old Spice the same way Topher's grandpa always did, and I'm so focused on stopping myself from panic-vomiting that I miss it when he speaks.

"What was that?" I ask after a beat, earning a mildly confused look from the man that quickly passes.

"I said my name is Wayne and it's nice to meet you, *finally.*"

The last part he says while glaring at Aaron, as if he had any say in the matter. "This one's been keeping you from us."

I don't correct him, but I'm overwhelmed with appreciation for Aaron the moment I realize he's taken the fall for this, too, even when he didn't have to. Even when he could've said, *I want her to come, she's just bizarrely opposed to meeting you guys for no apparent reason.*

The appreciation is quickly replaced by shame at the reminder that Aaron deserves far better than the tiny pieces of me I've been willing to give.

He shrugs at Wayne apologetically, a hardness in the set of his jaw that tells me he doesn't know what to do or say. He's watching me like I'm a skittish stray dog, liable to bite at any moment. I can clearly see the emotions warring on his expressive face: joy at seeing his father, fear of what it means for our relationship.

I can't offer him much. There's too much of me damaged and afraid and not worth sharing anyway. But I can offer him this, and so I do. I smile my best smile and brush the curls back from my face, holding the air in my lungs for as long as it takes to feel confident that my voice won't tremble, and then I let it out, squeezing his father's bicep affectionately and earning a grin in response.

"I'm so happy to finally meet you, too."

Chapter Ten

I never thought anyone could be chattier than Aaron.

That was until I met his father.

I finally retreat to our room when the ancient cuckoo clock by the fireplace announces blaringly that it's midnight, prompting Wayne and Jeremiah to finally take it down off the wall and find its nighttime mute button, or whatever it is those things come with that shuts them up. I take the momentary distraction as my opportunity to give an Irish goodbye and disappear without a word.

When our door is shut behind me, I pad across the worn-down carpet and lock myself inside the bathroom, pressing my back against the door and sliding down to the cold tile. I rest my forehead against my knees, dragging in breath after raggedy breath, trying to stop the world from spinning.

It takes a gargantuan effort to be somebody you're not. To stand in the midst of something that makes you so terrified and, when the fear does not subside, to do the thing anyway. I dissolve into an earthquake of anxiety-induced full-body shakes, teeth chattering as if I were knee-deep in snow. All my false brevity has expired, and in its wake I become who I really am: an echo of a woman, void of all the things that once made me the person I pretended to be tonight.

Before Topher's hands ever marked my body, I was the life of the party. I was the girl who could talk to anyone, from the two-year-old standing next to me in line at a grocery store to the entire extended family of the boy I dated when I was fifteen. I was vibrant and unabashedly myself, a force to be reckoned with by all accounts from my friends and family.

Piled up on the sofa tonight, participating in a lively game of charades with a roomful of people who love Aaron the most, I tried to dig deep and access that girl. I went into the basement of my soul and found the old box of my personality traits and put it on like a Halloween costume that's two seasons too small. I laughed and I bantered, and I watched as my performance lit Aaron up from the inside out, his face growing animated and relaxed when he saw me acting out the iconic pranks from *Home Alone* alongside his sister to the delight of Wayne, who guessed our movie immediately when I took an imaginary staple gun to my butt cheek.

I've taken too much from myself. I know it because now, as the adrenaline wears off and the past twenty-four hours—or more accurately, the past eleven years—catch up with me, I feel hollow inside.

Dragging my body off the floor, anger at myself for being so weak begins to build. I stumble toward the standing shower, cranking the water up until steam billows out. I strip off my clothes and sit under the blasting stream of water, hoping the heat will do something to stop the shaking.

When my fingertips have withered into raisins, I dry myself off and finally unlock the door. In the light falling onto the bed from above the vanity, I see Aaron is already in bed, shirtless with one arm propped behind his head as he watches me. A soft smile tugs at his lips as his gaze travels up my towel-wrapped body, but it quickly falls away when he sees my expression.

"What's wrong?"

"Nothing," I whisper, too quickly for it to be the truth. I pray that he will just let it slide, but if I know Aaron, there's not a chance in hell.

He studies me as I don my pajamas, a soft button-down and matching cotton pants. His dark eyebrows are knitted together, casting a shadow over his eyes. I turn the bathroom light off, shrouding us both in a blanket of darkness that hides any unwelcome facial expressions from one another.

When I climb into the bed and tuck myself warily under the covers, his arm reaches for me in the dark. "Come here."

I do as he asks, allowing myself to be swaddled in his strong embrace and tucked neatly against his chest. My fingertips must be cold when they rest against his chest, because he shivers under my touch.

"I'm so sorry about Dad showing up." His breath tousles the slow-drying curls atop my head. "I mean, I'm thrilled he finally got to meet you, but I never meant for you to be ambushed like that. Truly."

A sigh escapes my lips. "It's okay." I scratch softly at the smattering of hair on his chest while my mind races with all the unspoken pain simmering below the still surface of my exterior. "I like your dad. And Dani. And Jeremiah's an incredible cook."

"Yeah?" Hesitant excitement tips his voice up an octave. "They really like you, too."

He sounds so happy I only feel worse about being so miserable. I suddenly feel exhausted by the act, a yawn pouring out of me like a boiling teapot releasing some of the built-up steam. I decide to change the subject to something easier, because if we keep talking about his family's approval rating for me, I'm going to explode.

"Before you two got home, Jeremiah was telling me some interesting things about you in college," I begin, eliciting a shameful groan from him that rumbles against my ear. "About partying and drinking and *girls*—"

"I'm gonna kill him," he quips, tugging at the covers like he's got to get up and do it right this moment.

I pull him back against me, the laugh his embarrassment pulls out of me working wonders to add seconds to the doomsday clock of my anxiety.

"Relax. You know I don't care about that stuff. It was just funny to confirm my suspicions."

"Oh? And what were your suspicions?"

"That you were a wild child."

I feel the vibration of the resulting *harrumph* rumbling through his chest. I tilt my head up to study him in the faint moonlight filtering through the sheer curtains that cover the window in the corner of the room. He's smiling, but it's tight on his face.

"What?"

"It's nothing." A frustrated sigh passes through his full lips. He's looking past me, focusing instead on the hand he isn't using to hold me. He's picking at the frayed edge of our blanket. "I guess I was a little wild. It was hard because growing up Dad was always away, flying to some exotic location while I was at home with Mom and Dani, and every time he'd leave, he'd tell me the same thing. 'While I'm gone, you're the man of the house, all right? You gotta take care of your mom and your sister for me.'"

"That's a lot of pressure to put on a kid." My heartbeat stumbles over itself when I picture Aaron as a child, all mischievous boy energy and abundant love. The same man he is now in a smaller package. How much of himself did he have to deny in the process of making sure everyone else was okay?

He nods almost imperceptibly. "Sometimes it felt like the only time I got to be a kid was when I was fucking around with Chase out in the mountains."

"Is that why you didn't move to Arizona after college?"

"Yeah. I mean, don't get me wrong, I love my parents. And it would be nice to live closer to them. But in Loveless, I could live away from their expectations and pressure. And Dani settled in Denver after she got her degree and married Jeremiah, so I'm still close enough to her that we can be a part of each other's lives."

"So how'd you end up teaching, then?" I draw phantom shapes on his warm skin. "Seems like a big switch to go from rebelling against responsibility to being in charge of a buttload of children."

He snickers and I pop my head up. "What?"

"Nothing. I just like it when you use 'buttload' as a unit of measurement."

I smack his chest gently and lay my head back down.

"I don't know." He hesitates like he absolutely *does* know but doesn't want to say whatever it is. I wait patiently, leaving an expectant silence in the room for him to fill. "I picked teaching because what else are you going to do with a generic biology degree? And at first, I guess I was just one of the kids, really. Still am, most days."

He says the last part with a chuckle that draws one from me, too. I'm picturing the island of lost boys in *Peter Pan*, with all their chaos and mess and poor leadership.

"But since meeting you..." The words are a whisper, a nervous opener. He pauses, leaving space for me to stop him from what comes next. I don't know why, but I find myself waiting with bated breath for what he's about to say.

"Since meeting you, things started to slowly change. I found myself wanting to step up and be the kind of man you deserve, and that bled into all parts of my life. Even teaching."

I don't know what to say, so I remain silent. I sit in the quiet, the air thick with longing, and focus on taking steady, measured breaths until a familiar gentle snore escapes his lungs. His hand goes limp where it rests on my back, and I lift myself up so I can see his face. His jaw has gone slack, that soft snore the only evidence he's alive. He looks so peaceful, the exact opposite of how I feel with my heart hammering against the walls of my chest.

I ease myself out from his embrace, crawl out of the bed, and shove my feet into my slippers. It feels like the walls of the suddenly too-small room are closing in on me, and I need to get out. I need to get air.

Every floorboard feels like a land mine as I tiptoe quietly down the hallway, expecting to find their father asleep on the couch. When I exit the inspirational wall art capital of the world, I'm surprised to come upon an empty couch, still made up with the sheets we found in the linen closet. I quickly scan the room, my heart in my throat. The door to the screened porch is slightly ajar, and I silently curse that my planned asylum is occupied.

Doing my best to tread quietly, I move closer to the cracked doorway and the soft hum of voices trickling through the gap. I recognize the baritone of Wayne's voice almost immediately, followed by the lilting tone of Dani's. They're chatting animatedly, I can see as much from my vantage point, hunched over and tucked against the fireplace to remain out of sight in the darkness of the living room.

"I like her; she's got some spunk to her that that boy needs." An amused chuckle punctuates Wayne's words. "But what do you think? You've spent more time with her than me."

I can only see the side of Wayne's face from where I'm squatting, but I have a full view of Dani's as she turns to him with a thoughtful expression.

"She's really guarded." She bites her lip as she measures the words she wants to say. "Aaron didn't tell her ahead of time that it was his sister she'd be spending the weekend with, and when she found out, she looked downright panicked. And then when you showed up, well, I thought she was going to die right on the spot."

Thanks a lot, Dani. I groan internally, unable to see what Wayne's reaction is to this revelation.

"But seeing them interact, seeing the way Aaron's hot-air balloon of a personality lifts her up at the same time she tethers him to something steadier..." She hums, the hint of a smile soft-

77

ening her stunning features. "I don't know, Dad. It's just really special."

"You think our boy has finally found the one?" He asks like he already knows the answer.

"I do," she says, and it's the last thing I hear before the roaring in my ears blocks out all other noise.

It all crashes over me at once. The last few months of Aaron steadily showing he wants more even as I dance around the inevitable discussion. Meeting his sister and his father unexpectedly and pretending I can be the woman they need me to be, all upbeat and friendly and perfect. Aaron's words as he drifted off to sleep, like I'm some occasion he's trying to rise to rather than the other way around. Hope that I could be who he thinks I am ballooning in my chest till it's so tight there's no room for my lungs to let any air in.

That hope sours in my stomach, because where there is hope, there can be love and where there is love, there is a noose and as it tightens around my neck, I feel like I'm going to be sick, and even though the chicken parmesan was delicious the first time around, I have no desire to taste it on its way back up.

Before I can think about the implications of my decision, I pull my phone from the pocket of my pajama pants and open my text messages, knowing Eden keeps her sound on when I'm out of town in case someone from the bar calls her with an emergency.

This is an emergency, a red alert if there ever was one, and I type out the message with trembling fingers before hitting send and locking my phone. I retreat as quietly back down the hallway as I can, mentally begging each weathered floorboard to keep its shit together long enough for me to pass without them squeaking.

Aaron is fast asleep in the bed, still unaware of my absence. I gather my things in stealth mode, staring at him the whole time for any traces of movement. By the time my phone buzzes with a text from Eden, I have my bag slung over my shoulder and my slippers swapped out for boots.

Eden: On my way.

I send a silent *thank you* up to the universe that I have a best friend who loves me enough not to question why I'm asking her to drive an hour to rescue me in the middle of the night. I know she'll want answers when she gets here, and at this point I have to find a way to give them because it's eating me up from the inside out, but for the moment the fact that she's in her car and driving in my direction is enough to drive me to tears.

I spare a final glance at Aaron's sleeping form before tearing my gaze away. It hurts so badly to leave him, but it'll hurt more if I stay. I start back down the hallway, managing to reach the front door without the floors betraying me. I watch for movement coming from the screened-in porch as I slowly tug the front door open just wide enough for me and my bag to pass through, thanking my lucky stars when it doesn't let out its telltale squeak.

I hold my breath as I stalk across the gravel toward the canopied driveway that will take me away from here, grateful for Wayne's booming laugh that covers the sound of my retreat.

It's not till I'm safely distanced from the lakeside cottage and its inhabitants, walking determinedly up the road in the direction I know Eden will come from, that I let myself begin to weep. Sorrow for myself, which I rarely entertain, blooms in my chest and fills my eyes with hot tears. And on its trail follows the bloodhound of shame, white-hot flames of it burning up my soul when I think of Aaron and how he will feel waking up alone.

Chapter Eleven

"Zoey, Christ," Eden whisper-shouts. "It's forty degrees and you're in pajamas!"

I roll my eyes, slipping into the car while purposefully ignoring the puff of steam my ragged breath produces. Once I'm settled in the warm cocoon of her CR-V, the heated seats begin unraveling the tension coiled in my spine. She pulls a three-point turn that Mr. Turner from drivers' education would be proud of, and then we are climbing back up the mountain and away from my mistakes.

She's playing the *Ledges* album by Noah Gundersen, my all-time favorite. His voice is the only sound in the cabin of the car for so long I half lose my nerve to tell her the truth whenever she finally asks. Though I know she won't ask, at least not with her words. It'll be with her signature look of understanding and empathy that she will crumble all my defenses.

The minutes pass and I feel my soul drawing in on itself, like the ocean right before a tsunami wave crashes over a portside city and leaves nothing in its path. I'm afraid that once I open the floodgates, there will be no survivors in my little village, least of all me.

I stare at her engagement ring glinting under the streetlamps we pass. It seems so at home there on her finger, like it was always meant to be. I used to stare at my hand in high school and imagine the day Topher would propose, my delusions of forever conveniently failing to take into consideration all the reasons that would be a terrible idea. How could I have wanted a future with him when I was already so miserable in my present?

The car rolls to a lurching stop at the bequest of a red light. I'm so used to Eden's delayed attempts at breaking that I just let my body flop back heavily into the seat. I can't even be bothered to give my usual chastisement, which is what finally draws her undivided attention to me. She and I both know something is wrong if I'm not commenting on her driving skills. Or her lack thereof.

She's still studying me long after the light has turned to green, but it's the middle of the night and we haven't encountered a single other soul on the road since she plucked me up like a hitchhiker, so she slides the gearshift into park and turns to face me head-on.

As I suspected, not a word is spoken. Her face is wide open, every emotion on display. Concern, fear, and confusion are all at war with each other, fighting to stake the ultimate claim on her expression. When none of them are able to secure a victory, one delicate eyebrow lifts incrementally. That's my cue.

My face grows hot under her stare, and I let my gaze fall to my lap, clicking my nails together as if I can somehow communicate to her in Morse code all the things that must be said. When I finally get over the hill of my own embarrassment, I find myself staring down the thing I've truly been dreading: the mountain of fear that she will be hurt by what I've kept from her. That she will blame herself.

Because I know Eden. I've known her my whole life. And this is the only secret I've ever kept from her for longer than a gift-giving season. She will be confused as to why I didn't feel I could trust her. She will wish she could've done something, anything, to stop it from happening.

I know because I've wished the same.

"Does Aaron know you left?" The question is a fracture in the ice she's trying to break for me.

I give her an appreciative half-volume smile before shaking my head. "No."

"Did he hurt you?"

There's a broiling rage just below the surface of her disbelief. I shake my head even harder, hoping my eyes convey the sincerity of my words. "No. *God*, no."

She sucks in a relieved breath and lets it out slowly before reaching for the hand I've left resting on my lap. It's clammy and trembling, but she doesn't seem to mind. She just wraps it up in hers and rubs her thumb steadily across the pale, dry skin of my knuckles.

"What happened?"

I draw my bottom lip between my teeth, looking her fully in the eye as I fall apart.

I don't know how long l cry for, but she doesn't make any attempt to stop me. It's long enough for the entire album to cycle back around to the beginning, her Spotify set to a loop. When I'm finally able to suck in a breath, the words all come out in a whoosh.

"Do you remember that time my ribs got bruised in high school?"

A deep valley forms in the skin between her eyebrows, but she nods. "You got kicked by that horse. Your parents pulled you out of riding lessons after that."

"The horse never kicked me."

"What do you mean, the horse didn't kick you? You went to a hospital, Zo. I *saw* the bruises."

"*The horse* didn't kick me," I repeat, quieter this time and directed at our joined hands. "Topher did."

"Topher did what?" She asks it as if she's misheard me. As if she's begging me to tell her a different truth, a better one.

I wish I could.

"At first, it was nothing major. A shove here or there. He'd grab my arm a little too tight or just say something nasty to me. I'd tell myself it wasn't really him. He got into steroids really heavily after he joined the wrestling team, and it did something to his brain. At least, that's what I thought at the time. Now I think it probably just unleashed what was already there."

I'm not sure if she realizes her mouth is agape. She gets the worst chapped lips of anyone I know in the winter. She single-hand-edly keeps Burt's Bees in business with all the vanilla lip balm she buys. I can tell the weather is already getting to her because there's a split up the side of her bottom lip. I stare at it instead of her eyes, trying not to come completely unraveled.

"He started stealing liquor from his grandpa's cabinet and refilling the bottles with water. The more he drank, the more I saw that rage build in him until it was so close to the surface it leaped out and touched me. We were having sex, and he slapped me across the face and called me a whore."

She's starting to cry, so I close my eyes because I can't handle both of our pain. I can't even manage my own.

"It just kept getting worse, and I was telling myself that he didn't mean it. It wasn't him. I blamed it on the steroids. On the alcohol." I squeeze my eyes so tight stars explode across my vision. When I finally open them, it's no better. Now the entire galaxy swirls in the pool of tears, blocking my line of sight. "God, Eden, I was so in love I wouldn't leave him. I just took it. I even convinced myself I deserved it.

"I don't know what I did to piss him off so bad, but that night he was worse than I've ever seen him. He was convinced I was cheating on him. Kept saying the guys on the wrestling team were talking about fucking me and if I kept being such a slut, he'd be tempted to let them. I never cheated on him, Eden."

She takes hold of my shirtsleeve like it's a life raft and she's drowning. Or maybe I'm the one who's drowning and it's her who's trying to save me. She uses her other hand to tip my chin up until I'm facing her. She speaks through a torrent of tears. "You could've fucked the entire school and he'd still never have a right to touch you, Zo."

My shoulders crumple as I feel a piece of blame I didn't even know I'd been holding on to slowly detaching itself from me, leaving a jagged edge where it tears off.

"He shoved me to the floor, and he kicked me. Again and again and again. Even when I begged him to stop. Even when I couldn't draw in enough air to keep begging."

She unbuckles her seat belt and lunges across the car, wrapping her arms around me as best she can in this position and stroking the back of my head. The sounds of our sobs run together the same way the lines between our pain so often blur, leaving it feeling like they belong to both of us at once. It makes the burden a little lighter even as the memories are weighing me down.

"How did I not know?"

"Because I didn't want you to."

She sits back and stares at me in disbelief, her porcelain skin blotchy and emerald eyes swimming with a million questions. I do my best to shrug at her, but it's haphazard and more of a convulsion.

"After I broke things off with him, he'd drive by my house at night and rev his truck so I'd know he was out there. So I'd know he still had control. I hated myself for staying, but a small part of me hated myself for leaving, too. Because I still loved him. That's the part they don't tell you about. Even under all that fear, there's still love. It's the last thing to go."

I wipe my eyes, sucking in a breath and shaking my head to clear it. "I never wanted to feel that way again, and so I made sure that I didn't. Dating is fine, as long as there are no strings, because strings are what you get tangled in when you try to get away, and I could never allow myself to be trapped like that again."

Eden bites her lip like it's going to speak without her permission. For someone who measures every word so carefully, that must terrify her. I sit back in my seat and face forward, watching the traffic light turn from yellow to red, red to green, then back to yellow once more.

"Aaron brought me to the cabin to spend the weekend with his sister and her husband. He told me they were just friends of his because he knew if I thought I was meeting the family, I wouldn't come."

"Oh no?" Her tone tells me that she isn't sure it's actually that bad.

"And then his dad showed up."

"*Oh no.*"

There it is. "Eden, I can't be that girl. I can't meet the family and dote on the guy and pretend I'm capable of giving him everything he's asked for."

"What exactly has he asked for?" I can see her studying my profile out of the corner of my eye.

"Me." I whisper it like it's a secret. Like it's fragile.

She makes a clicking sound with her tongue before a sigh tumbles out. "Maybe I should refer you to Stephen. You have issues that require a professional."

I whip my head around to face her, the shock on her face just as apparent as mine that she would pull a me-style move like that. I find myself doubled over with laughter that quickly infects her, and soon we're belly laughing with an intensity that only comes after crying for so long. Manically, as if your life depends on it.

"Stephen would hate me," I reply when I'm finally able to get some air. I roll down the window and let the crisp night seep into the car, hoping all the sadness will find its way out. An even exchange. "You went to therapy to understand why you were the way you were. I know exactly what's wrong with me. I'm just not sure if fixing it is worth it to me."

The look she gives me is one of both compassion and a healthy dose of *come the fuck on.*

"Listen, if anyone gets how hard it is to do that work to heal yourself, it's me." She holds my gaze. "But if you don't, it'll just catch up to you eventually anyway. You can only run for so long."

"I can't even run for five minutes."

"Exactly."

A horn blares from behind us, startling me so badly my heart jumps straight past my throat and into my mouth. Eden lets out a scream before logic kicks in and she shifts into drive, pulling forward through the intersection. The pickup truck that just took ten years off my life seizes the opportunity to zoom around her like the driver could've done in the first place.

Her scream dissolves into a fit of giggles while I glare at the truck's taillights as they grow smaller and smaller in the distance, wishing not for the first time that I knew an ounce of witchcraft and could use it to curse the day the driver was born.

Eden turns the volume back up on the radio, Noah's voice numbing the anger until it's just a faint throb at the base of my neck. She reaches for my hand once more, holding it through every chorus and verse and bridge, till we find our way home to Loveless.

Chapter Twelve

I 've been lying in bed with my eyes closed for an immeasurable amount of time, hoping if I can feign sleep for long enough it really will come. Hoping perhaps I can convince myself that I'm not listening for the vibration of my phone receiving a call. That I'm not hoping it's from Aaron, wanting to tell me he's forgiven me before I've even apologized.

But my phone doesn't ring, and slowly the orange-tinged sunlight of a new autumn day finds its way in through the gaps between my curtains. I roll away from the windows with a groan, covering my head with a pillow that smells like Aaron. Spice and sweetness and warmth. My throat grows thick with the scent of it and the fresh round of tears it inspires.

I don't know how I became this person. For the better part of nine years I managed to keep every man at arm's length. I enjoyed them until I didn't, and then I went on my merry way. But from the day Aaron walked into the bar to order lunch for him and Chase, he's been slowly embedding himself underneath my skin, and now he's metastasized to my bloodstream. He's everywhere.

No, not everywhere, I tell myself. *I haven't let him take over my heart. I don't love him. I can still walk away unscathed.*

The tearstains on my pillowcase beg to differ, but I ignore them and climb out of bed, resigned to the fact that I've pulled my first all-nighter since the time three winters ago when I got snowed in at the bar with Gary and we sampled every offering on the shelf until the snowplows found their way downtown.

Two large scoops of Rose's medium roast dumped into my coffee maker seems like a good place to start. I pour water up to the fill line and flip the switch, only noticing after the first few gurgling drops of the aromatic liquid find their way through that I've forgotten to put the pot underneath. I grab it from the dishwasher without checking if it's clean and shove it into place, watching it fill through glazed-over eyes.

It takes two cups before I feel like I'm above water again, though now my skin buzzes like it's got a direct feed to a live wire. I sink into the cushions of my green velvet sectional and tuck my feet under a blanket, suddenly wishing Bagel were here to sit on my lap and warm me up, something he'll do as long as I don't pet him or make eye contact.

Maybe I should get a cat.

The doorknob begins to rattle before I can fall too far down that rabbit hole, jolting me from the trance I'm in. It turns and the door swings open, revealing a morose Aaron balancing a petite peperomia plant in a terra-cotta pot on his palm.

"Eden texted after she dropped you off, so I wouldn't worry."

He's still standing on the doorstep, warily taking in the scene. I imagine what it must look like to him, me in the same pajamas I wore last night for my grand escape, sitting cross-legged on my couch with the third cup of coffee in my hand, staring at a television that isn't turned on. My hair was an absolute rat's nest when I woke up, so I strung it as high up on my head as it would go and secured it in place with a thick navy-blue scrunchie. I swipe at my eyes, hoping he can't tell how much I've been crying while also knowing there's no way in hell. The bags under my eyes are so plush I could prob-ably take a nap on them.

"I gave you that key for emergencies, so if I slipped and fell in the shower, the medics wouldn't find me naked," I say in an attempt at being lighthearted. "I'm alive. You could've just knocked."

He just gives me a tight nod and presses his lips together, clearly not in the mood for jokes.

"I would've brought you a bouquet, but you hate cut flowers," he says, gesturing toward me with the peperomia, little vines of tightly clustered, button-sized leaves bouncing with the movement. "So I stopped by that nursery you like and got this instead."

"I ran away in the middle of the night, and you brought me a plant?"

He shrugs, looking sheepish. "I just wanted to say I'm sorry."

I realize he didn't get what I was trying to imply. And I feel ridiculous having this conversation across the room, so I stand and pad over to him, taking the little pot out of his hand. "I didn't mean that I'm not glad you're here, just that of the two of us, I'm the one who should be apologizing."

The corner of his lip twitches, and he plucks the plant back out of my hand. "Well, glad we agree. Thank you so much for the apology plant. I've been wanting one."

I offer him a sardonic smile and step to the side, gesturing for him to finally cross over the threshold and get out of the cold morning air. A young couple pushing a stroller carrying a babbling toddler catches my eye as I swing the door shut, and I try to return their friendly wave with an enthusiasm I don't feel.

Aaron sets the plant on my coffee table, then lowers himself onto the couch, perched so close to the edge I'm afraid that voluptuous butt of his is going to slip right off. I haven't seen him this nervous to be in my house ever, not even the first night he came over. Granted, I did a lot to put him at ease that night.

The memory brings a flush of heat creeping up my neck, but not the usual one of desire. This time it's full of shame. Guilt that I've made him this uneasy. Regret for how far from that first night we've fallen.

I sit next to him on the couch, reaching around his midsection and pulling him down with me into the cushions. It's awkward and uncomfortable, but he's close and that's all that matters in the moment. My lower back can yell at me later.

"What did I do wrong?" he asks, sounding more like a child than the man I hold in my arms.

It's the question that kept me up last night, not because it needed asking but because it didn't. Because truthfully, he didn't do anything wrong. Should he have kept it from me that we were spending the weekend with his sister? Probably not. But can I really blame him for taking such drastic measures after I've made the hoops he has to jump through so impossibly high? I'm beginning to think it'd be unfair. The truth is, he's not the man who should be apologizing for the way things have happened between us. But the one responsible is thousands of miles away and not any sorrier than he was the night he threw me to the ground like an animal instead of a woman he supposedly loved.

"You didn't," I whisper, my voice cracking on the words. I look up at his face, and suddenly I'm so overcome with embarrassment I can't think straight. I can't believe I've let him peek behind the curtain of my resolve and see this shrunken and shameful part of me. His gaze is deep and soothing, like stepping into a bath of Epsom salts.

"Then what's going on, Zoey?" His voice is pleading, desperate to understand why I keep taking one step closer just to turn around and run ten yards away. "Just talk to me. Let me be there for you."

My spine grows rigid at his words. The flow of air halts in my lungs. Just as I feel my heart stretching toward him, my better senses come careening downward with a hand clenched around the organ to shove it back into my chest where it belongs. Needing him is exactly what will get me hurt, ensnaring me in the cage of dependency.

I'm scrambling, desperate to find a way to answer him that will satisfy his questions but deflect them from hitting home. I study his face, questioning and hopeful, and I let my lips crash into the soft landing of his in a desperate attempt to keep us both afloat.

The taste of mint overwhelms my senses when he draws me in, tugging at my bottom lip with a soft drag of his teeth. He threads his fingers through my hair, unraveling my top knot and dropping the scrunchie to the side. His touch is reverent, cradling my head in his hands as he ebbs into the kiss and flows out of it, taking my anxiety away on the tide.

I flatten a palm against his chest, feeling the familiar thrum of his heartbeat hammering against my touch as I push him onto his back and follow him down. I'm straddling his tapered waist and trailing kisses along his jawline, finding the tender outcrop of his ear where I nibble at his earlobe until he sighs. The hint of stubble scrapes against my sensitive skin when I press my lips tenderly against his throat. I'm tugging his long-sleeved shirt up from his waist as I nip at his collarbone when two strong hands clamp down on my wrists and hold me in place.

I look up at him, confused and a little drunk on his presence, sobering instantly when I see the pained look in his eyes. I rock back on my heels, leaving him sprawled on his back, eyes the same color as my cushions.

"What's wrong?" I ask quietly because I'm not sure that I want to hear the answer.

His eyebrows are screwed together so tightly they almost become one. He drags a hand over his face and groans softly. It sounds like a wounded animal, the noise threatening to bring the tears back with a vengeance.

"I'm not going to have sex with you, Zo."

I balk, scrambling another foot away from him on the couch. He sits up, looking so incredibly sorry for the waves of rejection he senses washing over me.

"You're not here with me, mentally," he explains, clasping his hands together like he's in prayer. His eyes close slowly and remain that way for too long, before finally fluttering open with walls shielding the emotions normally filling his irises. "Sometimes it feels like you just use sex to avoid actually talking to me."

It rings too true for my liking. I reel backward from the emotional blow, clutching at my chest to relieve some of the sting. "You need to leave."

"Come on, Zo, just talk to me for once." He leans forward, reaching for me.

It's too late for that.

"I want you to get out of my house."

"Don't be like that, Zoey. Please. It's me."

"I know it's you," I say, meaning more than he could possibly understand. Then I lock eyes with him and hold myself stock-still, hoping he will feel my next words like a physical push out the door. "Now go."

It finds purchase, and I regret it almost immediately. But I'm not a woman to go back on her word and he's already walking away, pausing only to look at me over his shoulder.

"I can't keep doing this." The words are filled with remorse, his warm voice so thick with emotion it sounds like tires on a gravel road. My heart begs to go to him even as I picture myself growing roots deep down into the couch that hold me in place.

"What are you saying?"

He shakes his head at me, slowly at first and then quickly like he can't believe what he's about to do. "You know what I'm saying."

He pulls something from his back pocket, and I watch with disbelief as he unlaces my house key from its ring and sets it on the television stand, patting it once before walking out the door.

It takes until the count of fifteen for me to be confident that my shaky legs will hold me up. Once they feel safely solid beneath me, I retrieve the key, curling my fist so tightly around it that the rough edges will no doubt leave an imprint on my skin. I stumble across the room, drag the sliding glass door open, and step out onto the cold grass of my backyard.

Scanning the yard, I find one of Penny's holes on the far end next to the fence I share with the sweet old lady in the house behind me. She's probably looking out her second-story window at me kneeling in my pajamas on the earth still wet with dew, wondering why I'm dropping some shiny metal object she can't make out from so far away and shoveling the scattered dirt back over the hole in which I've planted it. She's likely puzzled as I stumble away without bothering to dust the dirt off my knees and hands. I wonder if she'll keep an eye out for what kind of life will sprout up from the earth, born from such messy circumstances.

Chapter Thirteen

I contemplate calling Eden but decide I can't risk waking her after forcing her to come pick me up in the middle of the night. Instead I drag myself into the shower and let the scorching water do its best to thaw me out. It takes double the normal amount of conditioner to get the tangles out of my hair. When my fingers can finally run through it freely, I just sit under the stream and stare blankly at the various shades of brown in the shower tile. Even after the water is as hot as it can be and my skin is an angry crimson, I'm still frozen inside.

I bundle up in several layers to compensate for my lack thereof last night before making my way to the kitchen to see what's available for me to cook. I've just unloaded all the necessary ingredients to make my grandpa's sausage gravy and biscuits when my phone lights up on the counter. When I pick it up, Rose's name flashes across the screen alongside a photo of her with Cleo perched on her shoulders, their expressions a matching set of disdain. I took the photo without her knowledge at a community event in the spring, and it's still my favorite candid shot of the two of them.

I accept the call and begin returning the ingredients to my

fridge, my stomach agreeing that we're well overdue for a pastry run from 8th & Main.

"Hey, Rose." I pinch the phone between my shoulder and ear so I can move the full gallon of milk with both hands. "I was just about to come see you."

Or at least I am now. The order of events isn't really important.

"Well, that's good," she says nervously, her normally singsong voice sounding more like the movie score for an ominous scene. "'Cause the police are on their way to your bar."

"What now?" I groan, slipping on a pair of tennis shoes.

"Better if you see it in person."

"Be there in ten." I end the call, locking my door behind me and trying not to be sentimental about the damn key I'm holding and how I buried its twin in my backyard.

Can this day get any worse?

Yes, as it turns out, it can.

As I'm approaching Nomads, I see Rose standing in front of the door with her hands perched on her hips, belly round and protruding from her jacket. She's staring at the large window that allows what little natural light we have into the bar, except now it's letting in a breeze, too.

I whip into one of the parallel spots out front, not caring if I'm taking prime parking for Chase and Rose's businesses that are actually open on Sunday's. I'm too preoccupied with the gaping hole in the window of my bar, thousands of tiny shards of glass littering the sidewalk in front of it. The midday sun reflects a rainbow off their jagged edges. It'd be beautiful if it weren't so devastating.

I'm stepping out onto the sidewalk just as the heavy oak door to Nomads pushes open and Officer New-in-Town exits the building.

He tips his hat when he sees me just like I'd expect a good ole Southern boy like him to do. A broad, admittedly gorgeous smile spreads across his face but fractures when it catches the scowl on mine.

"Zoey, good to see you again." His drawl is as strong as ever. Rose is looking at him with wide eyes and a jaw dropped so low I almost reach out and pick it up off the floor for her, lest she cut it on the shards of glass.

"Officer, wish I could say the same."

The corners of his lips twitch, but he looks over his shoulder toward the window and then back at me, shrugging like he gets it. "None taken." He pulls a little notebook out of his pocket and scans what he's presumably written.

"I didn't say no offense."

He and Rose both send shocked gazes my way, but his is the first to dissolve into amusement. Rose, however, is aghast.

"Zoey, Jesus." She smacks my shoulder. "He's here to help."

I roll my eyes at no one in particular before training them on Kit. "Funny, no one started messing with my bar until you moved into town."

He doesn't honor that with a response, and his lack of a quick quip makes my own unnecessary maliciousness all the more glaring. I shift my weight from one foot to another, staring at the glittery glass on the ground.

"Sorry about that; it's just been a really bad day."

"Understand that." His smug smile has returned when I glance up. The damage to his nose is even more apparent in the daylight, and I wonder how he broke it. Topher's looked like that, the result of a fight he picked with the wrong freshman in the bathrooms of our high school. He was too stubborn to go to the doctor, and it never set correctly as it healed. "Mind if I make it worse?"

My train of thought is effectively derailed. Even Rose manages to wipe the obvious adoration off her face and replace it with confusion. "Come again?"

He gestures over his shoulder at the shattered window with his pen, clicking it for emphasis.

"See, someone shattered your window last night," he says, and the irritated moan that comes out of me as a response is entirely involuntary.

"Yes, Officer, I can clearly see that."

"It's Kit," he says firmly, winking at me. I hear Rose gasp to my right but refuse to look at her and see the effect this man has on her. She's a married woman, for Christ's sake. The pregnancy hormones have gone to her head. "And yes, I know you can see that the window is broken. But what else did you notice?"

I'm not in the mood for the guessing game he's playing. My stomach is growling for one of Rose's pastries now that I'm within smelling distance, and my eyes are burning from lack of sleep and an overabundance of tears. He must see that I'm at the edge of my rope because he quits trying to give me directions to whatever point he's trying to make and decides to just escort me there himself.

"The glass is all on the outside, on the sidewalk, see?" He points with the pen again at the rainbow of sharp objects between us.

"Yes, and...?"

He huffs, looking from me to Rose and back again. I'm glaring at him, and Rose gives a little shake of her head that I can just see out of the corner of my eye; clearly neither of us are following.

"If someone were standing on the sidewalk and threw something at your window, the majority of the glass would be inside your bar, along with the weapon of choice." He points to the ground behind me, and I turn around, seeing a rock the size of my fist resting in the bed of flowers around the tree planted in the sidewalk.

"They were inside my bar?" I shake my head. "But how? The security system would've been on. Eden always makes sure it's on."

She's been religious about safety for as long as I've known her, but it reached a whole new level when she moved here after everything with her stepfather. I guess once you realize the people you trust most in the world are willing to hurt you, it's not hard to believe that everyone else might be, too.

"The door was unlocked when I arrived. Maybe you should call Eden and make sure something didn't come up and she just forgot," Kit says.

I pick up my phone and select her name from my favorites, placing it on speakerphone so we can all hear her response. It only rings twice before she picks up.

"Hey, Zo, are you okay?" Her voice is so full of concern that for a moment I'm embarrassed. Rose's eyes flash to me with a question I avoid by glancing at Kit, only to find him staring at me with an intense curiosity in what I can now tell are hazel eyes. My cheeks grow warm, and I transfer my gaze to my feet, where there are no questioning eyes to return the favor.

"Yeah, I'm good now," I murmur, hoping the other two witnesses don't catch that part. I contemplate switching her off speaker but it's a decision I've made already and if I go back now, it'll be even more obvious that something's amiss. The less people I have to explain things to, the better. "I was just calling to see if you turned on the security system before you left last night."

The line goes silent for a moment before I hear a groan that has my stomach flipping over itself.

"I'm *so* sorry, Zo." A low buzz of chatter fades into the background when she walks out of wherever she's at to go somewhere quieter. "I didn't get to work on end-of-month invoicing until after we closed because it was so busy, and then your SOS text came while I was still finishing up. I must've forgotten to turn it on before I left to come get you."

I pinch the bridge of my nose to abate some of the pressure there. This day is wearing on my already fragile psyche, and it's not even lunchtime yet. I'm overwhelmed with the urge to get in my car and drive over to Aaron's so he can wrap me in his arms and I can forget all that's happened today.

Except I can't do that *because of what's happened today.*

"Why? What's wrong, Zo?" Her voice startles me. I'd almost forgotten she was on the other end of the call. "Did someone slash more tires?"

I shake my head even though she can't see me. "No, someone threw a rock through the window. From inside the bar."

"They did *what?*" Panic and guilt pitch her voice so high it becomes shrill. "Oh my God, Zo, I'm so sorry. This is all my fault."

Kit is nodding and I scowl at him, hand on hip so he knows I mean business. "It's not your fault, Eden, it's mine. I'm the one who made you perform Uber duties in the middle of the night."

"But still, I should've remembered to turn the alarm on. I always turn the alarm on."

"I know you do," I say softly. I hate for her to beat herself up about this. I suddenly wish I'd never even told her. I could've lied and said a tree branch fell and took out the window, sparing her the guilt trip. "It's really okay. I'll take care of things. Enjoy the rest of your day off."

"No, we're just at the Raven. I'll have Chase drive us back, we'll be there in thirty minutes."

"Tell her I want one of their chicken salad sandwiches!" Kit says.

"Who's that?" she asks. I can practically hear the alarm bells going off in her brain. *Ironic, that.*

"It's the rookie officer I was telling you about."

"Oh yeah, I met Kit Friday night. He came in for a beer with Tomas while you were out. Tell him I'll be right there with a sandwich for both of you."

He does a little fist pump and shouts, "Yes!"

"Me too!" Rose pipes up. Eden mumbles an acknowledgment,

and before I can stop her, I hear her ordering three chicken salad sandwiches and lemonades to go.

"See you soon!" she says. "Sorry again, Zo."

The call ends and I'm left with two people staring at me who look as hungry as my stomach feels.

"I'll go have Mitch plate up some pastries for everyone." Rose points toward the coffee shop. "And then I'll have him run home and grab some plywood to board up your window until you can get insurance to replace it."

"These historic buildings have pretty specific window requirements. Might be a minute," Kit adds unhelpfully.

Her face softens as she looks at him and smiles. "Yeah, you're right." She turns on her heel as gracefully as she can at seven months pregnant and marches back to 8th & Main.

"So, you called for a rescue Uber from your coworker in the middle of the night?" Kit wiggles his eyebrows at me. "What kind of debauchery were you getting up to?"

My exhale comes out as more of a huff. "She's my best friend, and none of your business."

"Things not working out with the boyfriend?" He leans against the doorframe and crosses his arms over his chest. He looks so smug the blush on my face intensifies, spurred on by his verbal jabs.

"What makes you think that?" I try not to sound as prickly as I feel but fail miserably.

He shrugs, that half smile still playing on his thin lips. He's got nothing on Aaron's pillowy, delicious mouth. The thought causes a pang in my heart where normally there'd be uninhibited longing. I shake my head to clear it.

"It's just that, normally, if you were somewhere in the middle of the night and needed help, you'd call a boyfriend for that." He considers my reaction, scanning my face for a twitch or a flicker of something he'll recognize. He must come up empty because he presses on. "But you didn't. So either he was incapacitated or you two broke up."

I scoff, pushing past him into Nomads in search of a broom to begin cleaning up the glass. He watches me reach into the utility closet at the other end of the room and grab a broom and a dustpan. I hold his gaze on my return, determined not to back down.

"You know, if it were me, I'd come get you in the middle of the night."

"Not if you were the one I was running away from."

I regret the words as soon as I say them, but they're out there and he's already latched on to them, mulling them over as he calculates his response. It's so easy for him, this back and forth. I can tell he's used to getting what he wants. In another life I would've loved this. I lived for it. Because men like him never ask for anything more than someone pretty to wear on their arm, and that's an easy role to fill without losing any piece of myself in the process.

In this life, though, I've spent the morning making a series of mistakes I deeply suspect I'll be paying for forever. In this life, Kit is getting on my last nerve.

"Hey, Zo, sorry about your window!" Mitchell calls, breaking whatever mental standoff Kit and I are having. I look away from his unwavering smirk over to Mitchell, who's ambling down the sidewalk with a to-go cup in one hand and a measuring tape in the other. He offers the coffee to me after nodding his acknowledgment at Kit.

"That's a lavender latte, little something to cheer you up." He smiles down at me. Mitchell is tall and all sharp angles with a mop of curls on his head that matches the one I've noticed forming on Cleo's as she gets older. "Don't worry; Rose made it, not me. So it's actually good."

"Thanks, Mitch. I appreciate that." I take a sip of the sweet, floral liquid, and a hum of satisfaction forms at the back of my throat.

He gestures at the window with the measuring tape, and I focus on the movement so as to ignore the fact that Kit is still staring at me. "Figured I'd take some measurements before I head home and grab the boards to cover it up."

"Go right ahead." He smiles and passes me by, breaking Kit's line of sight. I sigh from relief, grateful for any reprieve I can get.

Chapter Fourteen

"**R**ed or white wine?" the waspish event coordinator asks.

"Yes," I reply.

She and Eden exchange a glance while Chase just chuckles. I'm only mildly disappointed when she hands me a glass of white wine, ignoring my not-so-subtle request for both. I take a sip of the chardonnay, pacified by its buttery flavor.

"So," the coordinator says, eyeing me warily before training her gaze on the happy couple. "Will it just be the three of you or are there any parents joining the tour? Often we find that anyone helping financially with the big day likes to be included."

The tall, willowy woman sporting a tightly bound chignon clearly misses the full-body wince her mention of parents elicits in Eden, but I don't. I gulp down a mouthful of chardonnay and sidle up to my best friend, looping an arm through hers and smiling witheringly at Barbara or Clarice or whatever wannabe posh name she told us to call her.

"I'm the mother of the bride." I offer a proud, unwavering smile while patting Eden's arm.

She freezes, looking at Eden and Chase like she's waiting for the punch line. To his credit, Chase manages to maintain a serious expression. The rigidity in Eden's spine eases, and she relaxes into me with a grateful smile and a sidelong glance.

When no one follows it up, Hillary or Janice or whatever clears her throat and plasters an artificial smile on her face, teeth the same shade of white as the string of pearls around her neck.

"Well then, if this is all, let's begin the tour."

She wiggles her fingers in a half-hearted gesture for us to follow. An impractical pair of stilettos carries her precariously down the cobbled pathway. The *swish-swish* of her pencil skirt brushing against her legs highlights each step.

I bump hips with Eden, resting my head against her shoulder before the unsteady walk makes it impossible to maintain the position. She offers me a soft grin that doesn't reach her eyes, the evergreen orbs full of shadows brought on by the event coordinator's comment.

"Thank you," she whispers, gaze scanning the rolling hills of the vineyard we're touring as a possible venue for the wedding. Chase is chatting easily with Millicent or Allegra or whatever. The man could make a friend out of a fence post if left alone with it long enough. He's covering for his bride-to-be, giving her a chance to recover. My gaze flickers to where their joined hands swing back and forth between them, his thumb stroking hers reassuringly.

"Anytime, *daughter*." My wink earns a giggle, and just like that the clouds part in her eyes and light fills them once more.

"Max two hundred guests if you want an indoor ceremony in the barn, three-fifty if you're open to an outdoor location, of which we have two options."

Eden shakes her head, eyebrows furrowed. "We're actually looking for something a lot more intimate." Chase winks at her before catching my eye on her other side. I scrunch my nose in mock disgust, which he ignores. "We only have fifty guests, tops. We don't want to feel like we're swimming in the place."

"Oh," the wasp croons theatrically. "Well, that's not much of a party!"

Eden pinches her lips together but doesn't honor that with a response.

"Anywho"—*who actually says that out loud?*—"your guests will be treated to a gorgeous spread during cocktail hour while you and the hubby"—*again, cringe*—"take photographs with the wedding party. We have decor-included packages for every budget, starting at ten grand. We even offer ice sculptures!"

Chase and I simultaneously choke on our own spit. The fact that it's both of us sputtering rather than one makes it that much harder to play it off as a cough. Eden still has that tight-lipped expression frozen on her face, but I'm well enough versed in her emotions to see the glint of panic in the twitch of her eyebrow.

We step into a barn that's more of a mansion, where two white-coat-wearing chefs have a gorgeous spread of exotic cheeses and various labels of wine from the vineyard arranged on a live-edge oak table. It's like something out of a movie, right down to the curled-up mustaches on their aloof faces.

"We will let you three enjoy the taste-testing portion by yourselves so you can discuss any questions you might have. I will be just outside with Jacques and Peter if you have any questions." With that, Gianna or Portia or whatever takes her leave from the rustic farmhouse, along with her chef/henchmen.

"It's a no for me," Chase mumbles around a mouthful of gouda.

"No kidding," Eden huffs, uncorking a bottle of merlot and pouring each of us a glass. "Is it just me, or is that woman insanely out of touch with reality?"

"Not just you." I take the glass she offers. "Did anyone catch her name?"

Chase removes his baseball cap and runs a hand through his brunette waves. "Francesca, I think?"

I groan. "Of course it is."

105

Chase laughs, wrapping an arm around Eden's waist and raising his glass to me. "Thank you for being Eden's mom today. Mine had a work conflict and was so bummed she couldn't make it."

"What can I say? It's just the kind of girl I am."

"Speaking of which," Eden adds, gesturing around us at the exposed wooden beams and grand oak tables. "This seems much more like the kind of wedding you'd want than me."

"Except I don't want a wedding."

"Oh please, you and Aaron are going to be married in no time." Chase waves his hand dismissively. His statement is followed by radio silence as Eden and I exchange a tense glance, trying to gauge how much can be said. His gaze darts back and forth between our faces. "What? What's that look?"

"Aaron and I broke up."

"You and Aaron *what*?" Chase glances from me to Eden, who grimaces. "Since when?"

"Since I ran away in the middle of the night after he introduced me to his family." I take the bottle of merlot from Eden's hand, pouring myself a refill. Thank God I'm not the designated driver.

"Yeah, but I thought he texted Eden and said he was going by your place to apologize? He even sent her plant options to choose from." Chase crosses his arms, his abandoned glass of wine sitting untouched next to the empty plate of cheese he demolished.

I shrug, unable to meet his eyes. I know Chase loves me; we had an established friendship before he fell in love with Eden that has only grown stronger since. But Aaron is his lifelong best friend. If the situations were reversed, I'd have a hard time picking Chase's side over Eden's.

"It's okay, Zo. We don't need to have this discussion. It's not really any of our business," Eden offers, trying to give me a way out. Chase's brown eyes grow wide with surprise. I doubt any of us thought we'd see the day where Eden would speak up so I, of all people, don't have to. Talk about a role reversal.

"It's fine." I try to shake my head like it's no big deal, but my heart's not in it. "We just want different things. It'll be okay. It's for the best really."

Eden worries at her lower lip. Chase's expression softens as his gaze flicks from me to Eden before he nods his head in understanding. "Been there. Don't worry, you two will figure things out. You have to. You're soulmates."

"Chase Taylor, I never pegged you for a romantic." I pluck a grape from the bundle on the table, popping it into my mouth so I'll stop drinking wine. If I have too much more, I'll find myself curled up on this rustic barnwood floor, crying my eyes out. Francesca would never tolerate such behavior.

Chase hooks an arm around Eden's neck and plants a firm kiss on her freckled cheek, the skin there flushing red from the wine and affection. She glances at him adoringly, and the emotion they exchange in that moment is so intense I can feel it from the other side of the table.

"What can I say? I'm feeling inspired." He nuzzles her neck, eliciting a sickeningly sweet giggle. Warmth blooms in my chest, joy for my friend overwhelming any jealousy and sadness that might've taken root otherwise. "Also, this place is very not us and way out of budget, so I say we run away before the scary lady returns and tells us more about ice sculptures."

"Deal," Eden and I say simultaneously. Chase pockets another handful of untouched cheese I'd arranged on my plate and presses a hand against mine and Eden's backs, urging us toward the fire exit.

I let myself be led away, trying to leave my thoughts behind at the table with the gorgonzola that no one touched. Trying to believe what it is I'm telling them. That this is the best possible outcome for both parties. That Aaron will be happier when he doesn't have to deal with me.

His words from that night in the cabin run through my head on an endless loop. If we didn't break up, he'd spend forever thinking I was this idealized version of myself, a perfect woman he had to change himself to be worthy of. He'd never be able to see the situation clearly or understand that when he holds me, he's holding the broken remains of a woman left behind by a man who only knew how to handle women with cruelty.

I've been trying to don the mask I wore successfully for years. The Zoey this town knows and loves. A workaholic, no-nonsense woman with a weak spot for beautiful, aloof men. It feels like it doesn't fit anymore. My heart has swollen up from the beating it's taken the last few days, the last few months really, and the mask is two sizes too small. All the suppressed memories of Topher surfacing like bodies in the water of my brain have left me reeling and unsteady on my feet.

It'll just take time, I reassure myself. In a few days, a few weeks max, the swelling will go down and my heart will feel normal again. Even if I can't go back to who I was before I knew Topher, I can at least return to the safety of the facade I built before Aaron took a pickax to it.

I climb into the back seat of Chase's Silverado, looking out the window just as Francesca peeks her head through the emergency exit door. Her overly Botoxed forehead scrunches up in surprise as best it can when the truck rumbles to life. I flip her the bird, knowing she probably can't see it through the tinted windows, but hoping desperately that she does. For wearing impractical shoes and looking down her beak-like nose at us and for making Eden remember her lack of parents on a day that should've been joyful.

Fuck you, Francesca.

Chapter Fifteen

Safeway is blissfully empty when Monday morning rolls around and I have to go stock up on buns after our delivery guy forgot a pallet at the warehouse. I'm emotionally hungover and feeling like I've been hit by a truck, but it's either this or we're bunless until Wednesday's truck arrives. My contacts have been driving me nuts after too many accidental overnight wears, so I've foregone the pesky things and opted for my glasses instead. Between that, my linen overalls, and my unruly curls barely contained in a tortoiseshell clip, I'm grateful for the lack of witnesses in the store.

"Weird location for a first date, but I'll take it."

I whip my head around at the familiar drawl so quickly my glasses fly off my face. I hear but can't see them clatter across the linoleum. A blurry but undeniably male shape squats down to pick them up, offering them to me after rubbing the lenses with the corner of his shirt. I grab the glasses from him and return them to their rightful location, bringing Kit's features into focus.

The scent of hair cream comes off him in waves, smelling like sandalwood and a hair salon all wrapped up in the tousled brunette locks atop his pretty head. His ever-present cocky grin is looking especially smug in the fluorescent lighting. I glance at his cart, finding a predictable cast of characters. Preworkout and protein bars are strewn about next to an impressive stack of chicken breasts and an industrial container of rice.

He follows my line of sight, one of his eyebrows shooting upward when his gaze rises to meet mine. A flicker of movement on his chest catches my eye as he flexes his pecs. "You like a man who works out?"

There aren't enough words in the English language for me to express to him just how much I do not like a man who thinks working out is a personality trait, so I settle for a withering stare and a shake of my head. He pouts as much as his thin lower lip will allow him, the jutting of his chin making that sharp jawline even more prominent.

"You're a tough nut to crack, Zoey Allen." He perches his elbows on the push bar of his cart, folding his hands together so he can rest his chin on them. "Lucky for you, I like a challenge."

He's so predictable that it's almost endearing. He's exactly the type of man I would've found myself wrapped up in and underneath not too long ago. A man who makes it clear how attractive he finds my body while wanting nothing from my heart. An easy ask. A painless one. So why does it do nothing but exhaust me now?

"I have buns to buy, so either leave me alone or try to keep up."

Shock passes over his face. I catch a glimpse of it before turning back to my cart and pushing onward toward the bread aisle. It's not long before I hear the distinct squeak of a wheel following closely behind me.

"I honestly didn't think that would work."

The corner of my mouth twitches toward a frown. "Oh come on, don't let your asshole confidence falter now. It's unbecoming."

"Ouch." I glance over my shoulder, and he has a palm splayed against his chest. His admittedly broad, muscular chest. "You wound me."

I roll my eyes and return to the task at hand, eyeing the nearly empty display of hamburger buns with a touch more exasperation than reasonable. One hand planted firmly on my hip, I roll my head back and let out a groan that can probably be heard three aisles over.

"Look, as much as I'd love to hear you make that noise, I'd rather wait till we're in the comfort of my bedroom." His eyes are sparkling with amusement and more than a hint of lust.

I'm surprised angry gashes don't bloom across his skin with the daggers I'm shooting his way. "You're going to be waiting a long time."

"Finding everything okay?" a cherub of a boy asks, cheerily unaware of what he's interrupted. He looks so young I would think he should be in school this time of day instead of working. His cheeks are round and rosy, a polite smile causing them to swell. His adolescent face is in direct contrast with his six-foot-tall body, towering over me and even edging out Kit by an inch or two. He's dressed in black from head to toe, with knee pads strapped on like he's going rollerblading. He's tugging a cart behind him stocked to the brim with carbs. Inconveniently, not the carbs I need.

"Actually, I'm here for hamburger buns for my restaurant and you seem to be nearly out. Do you have any more in the back?"

"I don't know!" He gives me a cheery smile. "I'll go check and be back in a jiffy."

He's far enough away that I doubt he can hear it when Kit mumbles, "Did that large child just say 'jiffy'?" I turn to him and shrug, equally surprised. He studies me for a moment, his hazel eyes looking like a forest floor full of amused swirls of brown and green and gold. He holds the stare for a beat longer than is comfortable before clearing his throat. "Anyway, this works out. Now we have more time to chat."

Curiosity gets the better of me, winning out over my annoyance. I don't know what it is about him that irks me; whether it's the awareness that he was once exactly my type, or the reality that some unevolved part of me still thinks he might be. Probably a combination of both. "What would you like to chat about, Kit?"

"I don't know, the weather? Sports? Ole Miss, my alma mater, just won their fifth game in a row. We're undefeated this season." I make snoring noises at him. The annoyance is taking the lead again. "Okay, so no sports. Oh, I know! We could talk about why you broke up with your boyfriend?"

My spine goes rigid, and my cheeks flare with prickly heat. "What makes you think we broke up?"

"You called your friend to come rescue you from him in the middle of the night." He levels a hard stare on mine, grabbing a bag of plain English muffins off the shelf and tossing them into his cart without even looking. "That doesn't exactly scream *happy couple*."

"I believe I said I'd be running away from *you* in the middle of the night, not Aaron." I stare at my chipped fingernail polish, picking at a large periwinkle chunk until it finally flakes free.

"It was a hypothetical 'you' in response to my comment about being your boyfriend. Context clues, baby." When my gaze flickers upward, he's still watching me, smug as ever. "So, what happened?"

"You're awfully keen on inserting yourself where you're not wanted, you know that?"

"I'm a cop." He flashes his badge before tucking it back into his jeans pocket. "Comes with the territory."

Another groan forms at the base of my throat, but I catch myself before letting it get too far, not wanting to invite another comment on our potential sex lives. I don't know why I feel so protective of Aaron, like telling Kit what happened is somehow betraying his trust. I remind myself this is good, chatting with a handsome cop in the middle of Safeway. Maybe moving on is the only way to shove every memory of Topher back into the dusty filing cabinet in the recesses of my brain from whence it came. Tears burn the back of my eyes when I realize I'll have to add a cabinet for Aaron, too.

Nope, not going there. Not in a grocery store, and not in front of

Kit. I swallow the lump in my throat. "Let's just say I have commitment issues."

"Weren't the two of you together for like a year?" One manicured eyebrow quirks up. He must read the obvious question on my face because he throws his hands up in a display of innocence. "It's a small town; people talk."

All I can do is sigh. By *people* he probably means Tomas. No more free beer for the gossipy sheriff. "What's your point?"

He shrugs. "Just sounds a hell of a lot like commitment to me."

I open my mouth to object, to say it was just casual, but I press my lips into a firm line instead. I'm beginning to sound stupid even to myself. "He was ready for the next step. I was happy to stay where we were." I stare at my feet, those damn tears pricking the backs of my eyes. "I don't know if I'll ever be ready for that."

Kit claps a firm hand onto my shoulder, squeezing it when I look up at him. He clears his throat when our eyes meet, letting his gaze fall away first. "Can't say that I blame you. I'm never getting married again."

"Again?" The shock helps keep the tears at bay, if only for a moment. I suck in a shuddering breath, appalled at myself. I am not the type to cry in public. I reserve my tears for late-night car rides with Eden and hot showers where no one can hear my sobs.

If he sees the glassiness in my eyes, he doesn't comment. He drops his hand from my shoulder, gaze far away. I immediately miss the feeling of a warm body, any body, touching mine. "I was in the military before I moved here. I was like everyone else in my hometown, desperate to get out with no way to leave, so I joined the Air Force. Married the first girl who batted her eyelashes at me in a bar. She cheated on me while I was deployed overseas."

He says it all so matter-of-fact it almost sounds rehearsed. He sees the frown on my face and plants a thumb on each side of my mouth, tugging the corners of my lips upward. "Relax, I'm fine.

Lesson learned. Marriage isn't for me. I just wanna have a good time with no strings attached."

It sounds so much like my inner monologue it's physically painful to hear out loud. Do I sound that cynical? That obviously hurt? God, I hope not.

The man-baby returns carrying my buns in a crate. He asks how many packs I want and I tell him all of them, so he just drops the crate right into my cart. I thank him and turn to leave, lost in thoughts about Aaron and how this must be what he thinks when he listens to me ramble about wanting to keep things casual.

Thank the universe he left me, for his own sake.

That squeaky wheel breaks through the self-loathing soundtrack of my thoughts. Kit joins me in line for the checkout behind an elderly woman hunched over a cartful of Ensure and Activia. She's giving the cashier hell about an expired coupon, and I lock eyes with the poor guy behind the counter, sending my sincerest apologies to him through telepathy. People in the service industry have to stick together.

"So that was a fantastic first date. When can I see you again?" Kit asks cheerfully, bumping my backside with the front of his cart. I glare at him before directing my attention to the candy rack.

"We literally just discussed how we both aren't interested in serious relationships." I grab a pack of peanut M&M's off the display, tossing them onto the belt alongside my buns.

"Exactly. We're perfect for each other."

I scoff, looking first at my candy and carbs, then over to his cart full of protein. "Doubt that."

The cashier finally gives in and overrides the coupon, deciding it's not worth arguing with someone who clearly has nothing better to do. The lady writes him a check, because of course she does, and he runs it through the printer before depositing it in his cash drawer and handing her the receipt. When she finally hobbles away, the relief on her face is evident.

"Fun way to start your day, huh?" I ask, taking the M&M's when he offers them instead of letting them go into a bag with the buns. I rip the corner open and pop one in my mouth. Breakfast of champions.

"I just try to tell myself we'll all be there one day," the man replies. "Fifty dollars and seventy-eight cents, please. Cash or card? Or will you too be using the ancient form of payment known as personal check?"

I scrunch my nose in disdain at the same time laughter bubbles up, turning the sound into an accidental snort. My skin flushes with embarrassment as the sound echoes back to me. "Card." I insert the chip and wait for it to yell at me that it's done.

"Thanks for shopping at Safeway." He offers a tired smile. "Have a good day."

"You too." I smile sympathetically in return.

I'm pushing the cart toward the exit and chewing on a candy-coated peanut when I hear Kit call after me. I turn around to look at him, but I don't stop walking away. It's too early in the morning and I'm too emotionally fragile to be entertaining these kinds of conversations with him, especially standing close enough to get high off his hair cream fumes.

"You didn't tell me when our date is!" he shouts. The clerk looks up at me expectantly. This is clearly the most entertaining thing that's happened to him this morning. I almost offer him a job at the bar. Where there are drunk people, there are infinite sources of entertainment.

Kit is still watching me, a half smile playing on his lips. The cockiness dripping off him is so thick I'm tempted to run back and put a *Wet Floor* sign next to his feet. It reminds me of Topher, I realize with a start. Not at the end, when his confidence had devolved into possessiveness, but at the beginning. For a moment I can see him appearing on the other side of my locker door when I slammed it shut, eyes nearly black and bearing an intensity my seventeen-year-old self had never come up against before. I can feel the quickening in my gut, like fluttering wings. It was a thrill back then.

Now it's a warning sign.

"Oops," I reply, shrugging as if to say, *What can you do?* "See you around, Officer."

I see his smile falter a fraction but don't wait for his response, disappearing behind the soft *swish* of the automatic doors.

Chapter Sixteen

"**A**re we sure a cold drink is the move for a fall menu?" I ask. I know Eden knows what she's doing, but I'm shivering just looking at the drink she's preparing.

"I think the broken heater has gotten to your brain." An aggressive huff blows a long bang off her face so she can see clearly as she settles an apple slice onto the martini glass rim. "Believe it or not, most cocktails are in fact cold."

My teeth are chattering slightly, so I nod instead of replying. The heat went out sometime in the middle of the night, leaving both the bar and Gary's apartment uninhabitable. We closed for the day to patrons but bundled up in our finest parkas to work on fall menu design. The food menu is complete, and now that our bellies are full, Santi, Gary, and I are piled up on the barstools in desperate hopes of obtaining alcohol-induced warmth.

"Thyme? Why the hell are you putting thyme in a cocktail?" Gary asks. Eden doesn't honor him with a response. For a man who orders the same dinner with the same beer every evening, menu tasting isn't as fun as it is for the rest of us. Still, he insists on being involved, *"Lest you all turn my rugged bar into some hoity-toity lemonade stand."*

I don't bother reminding him it's my bar now when he says things like that. I know better than most how things that were once yours stay with you long after most people think you should've let them go.

Eden lays bar napkins in front of each of us, setting three rosy-pink cocktails on top of them. I take a sip of the liquid as she explains the recipe, excitement dancing in her emerald eyes. She may not be as much of a workaholic as I am, but when it comes to inventing new ways to get people drunk, she shines.

"It's gin, lemon juice, agave nectar for some sweetness, and then sparkling apple cider. The thyme helps round out the gin." She says the last part pointedly, gaze locked on Gary. To his credit, he appears pleasantly surprised.

"It'll go well with the fish," Santi comments. I nod my agreement, taking another swig. Eden smiles at him and then looks at me, waiting for my approval.

A chuckle vibrates off my lips. "You know I have a weak spot for gin." I swear her face pales a little as she no doubt recollects the time she had to wash my vomit-soaked hair after a night when I overindulged in gin and tonics. It's a memory that used to make me cringe; now it makes me nostalgic for college and simpler times. "It's just very cold."

She lifts the drink from my hand and swallows it in one long gulp. When the glass is empty, she lowers it to the metal countertop and burps. "I'll make you an Irish coffee."

"Yay!" I give her a round of enthusiastic applause.

She gets to work setting the coffeepot to brew. When it finally gurgles to life, she loops a finger around the neck of the gin and returns it to its rightful place on the display shelf. She settles the apple cider back into the fridge and bumps it shut with her hip. When she grabs the bundle of thyme sprigs, Gary lets out a sputtering cough that's almost a laugh.

We all look over at him, startled. His gray eyes dance between our faces like he's trying to gear up for something. "Why do you think she's making us all these drinks?"

I stare at him, not blinking. I have no clue what he's getting at. "Because we're menu tasting?"

He shakes his head, glancing around me at Santi like he might know the answer. He's wheezing now from his barely suppressed laughter. Eden's standing across from me, frozen in puzzlement. Santi must look as clueless as the rest of us because Gary gives up with an exasperated grumble. "Because she's got a lot of thyme on her hands!"

A chorus of groans fills the room. Santi grips his gut like the terrible joke has induced nausea. Eden, emboldened by alcohol, throws the bundle at Gary, tiny sprigs of thyme going everywhere.

"Now who's got a lot of thyme?" she taunts.

"Children, children," I interrupt, stifling a giggle. "You're wasting thyme!"

"I hate you all," Santi moans.

By the time Eden's got my coffee prepared, smelling like she heavy-handed the Bailey's, Gary and I have crumbled the herb up and rubbed it thoroughly into Santi's buzz cut.

I take a sip of the hot liquid, feeling it melt the ice that has encased my bones. I'm not sure if I'm imagining it or if I really can see my breath in here. I wait for Santi to finish dusting the thyme out of his hair before asking him, "When did the repair guy say he'd be here?"

"Around two o'clock." He settles back into his seat, taking a sip of his cocktail calmly like the last five minutes of shenanigans never happened. Too bad there are still tiny sprigs of thyme littered across his shoulders like dandruff.

I check my watch and then let out a heavy sigh. "We'll be day-drunk by then."

"*We?*" Gary and Santi ask simultaneously. Eden doesn't chime in, just glances up from the double shot of Bailey's she's pouring into her own mug of coffee.

"We," I repeat, gesturing to Eden and myself. She winks and brings her coffee to her lips.

Santi shakes his head, the corners of his lips twitching. "Have you heard anything else about the vandalism?"

"Nope." I pop my lips on the *P*.

"Tomas said they still think it might be kids just messing around, since there was nothing stolen when they broke the window. Doesn't take a mastermind to open an unlocked door," Gary adds. Eden winces and color fills her cheeks. I offer her a sympathetic smile, trying to ease her guilt. No matter how many times I tell her not to blame herself, I know it's her natural instinct to do just that.

In reality the fault is all mine. The cherry on top of all my shame for what happened that night.

"You don't think it could be any of the new guys, right?" Gary pipes up. "Did you run background checks on any of them?"

I shake my head. "Santi vouched for Mateo, and you said you'd known Eric since he was 'knee-high to a grasshopper' so I considered that my background check."

"What about Marcelin?" Gary asks.

"Marcelin wouldn't hurt a fly," Eden interjects. She has a soft spot for anyone marooned from their family, rooted in her intimate familiarity with the situation. Gary raises his eyebrows but doesn't comment, looking from her to me and then craning his neck to lock eyes with Santi.

"He's pretty quiet. Mostly keeps to himself," Santi says. "But I see him in church every Sunday."

"That doesn't mean much," Eden scoffs, forgetting which side she's on. When she feels us all staring at her, she shakes her head to clear it of whatever memory is giving her that solemn expression. "All I'm saying is I don't think it's Marcelin. It's probably just stupid kids with nothing better to do, like Tomas said."

Just then, the front door rattles, startling all of us. We look at each other as if taking attendance, confirming everyone's here. I scoot off the barstool and land on two wobbly feet, the effects of my sampling catching up faster than I expected. The clock beside the office door reads just past noon. As I turn the lock on the door, I'm silently hoping it's the repairman coming by early to save us from the cold.

Two jade-colored eyes hit me like a splash of cold water to the face. Aaron either doesn't notice my shock or pretends not to, pointing at the *Closed for Maintenance* sign I printed out and taped to the door this morning. "Can I come in?"

I look over my shoulder at Gary, Eden, and Santi, who have all stopped talking and are watching our exchange intently. When they catch me looking, they break their respective stares and all resume a theatrical version of normalcy, complete with a whistled cartoon theme song coming from Gary.

"Erm, it might be better if we talk out here." I gesture beyond him to the sidewalk. If it's difficult to talk in a crowded bar, it's even worse in an empty one with three nosy coworkers. "It isn't any warmer inside. Our heat went out."

He simply nods and I join him outside, pulling the heavy oak door shut behind me. But not before I see three disappointed expressions aimed my way. *Bunch of gossips.*

"So." He crosses his arms over his chest. He's wearing a thick North Face jacket to keep out the cold, and I'm overwhelmed with the desire to unzip it and slip inside, wrap my arms around his waist and snuggle close. I shove my hands into my back pockets in an attempt to ignore the urge.

"So," I finally reply, realizing he hasn't followed the word up with anything else in all the awkward minutes I've spent imagining us entwined once more. I start to wonder what is going on in his brain before I quickly remind myself I probably don't want to know.

"I'm sorry for how I walked out on you. I shouldn't have left things the way I did."

I don't know what I expected him to say, but apologizing wasn't even in the top five possibilities. How he could think, even after all that I've done to screw this up, that anything is his fault is beyond me. I shift from one foot to the other, unsure where to go from here.

"This is the part where you apologize." He leans in to whisper the words. The spiced scent of him is so familiar as it envelops me, so intense that for a moment all I want to do is cry. I swallow back the lump in my throat, but I'm unable to speak. I know the second I do, the second I try to tell him how sorry I am and how right he is, I will break. I can't expect him to pick up all the jagged pieces and risk cutting himself on me.

He studies my face, waiting for the words to come. Waiting for me to tell him what I wouldn't that day, to tell him why I'm incapable of giving him the relationship he wants so badly. When seconds turn into minutes, the silence grows heavier until it's so massive I'm afraid I'll be crushed beneath it.

"Seriously, Zoey? After everything we've been through, there's nothing you want to say to me?" I stare at our feet because I can't face him, can't take the hurt working its way into every inch of his body. "We can fix this, Zo. All you have to do is tell me what's wrong, what you're holding back, and we can fix it. After everything we've been through together, don't you think we're worth that?"

I'm frozen in place, recounting every promise I've ever made to myself to rise above all of this. Above needing a man or even wanting one for more than a night. It rings so hollow in my brain, so empty of any conviction. My gaze rises to meet his, but it feels like I'm looking at him through a telescope from the other side of an ocean of pain and fear. I watch his expression harden when he mistakes my silence for indifference.

"Fine. If you want to sit there and pretend like the last year and a half never happened, like *we* never happened, then so be it. But I refuse. I love you so goddamn much, Zoey, and it's killing me. I don't understand why you won't let me be there for you. What secret could possibly be so bad that I couldn't handle it? How could it be worth losing everything we have, everything we are to each other?"

He steps closer to me and I can't breathe. My body knows he's right there; it desperately wants to reach for him and never let go. But my mind feels like it's so far away it can never be reached.

He's staring at me intently, as if he can get me to open up by sheer force of will. I realize he'll never stop trying, never stop hoping for me to change. He can't see how poisonous the plant he holds in his hands is; he's too distracted by the beautiful array of flowers.

"Everything okay here?"

I didn't even hear Kit approach. I turn to face him, hoping he'll take one look at both of our faces and go the fuck home.

Well, he's in his uniform, so he can't go home. But go the fuck away from *here*.

"It's fine, Officer; we're just talking," Aaron says. He sounds completely exhausted, like talking with me—or at me, since I haven't offered much to this conversation—has taken everything out of him. I want to shake him and say this is only the tip of the iceberg. If he thinks me not opening up is exhausting, he'd hate dealing with all the shit I keep bottled up inside.

"Is that true, Zo? Are you 'fine'?" Kit asks, turning to me. It's the closest thing to genuine concern I've ever seen from him, even more so than the two times he's been investigating literal crimes against me.

"Do you two know each other?" Aaron eyes Kit warily.

"Yeah, when people are vandalizing your bar, you tend to get friendly with the local police." It's the most words I've said since we've been standing here, and they sound more defensive than I intend them to. I'm desperate for Kit to get the picture that he is not wanted here.

My tone is picked up on, though not by the intended target. Aaron steps back, studying my face. "Get friendly?"

It takes a beat for the implication in his words to hit, and by the time it does I'm the last to know. A smile tugs at the corner of Kit's lips, but he valiantly tamps it down when he catches me glaring at him. I'm not usually one to be speechless, and this is exactly why. The one time I clam up, chaos ensues.

I look back at Aaron and see the anger flaring in his eyes. If you were just some stranger on the street, that's all you'd see. But I know him, and beneath that anger is a hurt so vast and deep I could drown in it.

I realize the only way he will ever let me go, the only way he will ever stop being hurt by me, is if I take away any last remnants of hope he is harboring for a future in which we are together. I suck in a deep breath and hold it, willing myself to be brave, desperately trying to slip that wall back into place around my heart so I won't feel the blowback from the shot I'm about to fire.

"Kit and I actually went out on a date the other day," I say through gritted teeth. I'm hoping Aaron just writes it off as shivering from the cold; otherwise he'll never believe the lie.

Shock passes over both of their faces, but Aaron's is the only one I can focus on. It's all I can see. Despite the defenses I've tried to put into place, I feel every bit of the pain I've inflicted echoing back to me.

He stills, so much so I'd almost wonder if his heart was still beating if not for the throbbing vein in his forehead. He looks at Kit —who's bracing like he's prepared to fight—then returns his gaze to me. He nods once, almost imperceptibly, and then pivots on his heel and walks over to Taylor's Landing. The door flies open with the offensively cheery chime of a bell and then falls to a close, swallowing Aaron up inside.

Kit clears his throat, and I whip around to face him, wiping at tears I hadn't realized were falling. He clucks his tongue at me, reaching out and scrubbing away a stray tear with his calloused thumb. His touch feels so wrong, like the worst kind of betrayal. But at the same time I want to fall into it, desperate for some kind of warmth to grant me a reprieve from the icy touch of guilt that trails down my spine.

"Next time you plan on using me, let me know ahead of time," Kit says, shaking his head at me. "I'll put on a better performance."

With that, he continues past me down the sidewalk like he'd never stopped in the first place, and I'm left alone, realizing my parents were right about getting what you ask for not always feeling the way you thought it would.

Chapter Seventeen

W hen I step into Nomads the following morning, I'm enveloped in a warm embrace. At least that's how the heater makes it feel. The repairman worked his magic, and the cozy atmosphere is just one piece of evidence testifying to that fact. The staggering invoice waiting for me on my keyboard is another. Turns out replacing a twenty-year-old furnace is a bit of a blow to the budget.

I thumb through the paper-clipped bundles of invoices Eden has filed away as paid, mentally adding up our bills for the week. The furnace, even after splitting the cost with Gary, easily doubles all our other expenses. For a brief moment I wish I'd just embraced the cold and turned Nomads into an ice bar like the ones I've seen on television.

Once the payment has been submitted, I shrug out of my coat and remind myself just the ability to do so is well worth the money. The *click-clack* of my boots on the hardwood echoes as I cross the floor to gather my watering pot from the supply closet. The rest of the crew will be here soon to begin prepping for the lunch rush. After closing for a day, I imagine we'll be slammed with all our regulars. Very few people on Loveless's downtown strip can stand to miss out on Santi's cooking for more than twenty-four hours.

My mind is on autopilot as I flit about the room, gathering what I need to do my daily plant watering. When the can is situated in the sink basin and I've started the flow to fill it, I return to the closet and grab the ladder.

"Shit." I feel the edge of a metal rung snag on my tights. I set down the bulky thing, stepping away and watching in horror as a string of fabric stretches between me and the ladder, leaving a run in my tights that climbs straight up my thigh and disappears under my sweater dress. "Great."

I'm muttering to no one in particular, cursing myself for trying to look cute for a job that involves so much physical work. It feels pointless most of the time, but when I woke up this morning and faced a bedraggled version of myself in the mirror, I decided to do what I could to make myself feel better. If I couldn't bandage up my bleeding heart, I could at least slap some lipstick and a dress on the package it comes in.

With a frustrated sigh, I hoist the ladder up again, make my way over to the edge of the bar, and set it up. The weight of the overly full watering can makes my walk back to the ladder more of a hobble. I heft it onto a rung and let it rest there for a second, willing the tension to flow out of my neck. It's funny how irritating the inconsequential things become when your mind is tiptoeing around a massive hole, trying desperately not to fall in.

My thoughts have been running in overdrive, an unforgiving loop of Aaron's eyes when I lied to him about Kit playing on repeat. Every time I remember it, white-hot shame pools in my stomach, making me nauseous. *It's for the best*, I try to remind myself. He would've given me all the time in the world to become someone I will never be. Severing that tie was merciful, no matter how cruel it felt at the time.

I draw in a deep breath and push myself forward, both mentally and physically, trying to leave those feelings behind.

What the hell?

I draw the leaves of my golden pothos between my thumb and forefinger, rubbing them gingerly. They break away even at the gentlest touch, their normally vibrant green fading to a rotten brown. I stagger backward, nearly falling from my perch on the top rung of the ladder. I grab the beam the vining plant has woven itself around, bracing myself.

Upon further inspection, I see that the sickness has infected not just the leaves but the vines themselves. How could this happen? Surely one day of cold weather indoors couldn't do so much damage.

Lowering the hanging pot down to me brings with it the scent of bleach, filling the air around the plant so thoroughly it burns my eyes. I test the soil, dampness coming away on my fingertips.

The exploratory personality of the plant has driven it clear across the beam until it dead ends against the wall on the opposite edge of the countertop. I'm horrified to find that every single leaf has gone brittle and brown, one firm shake away from crumbling and falling to the ground just like the leaves on the trees in the mountain range beyond town.

"Who did this to you?" I whimper, cradling the pot against my chest as if it were a child. Gary got it for me as a congratulatory gift when I purchased the bar from him. Back then, the tendrils of leaves barely spilled over the edges of the pot.

First Maddie's tires, then the window, and now my plant? This doesn't seem like the random acts of some angsty teenagers. As the pungent bleach combines with fresh tears to burn my eyes, it feels absolutely personal.

I suck in a sickeningly chemical breath and release it, counting out the seconds until my pulse slows back to a normal pace. I will not cow to the tactics of a bully. Never again.

I rest the pot on the top of the ladder alongside the watering can, hurrying back down to the floor. When I push through the saloon doors, they slap against their respective walls with more force than I intend. I yank a set of scissors off their hook on the cage Santi uses to display his utensils, running back to the ladder with them clenched in my fist despite every warning my mother gave me to do no such thing.

I slice through every vine as close to the soil as possible. The existing ones are dead and gone; there's no saving them now. But there's a slim possibility that I can save the roots, and I have to try.

When I've severed every lock of hair from my beautiful plant's head, I take the pot with me into the kitchen and lower it into the three-compartment sink. I swivel the faucet until it's right overhead and then I let the water flow, flooding the soil. If I can rinse it free of as much poison as possible and then replant it in fresh soil, it might have a chance to heal. To come back to life.

Tears are agitating my contacts, adding to the burning sensation. I have to use my sleeve to wipe them away or risk what's left of the bleach getting into my eyes. It strikes me as utterly ridiculous that I'm here, bent over the sink in my empty restaurant, crying over a goddamn plant. I cough out a laugh, a racketing sob escaping my chest simultaneously. The sound is almost animalistic in the way it is so stripped down, void of any veils to hide what I'm feeling.

The back door to the kitchen opens wide, an icy breeze cutting right through my clothes so easily I might as well be naked. I startle, turning to face this intruder, this plant murderer. But all I find is Marcelin, looking as shocked as I feel.

"Sorry, miss," Marcelin says, eyes flickering around the room to avoid landing on my tear-streaked face. "I came early to work; the door was not locked."

"It wasn't locked?" I stare at him, trying to keep suspicion from creeping into my expression.

He finally levels his gaze with mine, taking in the full effect of my distress. His eyebrows furrow as his lips flatten into a grim line. "You did not unlock it?"

I shake my head slightly, a shiver running down my spine. Marcelin is still leaning against the door, holding it open with his back. He must see the shake course through me because he steps forward into the kitchen, letting the door fall shut. He glances around like he's checking if we have company, shifting his weight when he realizes we're alone.

"Marcelin, someone poisoned my plant." I watch him carefully to analyze his reaction. That wrinkle between his eyebrows turns into a canyon of concern. His mouth opens and then closes like he's too surprised to speak. I relax, only slightly, into the metal lip of the sink.

"Your plant? Why would someone want to poison your plant?" He approaches me hesitantly, like I'm a bomb that might explode on him. When I don't, he closes the distance, peering around me into the basin. His eyes go wide as he takes in the damage. "Oh miss, I am so sorry."

When someone you trust hurts you, you develop an other-worldly skill for reading people's expressions. It becomes your life-line, the only way to gauge what version of them you are going to get. The twitch of an eyebrow, beads of sweat forming at their temple. They are the sentences that make up the manifesto. The difference between suffering and pleasure, all dependent on the intent behind someone's touch.

It is with a well-trained eye that I study Marcelin's face, searching for a flicker of something I might recognize. Topher carried his anger in his dark, lifeless eyes, wore it in the hard set of his mouth. Everyone's tell is different, but the feeling remains the same. Marcelin glances up at me, eyes round with genuine concern. His lip quivers like he wants to say something, *anything* to make the situation better.

My shoulders slump and I offer him the ghost of a smile. "I'm going to do everything I can to save it."

He mirrors my expression, a glimmer of hope tugging the corners of his lips into a grin. "You will," he offers, patting my hand tentatively. "Anything left worth saving in that soil will come to life for you. You have a way with these things."

He nods, more to himself than to me, satisfied with his assessment. He turns and makes his way to the lockers in the corner of the room. The dial of his lock rattles as he spins it to the correct string of numbers. When it springs free, he shrugs out of his coat and swaps it for an apron before sliding the lock back into place.

Even after the lock's wheels have stopped spinning, my mind continues in circles. If Marcelin didn't unlock the door, someone else had to. I know for a fact I locked it after the taste testing yesterday. I mentally retrace my steps, wobbly as they were from the alcohol and my argument with Aaron, trying to find the missing link. Surely I set the alarm. It's practically muscle memory. Lock the door, arm the alarm. Was I so lost in my own feelings that I missed such a crucial step?

"Where is everybody?"

I jerk my head up, following the sound of that voice. When a tall man waltzes into the kitchen with his blond hair tied back at the nape of his neck and an unruly mustache curling over his upper lip, I'm too shocked to continue racking my brain for answers.

"*Zander?*" I exclaim, startling Marcelin who has taken up his position at the dishwashing station, prepping as best he can around the potted plant in his way.

"The one and only!" He catches me midair as I jump up to throw my arms around him, squeezing me against his lean frame.

"Jeez, did you come straight here from the PCT? You *stink*!" I push away from him once he sets me back down, pinching my nose to block out the scent of too many days without access to a shower. Or deodorant.

131

"Missed you, too, Zo." He ruffles my curls, unbothered by the insult. "I got back into town two days ago, went camping with Chase to celebrate."

"You celebrated returning from six months in the wilderness by going...back into the wilderness?"

He nods, not seeing the irony of the situation the way that I do.

"To each their own, I guess." I shrug and turn around, pacing back over to the sink and retrieving what's left of my plant. Marcelin turned the water off to let it drain out, but dirt-soaked droplets still splatter across the tile floor.

"Is that what I think it is?" Zander asks, hands slapped against either side of his face to frame the round O of surprise on his lips. He looks like that Edvard Munch painting, just with more hair. "I never thought I'd see the day where Zoey Allen would kill a plant."

I roll my eyes at him but feel a pang of sadness at the reminder. "It's not dead."

He raises two unruly blond eyebrows, staring at the waterlogged stump with disbelief. "Yet."

"Does Eden know you're working today?" I shift the pot to my hip, not caring if it stains my cream-colored dress. "I'm pretty sure Maddie is scheduled to come in."

"Nah, I start back officially next week. Just wanted to stop by and say hey to the gang."

"Hey," Marcelin calls from behind me. Both Zander and I bite back a laugh, but he returns Marcelin's greeting with sincerity.

"So," Zander says, crossing his arms over his chest and resting against the steel freezer door. "Heard you and Aaron broke up."

"You and Chase haven't seen each other in months, and you had nothing better to do than talk about my dating life?" I'm deflecting; he and I both know it. But that doesn't stop me from hoping it works.

"Heard you're also already seeing some new cop that just moved to town."

So much for deflecting.

He's studying my face in that thoughtful way that only he can pull off without being creepy. Zander has always had this air about him, like he sees so much more than what's just on the surface. Whether it be of nature or of people, he can dive deeper with nothing more than a look.

I recognize it the moment he peeks behind the mask I'm wearing. His lips thin, pressing tightly together. So tight his mustache tickles his chin.

"Oh fuck, Zo." His arms come uncrossed. He presses a hand into either hip. "You lied about the cop."

I look away from him because I'm so flimsily put together and if I force myself to face the blatant disappointment on his face, I'll fall back apart. "It's better this way."

"Better?" He drags a hand over his face in exasperation. "Better for whom? Certainly not Aaron. He thinks you moved on in a week while he's left heartbroken from all this."

I force my gaze back to his when I'm certain I can hold back the tears. I find myself drowning in a blue sea of pity.

"Better for you?" He gestures toward the poisoned plant resting against my hip. "It doesn't appear that way."

I shake my head, knowing he couldn't possibly understand. "You can't tell him, Zander. Please. Things are over now between us; we can both just focus on moving past it."

"I'm not going to tell him, but you should. You owe him—and yourself—the truth."

He has no way of knowing how true those words ring, reverberating through the caverns of my pain. My lungs feel too small for the air they're meant to hold, as though Topher has managed to reach through the years and clamp two fists down around them. I pull in a strangled breath, willing my lungs to expand, to fight back against their captor.

"I'll see you next week, yeah?" Before he can respond, I'm past him and pushing through the double doors. I make my way to the office and lock myself inside. The shelf in the corner of the room takes a little clearing off, but soon there's a space just large enough to fit the pothos. After a change of soil when I get home tonight, everything will be alright. The process of regrowth can begin.

Chapter Eighteen

I can't tell if Zander's angry at me or just disappointed.

It's his first shift back tonight, and he's barely spoken two words to me. Not that he's an avid conversationalist by any means, but that's a low word count even for him. That coupled with the looks he occasionally throws my way as I interact with the customers tells me it's intentional.

"Did I tell you my granddaughter got engaged last week?" Gloria Engle is trying and failing to hold my attention as I serve her the custom-blended dinner Santi makes to accommodate her ill-fitting dentures. She comes in once a week, tells me all about her grandchildren, and if I stick around long enough, she'll start commenting on what she would do with it if her body looked like mine.

I'm trying to avoid getting to that point tonight.

"No, Mrs. Engle, I don't believe you did." I top off her glass of tea and place a stack of napkins next to her plate, knowing they'll come back crumpled and covered in bright pink lipstick. "Can I get you anything else?"

"I have told you repeatedly to call me Gloria." Her tone is stern, but her expression is one of affection. I know since her husband died, she's been lonely, with the rest of her family living on the West Coast. Tomas told me several deputies visit her once a week to rake up her leaves and nearly go into overtime just from listening to her talk. "The reason I bring it up is because you threw such a beautiful party for Eden, I thought you could help me plan one for my Breanna."

I offer her a polite smile, hoping to ease the blow of my rejection. "You know I would love to; it's just that things are so busy right now between the bar and helping Eden with the wedding, I don't have a lot of time to spare." I fish my phone out of my back pocket, pulling up the waspy event coordinator's contact information. "There's a lady, Francesca, she might be able to help you. She manages the events at the Pritchard Winery just outside of town."

I write down her name and phone number on one of the napkins, feeling guilty for passing Gloria off onto the prim and proper bitch. But I have to admit there's a small twinge of satisfaction deep in my gut at the idea of her talking Francesca's ear off.

"Thank you, baby." She runs a ring-laden hand through her silver-haired bob. I wink at her and take the opportunity to escape before she starts trying to convince me to show more cleavage.

I return the tea pitcher to a drain pad behind the counter, wincing internally when Zander puts as much distance between us as the bar allows. It's as though we are the twin poles of two magnets repelling each other. Eden offers me a sympathetic smile, but it does little to balm the wound of rejection.

"I just don't understand why he's so mad at me." It comes out in a low whisper so as not to alert Zander that I'm talking about him. He's struck up a conversation with a pixie of a woman seated in front of the pour spouts. She twirls a strand of white-blonde hair around a delicate finger, fluttering her eyelashes at him. "What happened is between me and Aaron; it's none of his business."

Eden blows out a quick breath between gritted teeth, like she feels bad that she's about to have to correct me. "Do you remember that time Jake Morton told me I was ugly and you took it upon yourself to spread a rumor that he wet the bed?"

"That was in the fifth grade."

"Would you do it any differently if it happened today?" she asks with a knowing smirk.

I can't help the wicked grin that spreads across my face. "Now I'd probably do more than spread a rumor."

"Exactly." Her gaze travels from me over to Zander, a glint of amusement appearing in her eyes as she watches the woman's obvious flirting fly right over his man bun. "Aaron is one of Zander's best friends. You can't blame him for not loving being caught in the middle of you two."

A resigned sigh escapes my lips. "I guess you're right."

"Always am." She finishes arranging an order of cocktails on her tray and hoists it up without jostling a single ice cube. "You'll find a way to fix it. DIY is your forte."

With that, she takes off for the table of college students tucked away in a corner booth. Her foot catches on a bowed floorboard, nearly pitching her forward, but she steadies herself at the last minute. She uses a free hand to brush an auburn strand back out of her face and shifts the tray of drinks. Not a drop of alcohol has spilled, and the table cheers.

It will never cease to amaze me how someone can be so clumsy with her own two feet yet so graceful when it comes to people's drinks.

Movement in the corner of my vision catches my eye. I turn to see Kit approaching, joining in on the commotion with a slow clap. He's not looking at me yet. His gaze is still trained on the table of students. I take the opportunity to study his face, that ever-present smirk and those tortoiseshell-colored eyes like two sides of a coin. Heads, he's aloof and smug. Tails...well, those eyes could almost convince me there's a warmth to him.

They flicker to me, hardening a fraction. In the low light of the bar, the shadows cast on his face emphasize the hollows beneath his cheekbones and the crook of his nose. As forward as he's been with me, I'm tempted to ask him how he broke it, but then I decide not to push my luck considering how our last conversation went.

"Can we talk somewhere private?" he asks, gesturing intermittently to each of the doors that lead away from the main dining room like he's offering me options. I scowl when he settles an index finger on the bathroom.

"My office," is all I say. I walk in the opposite direction he's pointing, not waiting to see if he follows. I don't miss the hard stare Zander hits me with, followed by a less than kind expression aimed at Kit.

When he pulls the door shut behind him, it lulls the noise from the bar to a dull roar. Cocooned in the muted bubble of my office, he feels too close all of a sudden, despite standing three feet away.

He's studying the room, and I fight the urge to squirm when he analyzes the corkboard of menu ideas and my senseless ramblings about marketing plans. Among the handwritten notes are random Polaroids of the staff I've taken at any number of events, from holiday parties to team-building activities to everyday tasks. His gaze settles on a particularly unflattering shot of Gary and I drinking straight vodka from an ice luge. Gary still hasn't forgiven me for making him do that.

I clear my throat, pulling his attention from the photograph. "What did you want to talk about?"

"You remember I pulled a few fingerprints from the bar after the rock-throwing incident." He scratches the back of his head. "After we ruled out all your employees, the only ones left were a few partials. It wasn't enough to find a match in the system."

I deflate, sinking into my desk chair. "Great, so we still have no clue who's doing this."

"I wouldn't rule out that it could still just be opportunistic teenagers." He squats down in front of me so our eyes are level. The cop mask settles over his face, the one that tries to comfort me rather than convince me to sleep with him. He's not particularly talented at either. "I did run background checks on the staff, just to be safe."

My heart lurches. "And?"

A little half smile plays on his lips. He shakes his head. "Other than a few too many speeding tickets for Mateo, you're good. Nothing to worry about."

I nibble at my lower lip, knowing after the plant incident that I'm not *good*. I don't know how to explain the feeling in my gut, but I'm absolutely certain it isn't kids doing this to my bar. A delinquent teenager, no matter how mischievous, didn't pick the lock to Nomads, hunt down our ladder, and then climb up and pour bleach on my plant. It just wouldn't make sense.

I've been meaning to tell Tomas, but he didn't come in last week for his regularly scheduled drinking session. Gary let me know he'd be back from vacation this Wednesday and I could talk to him then. It just felt too ridiculous to call the non-emergency line and say my plant had been murdered, so I've been sitting on the information until I could explain it in person.

"What?" Kit asks, attention focused on my lower lip. His voice interrupts my thoughts, jolting me a little. The movement catches his eye, and he forces his gaze upward, meeting mine. "What's on your mind?"

"Someone poisoned my plant."

He clearly wasn't expecting that, because he rocks back on his heels with a bark of laughter. "Are you sure you didn't just forget to water it?"

"I didn't forget." I clench the arms of the chair in my fists, straightening my spine. "Someone poured bleach in it. I could smell it."

The pothos, or what's left of it at least, is sitting in my bedroom at the house. I've replanted it and set it on my bedside table, as if I can bring it back to life by keeping it close to me. Every once in a while, I still catch a whiff of that chemical scent lingering in the air.

Kit scowls, his two perfectly manscaped eyebrows almost merging into one. "Do you know anyone who might hold a grudge against you or the bar?"

I rack my brain, trying to imagine who could possibly be doing this. Like all the other times I've done so this week, I come up empty. "No one that would be so determined as to break in and poison my plants. To slash Maddie's tires. Everyone I've ever kicked out for getting too drunk has been back the following week with a bouquet of flowers and an apology. People can't afford for the local bar owner to have a grudge against them."

He wipes a hand over his face as though he can manually refresh his brain to bring forth some answers. "You really need to consider getting security cameras. At this point we don't know what this person is willing to do, how far they will go."

I study the ceiling of my office, imagining a camera looking back at me. A familiar sense of paranoia laps at the edges of my thoughts, threatening to take over. Suddenly I'm seventeen again, staring at my bedroom walls while Topher's headlights pour through my window and cast a haunting glare over the lavender paint. It was his way of punishing me for leaving, of reminding me I'll never truly be free.

For so long after him, I lived my life looking over my shoulder. The fear he'd burdened me with became the filter that colored my world. I can't go through that again, I decide. All of this is so damn frustrating, but I refuse to let this person rule my life. The minute I start changing things as a result of their actions, they win.

They win, and I become trapped in that fear once more.

I draw in a deep breath and let it out slowly. "No." My gaze returns to Kit. "I will not let this person make me afraid. I'm not going to be forced to do anything by him."

"Him?"

"Her. Them. Whatever!" I groan, collapsing into the chair.

Kit stares at me, narrowing his eyes for a moment before shrugging and standing back up. He hooks each thumb through a belt loop and leans against the wall. "If you say so, Zoey."

I don't like the belittling tone, but I try to be grateful that at least he isn't arguing with me. After all, that's what I want, right? To get my way, no matter the cost? It takes everything in me to ignore the tightness in my chest when I think of Aaron, knowing he'd never let this argument go that easily.

Kit extends a hand to me, and I take it, letting him lift me from the chair. I try my best to leave those thoughts behind, but the throbbing lingers in my chest. I rub my hand just below my collarbone in the hope that missing Aaron is a knot in a muscle that just needs working out.

"If anything else happens, promise you'll call, 'kay? No matter how trivial"—he pauses for emphasis—"it seems."

I look up at him, suddenly very aware of how close we are, only a few inches separating us. I can feel the warmth radiating from him, and the smell of his hair cream fills my nose. His badge reflects back the light of my lamp, blurring my vision at the edge with its glow.

He hooks my chin between his thumb and forefinger, tilting it up. He doesn't hesitate before lowering his lips to mine, doesn't wait for a sign from me that this is what I want. All that matters is *he* wants it, and so he takes it.

His lips are hard against mine, tongue delving into my mouth without much grace. I haven't kissed anyone other than Aaron in almost two years, and I'd forgotten it could feel like this. I'd gotten so used to the heat and the passion and the *affection*, something I didn't know I'd been missing all these years.

I realize as Kit laces his hands through my hair and pulls me tighter to him that I'll be missing it for the rest of my life. Because when Aaron kissed me, it felt like every nerve ending in my body came alive. With Kit, all I feel is blessed indifference.

Chapter Nineteen

"**R**emind me again why I'm the one doing this when you have a perfectly good husband"—I level a hard stare on Rose—"who literally works in construction?"

She smiles, an apparition of a dimple appearing in her cheek, here one minute and gone the next. "Mitchell doesn't like to do any home improvement projects after working on other people's houses all day. Our floors have been half refinished for the past six months. I keep telling him he better get it done before the baby arrives."

An absent-minded hand travels over her belly. She's wearing a thin cotton T-shirt that looks like it came straight out of Mitch's closet, and even it strains to cover her stomach. A half-moon sliver of skin peeks out below the hem no matter how many times she tries to tug it down.

"Considering you're due in a month, I'd say the odds aren't in your favor."

She finishes taking a sip of her Dr. Pepper—pregnancy craving of late—before grimacing. "I'd say you're probably right."

I hum a response, turning to observe the chaos I've scattered over the carpet of her soon-to-be nursery. Since this baby is a boy, name still undetermined, she's decided to completely redo their spare bedroom rather than have the baby share Cleo's Pepto Bismol–pink space across the hall. The walls here are already a pale blue color, so the biggest project at hand is hanging the peel-and-stick wallpaper strewn across the floor in different stages of unpackaging.

Looking at the print of zoo animals in varying shades of beige, all I see is an adorable pain in the ass.

"And do you intend to help me with this?" I ask, cocking an eyebrow at her.

The incredulous expression on her face answers me long before her mouth does. "I'll be taking on a more supervisory role."

"Of course you will be." I expected nothing less. I'd blame it on the pregnancy, but Rose is best at dreaming up ideas while someone else executes. At least until it comes to her pastries. I take a bite of one of the almond croissants she prepared as payment, and it is executed perfectly. "How will I know if what I'm hanging is even? I can't hold up both sides of the sheet and a level."

She waves a hand dismissively. "I'll just eyeball it from here and tell you when it's good!"

I chew on the inside of my cheek, considering my options. "I think I'm going to call Eden. The bar shouldn't be too busy this early. Maddie will be okay by herself for a few hours."

"If you think that's best!" Rose shrugs. "Tell her there are pastries; that usually works with her."

A giggle rattles my chest. She's not wrong. I search for my phone, finally uncovering it beneath the first sheet of wallpaper I unrolled to examine how the backing works. I've already dialed and brought the phone halfway to my ear when I pause. "Is there anything else we might need before I call her?"

"No, I think that's about it." She takes another long pull from her straw, and I hear the telltale gurgling of a drink running dry. She shakes it, lower lip puffing into a pout when nothing but the rattle of Sonic crushed ice fills the room. "Maybe a Dr. Pepper?"

"I bet you're wondering why I've gathered you all here today," Rose begins.

I peek down at her under the arch of my outstretched arm. Eden cranes her neck from where she's wedged between the ladder and the wall, trying to show Rose she's paying attention without losing the firm grip she has on the final sheet of wallpaper I'm attempting to level against the ceiling.

"Well, you gathered *me* to do manual labor," I huff, turning back to the task at hand. "And *I* got Eden involved, so—"

"Nonsense." Her *s*'s carry the hint of a lisp, a result of her saying the word with her mouth wrapped around the straw of her soda. "It was all part of my master plan."

"And that plan was...?" I finally get the sheet into a position I'm satisfied with, looking down at Eden to get her okay that the print is lining up for her as well. She nods and I press down, adhering the wallpaper and immediately beginning the process of smoothing out all the resulting air bubbles with my scraper.

"We want to talk to you about Aaron."

"We do?" Eden asks, clearly not in on the plan. She passes the X-Acto knife up to me, and I cut away the excess, leaving a clean edge on the accent wall.

"Yes, we do."

I step down from the ladder and pull it back, freeing Eden from her cage so she too can join me in admiring our work. The pattern lines up all the way across, and it looks admittedly precious. The hand-me-down crib is a dark-stained wood that will stand out perfectly against the backdrop we've created.

Rose shifts uncomfortably in her chair, rubbing at a spot high on her belly where the baby has been kicking aggressively for the last half hour. When she speaks again, her voice comes out strained. "Aaron told me what happened with you two."

"He did?" I'm hedging, hoping if I can ask enough rudimentary questions, she will just let it go. There's a kink forming in my neck that has nothing to do with hanging wallpaper. "I didn't know you two were particularly close."

"Zo, how many times do I have to tell you that people tell me *everything*?"

Eden snorts, having been the topic more than once of that grapevine herself. I drag my gaze from the wall to Rose, her hazel eyes holding my stare for a moment before Cleo starts to stir in the other room, waking up from her nap. It breaks Rose's focus—and her resolve. "Okay, it's possible that after overhearing your phone conversation with Eden the day your window broke, I took it upon myself to press Aaron for answers the next time he came in to get coffee. He was looking very solemn, I might add."

I roll my eyes, reaching for another croissant so my mouth is too busy to say something rude. More unintelligible babbling reaches our ears, prompting Rose to move as quickly as her belly will allow her into the other room, coming back with a bleary-eyed Cleo on her hip. "I didn't have to press *that* hard."

"I'm sure," I grumble around a mouthful of deliciousness.

"What's really going on, Zo?" She sets Cleo down, and the toddler immediately charges toward Eden, wraps her arms around Eden's legs, and scowls up at her until she lifts the toddler into her arms. "Aaron can tell you're keeping something from him. It's obvious to anyone who knows you that this isn't just a simple case of you not being interested anymore. Hell, if I thought it was, I wouldn't have even brought it up. But I can tell you're hurting, and I hate that."

I'm hit with the distinct sensation of being a magician who's had their methods exposed to the crowd. I'm too stunned to speak, her words filling my throat with a fresh set of tears I refuse to shed. One glance in Eden's direction shows she's wearing the same concerned expression as Rose. Her eyes, however, are filled with a knowing compassion that nearly breaks me in two.

It's the thing I've hated most about trying to move past what happened with Topher. How one moment I can be completely fine, not on top of the world but at least not beneath it, and then the next I feel like I'm transported back to the nights that followed that brutal and final beating. I'm staring at the purple walls of my childhood bedroom, listening to the engine of his truck rev outside my window. To this day, when I see the color it's like he's here with me again, my heart still not sure that it's safe.

I know Rose isn't trying to make me suffer by bringing this up. Quite the opposite; she's looking at me like she can read clearly what's hidden beneath the surface at last. Like I'm a house she's driven past every day just to realize there's been a cemetery in the backyard this whole time.

"I just—" It's not as easy discussing it with her; not that telling Eden was *easy,* per se. But at least with Eden there was a foundational knowledge of all the periphery details, the ones she got a head start on by knowing Topher. "I dated this guy in high school." The pathetic sound of my own words reaches my ears. I half expect Rose to interject with something along the lines of, *That was forever ago, Zo; get over it already.* But she's not nearly as rude as my inner monologue, so she keeps quiet, studying my face while she waits for me to continue.

Eden reaches for my hand, weaving her fingers tightly between mine.

"He did things—*awful* things—to me. But no matter how bad they got, I stayed. I took it. I tried to change my behavior so that I didn't set him off, but even after I'd bent myself into a shape I didn't recognize, he found something to be mad about."

Cleo lets out a little whimper, like even she knows the weight of the words I've just said. She tucks her head into the crook of Eden's neck but reaches a hand out toward me. I grab onto it with the one not clutched in Eden's, rubbing her soft skin that still screams *baby* even as she's turning into a full-blown child before our very eyes. "Sowy," she says, her best attempt at the apology I never got from Topher.

It's that single little word that leaves me unable to hold back the tears any longer, their wet heat pouring over my cheeks in an uncontrollable downfall. My sweater sleeve does little to soak up the mess, but at least it functions as a shield so they don't have to see my face.

Eden uses the hand I've released to grab me and pull me into an embrace. I crumple against her, sobs racking my body in a magnitude 9 earthquake. She runs her hand up and down my back in rhythmic strokes, soothing me through the tears rather than attempting to stop them in their tracks.

A little hand comes up to pat my shoulder. "It otay."

This prompts a sound from me that's half laugh, half sob. I lower my hand to uncover my face. Cleo's peeking at me from under Eden's chin, a hint of a smile brightening her normally stony expression. "You're too sweet, Cleo," I say, finally drawing in enough air to speak.

"That's my girl," Rose says, holding her arms out for her daughter. Cleo goes to her immediately, perching high on her mother's belly like it's a bench made just for her rather than a home for her little brother. Rose runs a hand affectionately through the wild mane of curls atop Cleo's head, smoothing them back. She plants a kiss on her daughter's temple and then looks up at me, eyebrows furrowed. "Is that why you're so upset with Aaron? Did he do something to you like...like that."

She can't even bring herself to utter the words, and I don't blame her. I shake my head vigorously. "No, Aaron's been a perfect gentleman."

She looks from me to Eden, searching for the missing puzzle piece. Eden shrugs as if to say, *I don't get it either.*

I let out a frustrated huff, tired of trying to explain this even to

147

myself. "As you can see, I clearly have a lot of things to work through." I gesture to the tears on my face and my snot-stained sweater sleeve. "Aaron is ready for the next step, and I can't keep being the one to hold him back while I figure my shit out."

If I'm being honest with myself, I haven't exactly been doing a whole lot of *figuring out* anything. I've mostly been shoving it all down deep into the trenches of my heart and hoping it stays there, blaming the resulting heartburn on what I'm eating rather than the poison I'm keeping inside.

Eden's hard stare tells me as much, but she keeps the words to herself, for which I'm grateful.

Rose, however, does not. "Zoey, I love you, but that's a load of bullshit. And I'm only being that gruff with you because it's what you'd do if the situations were reversed. All you are doing when you cheat yourself out of a good relationship is letting that sick man who hurt you back then continue to do so in the present."

Eden nods sympathetically. "She's right, Zo. By holding yourself back, you're letting Topher win."

Leave it to my best friend to use my own thoughts against me without even realizing she's doing so. How often have I refused to do something, like the security cameras, simply because it feels like I'd be letting Topher win? At what point does all that avoidance become the very thing I've been running from: fear?

The minute that thought enters my brain, the pit of despair in my stomach sours, leaving behind a wave of overwhelming nausea. It's like someone has told me the sky I've always believed to be blue is in fact green. Not just any green, but the shimmering color of jade in a pair of eyes I can't bring myself to picture lest the tears come back with a vengeance. The discomfort is so strong, so monumental that I shove the thoughts away just to make space for myself. I tuck the revelation back into the trunk where it belongs and set it up on the highest shelf of my brain, forgetting I ever looked at it in the first place.

My throat is so sore from all the sobbing that I have to clear it twice before I trust it will work to form my next words. I check my watch, not really looking at the time so much as my disheveled reflection in the glass face before the digital display comes to life. "It's getting late. We better get to the bar before the dinner rush."

I walk out of the baby-blue room before they have a chance to respond, grab my purse off Rose's counter, and practically sprint to the front door. The slap of cold air on my face when I exit does wonders to bring me back to life, numbing my feelings in addition to my nose.

I'm lost in a haze of emotion as I pull out of her driveway. Barely three blocks from Rose's house, my heart lurches when I catch a glimpse of flashing lights in my rearview mirror. My gaze flickers to the speedometer. Even in my anxious state, I'm barely seven miles per hour above the speed limit. I pull to the side, expecting the officer to zoom past me in pursuit of the true criminal, but to my dismay the lights stay framed in my back window.

Shifting into park, I mutter a curse under my breath. It's so cold I don't dare roll down the window until I see movement out of the corner of my eye. The officer is outside my passenger window, likely avoiding the safety risks of standing by the road. I hit the button to roll it down, craning my neck to look up at the deputy.

Of. Fucking. Course.

"Kit, I wasn't even speeding." Not really. Not enough for it to matter.

"It's a little cold out here; can I get in?" he asks, ignoring my assertion.

I groan, but the breeze coming in from the open window is causing me to shiver, so I relent and unlock the door. The window is back up before he takes a seat next to me and shuts us into the warmth.

"I wasn't speeding."

"Seven over is technically speeding." He scrunches his crooked nose up as he delivers that fact. "But that's not why I pulled you over."

"Why did you pull me over, then?"

He jabs his pen in the direction I've just come from. "You ran that stop sign back there."

I jerk around in my seat, fighting against my seat belt to look out my back mirror at the intersection I'd been too dazed to realize I was crossing. Just as I look, Eden's CR-V comes to a stop at the correct spot before pulling forward. She slows as she passes me, mouthing, *What the hell?* before continuing on toward the bar.

My head makes a soft thud as it collides with the headrest. "Fuck."

"Yeah, that's what I said, too." I listen to Kit scribble out the details of my ticket on the pad in his hand. "Really should be careful in these neighborhoods; lots of pedestrians that could get hurt by a distracted driver like yourself."

"I'm not a distracted driver." My tone is sharp, and I immediately wince when I hear it play back to me. "Sorry, you're right. Just give me the ticket and let's get this over with."

There's a sound of tearing paper before he sets the slip in my outstretched hand. He follows it up with a swipe at my cheek, catching the remnant of a tear that hadn't fully dried. "Crying over a ticket? You didn't strike me as the type."

"I'm not," I grumble, crumpling the ticket in my fist. "Just a bad day, that's all."

Despite what I've just said, he grins. He really is handsome, if not a little bit obnoxious.

"I can think of a few ways to turn your day around."

Okay, *very* obnoxious. "No thanks."

He gives a convincing pout before tapping the paper in my hand with his pen. "Just think about it." With that, he presses a quick kiss against my cheek before opening the door and letting that frigid breeze back in. He bends over to look at me, one hand balanced on the top of my car door. "Drive careful."

Before I can reply, the door is shut and I'm safely wrapped in the warmth of my car once more. I watch in my rearview mirror as he walks back to the cruiser and climbs inside. He cuts the lights and flips on a blinker, passing by me and waving.

I wait until I see his taillights disappear around a corner before checking what my mistake is going to cost me, sucking in a quick breath when I realize the damage is going to be worse than I thought.

Friday night, pick you up from Nomads at 8.
We're going out.
    -K

Chapter Twenty

U nless you count the grocery store run-in, which I don't, I haven't been on a first date since Aaron surprised me with private dance lessons nearly two years ago. He certainly didn't need them, having grown up with a Puerto Rican mother who filled their home with music and dance parties. As I followed his lead and tried not to marvel at the way his tapered hips moved, he whispered stories of his childhood to me too quiet for the instructor to hear. He painted a picture of his father trying to lead his mother with two left feet and a lot of charm, of his sister inheriting that lack of skills but still dancing her heart out.

Remembering the heat of his hand at my back, the spiced scent of his cologne filling my lungs until I felt drunk on it, is enough to cause my heartbeat to stutter and skip. Under the guise of checking the bathrooms for toilet paper and soap levels, I'm hiding from Kit. It's nearly eight o'clock, and I have no clue how punctual he is, but this felt safer than being a sitting duck in my own bar. I wash my hands for the third time, my pale knuckles cracking from a combination of colder weather and too much soap drying them out.

I suck in a deep breath, a hand braced on each side of the pedestal sink. I've clipped the top half of my curls back from my face, leaving nothing to distract from the panicked look in my eyes. I don't know why it feels like some sort of betrayal to go on this date. My brain knows that it's over between Aaron and me, but my heart is struggling to keep up.

The door swings open, and I suck in a breath, straightening my spine and turning away from the mirror. My heart trips over its own beat when I see Aaron. For a moment I wonder if I've summoned him. If he's a figment of my imagination. But the scowl on his face is never something I'd dream up on purpose.

"What are you doing in the men's bathroom?"

I open my mouth to answer, but the words won't come out. So instead I just gesture to the soap dispenser and shrug like that explains anything.

His eyes darken, turning the same murky green as the ocean just before a storm arrives. He's never been one to grow facial hair, but a shadow of stubble is beginning to form along his jawline. I force my gaze away, knowing if I stare at his lips for too long I won't be able to stop myself from imagining them as they were on our first date, brushing against my cheek while his husky laughter buffeted my ear. Whispering stories of a family I'd never known but somehow felt a part of just from listening to him.

"The cop is out there, looking for you."

I jerk my head up. "It's not what you think."

He crosses his arms over his chest, eyebrows raised. "Oh yeah, are you not going out with him tonight? Because that's what he told Maddie when he asked for you."

The devastation on his face is like a dagger straight through my heart. Shame draws my gaze down to the floor, away from the mirror and his anguished expression and anywhere else in this room that reflects back to me the poor choices that I've made.

I watch as his feet stride slowly toward me across the dirty tile floor. His hands fall to his sides, and then, after a moment's hesitation, they reach forward and lock onto the pedestal sink in the very place mine were moments ago. I'm trapped mere inches from his chest, which is heaving with the effort of his breaths. He lifts one hand to my chin, tilting it up so we're face-to-face. I draw in a breath full of the familiar scent of him, feeling like I've finally reached the surface after too long underwater.

His eyes flicker to my lips so briefly I would've missed it if I could bring myself to blink. "Tell me it feels like this when you're with him, Zo. Tell me you feel like your skin is on fire when he touches you, like if he doesn't kiss you *right this second*, you're going to combust." He drags a rough thumb over my lips, leaving them buzzing from the sensation. "Tell me that, and I'll leave you alone. As fucking impossible as it feels, I will force myself to forget about us. About *this*."

A voice echoes from deep within the recesses of my mind, reminding me that *not* feeling like this is the whole point. That there is freedom in feeling nothing. But for the life of me I can't bring myself to put it into words he'll be able to hear. Standing here, caught up in his orbit, it's hard not to wonder if that voice knows what she's talking about after all.

He takes my silence for what it is: an admission. There's a nearly imperceptible nod, and then he steps back, gesturing to the door. "Then go. Have fun. And when you finally decide that you want more than the nothingness he can offer you, I'll be here. Because despite what you may think, Zo, you've always been worth the wait."

Aaron's words are still scrolling across my vision like closed captioning as Kit holds the door to a dive bar open for me. Dooley's is one town over— my only true competition, if you could call a smoke-filled room with two pool tables and a few barstools *competition*.

I toss a questioning gaze at Kit, who simply shrugs in response.

"I thought it might be nice for you to drink at a place that isn't yours for once," he says, sidling up to the bar and ordering us each a shot of tequila. I must look surprised, because he turns to me and adds, "To help you loosen up."

I hadn't even realized how tightly coiled my spine was until he said that, but as soon as I toss back the shot and bite down hard on a slice of lime, the tension begins to thaw a little bit. It doesn't melt altogether, but it's enough for me to relax into the moment and order another round from the bearded, heavily tattooed bartender taking our measure with a curious gaze.

"Thanks, man," Kit says, sliding his second shot over to me. "But I'll just take that Husky Lover IPA if you don't mind. Someone's gotta drive us home."

I look at the already empty glass from his first shot pointedly, to which he replies, "You know what they say, liquor before beer—"

"You're in the clear," the bartender finishes with a gruff smile, placing the draft pour on a bar napkin in front of Kit, who nods his thanks.

The tequila is still burning my throat when I speak. "So do you typically ask women out on dates instead of giving them tickets, or is that just a special punishment I received?"

He's wearing a black long-sleeve shirt that makes his eyes appear darker, the dappled browns dominating the greens and golds. They glimmer with amusement when he responds. "That was just for you. Can't go giving myself a reputation. Town's too small."

"A man as pretty as you? Surely all the women try to flirt to get out of their tickets." I call over to the bartender, asking if I can just get a whiskey sour next instead. "Or, at the very least, flash their cleavage."

He chuckles softly. "So you think I'm pretty?"

"I think *you* think you're pretty."

"That's not what you said," he corrects, then takes a sip from his beer. "And you're wrong. I *know* I'm pretty."

The liquor is warming me from the inside out, blurring the edges of my thoughts just enough to let my run-in with Aaron fade ever so slightly into the background. I try to slip into the woman I know I can be, the one who sits here with this handsome, overconfident man and gives as good as she gets, sowing the seeds of attraction in a field where nothing serious could ever grow. The persona is a thrifted sweater that's itchy and too snug in all the wrong places, but I force myself to wear it anyway.

"Those women over there know you're pretty, too." I gesture with my cocktail to a group of college girls eyeing him from the other side of the bar, not caring that I'm sitting right here. They're dressed in high-waisted jeans and flannels they've left unbuttoned but tied together just under their push-up bras. I remember when I cared enough about looking good to dress that impractically for the weather. I almost miss that version of myself.

His gaze travels over to them, resulting in a fit of giggles from the group. The resulting smirk tugging at his lips is aimed straight at me. "Zoey Allen, are you jealous?"

"Not in the least," I answer honestly, earning me a playful pout from Kit. I suddenly feel tired down to the marrow of my bones. "You can go flirt with them if you'd like; wouldn't bother me at all."

He shakes his head, a darkness passing over his face that takes me by surprise. "I might do no strings, but I don't do cheating. Not my style." I must make a face, because he follows that up with, "What's that look for?"

I shrug. "Nothing. Just that men like you don't normally come with a whole lot of morals. It's refreshing."

He mocks offense, one hand slapped against his chest. "Men like me? What ever do you mean?"

"You know, all cocky and self-assured and *pretty*."

It earns a laugh, but his expression quickly grows serious. He orders another beer, which the bartender brings over before resuming his position at the dish rack, continuing to polish the same glass while pretending not to eavesdrop on our conversation. I can't fault the man for it; there's not much else going on in this place to keep him entertained.

"You can blame my ex-wife for that."

I tilt my head in Kit's direction, letting my gaze roam over his face. I remember him mentioning she'd cheated on him, which hurts badly enough in a casual relationship, let alone a marriage. I can't imagine what that type of betrayal does to a person. Though apparently it has similar results to what Topher did to me. I suppose pain is all the same at its core, no matter what form it takes on when it comes for you.

I used to think my suffering was unique. Then I heard Chase talk about the loss of his father, or Aaron discuss the pressures of growing up with his dad gone so often. I watched Eden walk through unfathomable trauma I couldn't possibly imagine surviving, let alone thriving on the other side of it the way she has. Seeing the ripple of hurt under Kit's skin as he mentions his ex-wife, I'm beginning to realize at some point or another we all fall victim to tragedy. It's the universal truth, even more so than love.

He studies my expression, finding something there that he recognizes. "Would you like to get out of here, Zo?"

I simply nod, and he pulls a wad of cash from his wallet that he settles next to his empty glass. "Thanks, man," he says to the bartender, who mumbles his appreciation and gathers the glasses as we shrug back into our coats and return to Kit's car.

We drive in silence through the dark roads that wind back into Loveless. There's a heaviness in the air, a recognition. Like for the first time we've seen each other clearly, and we were surprised at what we found.

He pulls into the driveway of a small brick home in a quaint neighborhood at the edge of town, where the yards stretch wider between properties and the trees block your view of the neighbors. I don't know where I pictured him hanging his hat each night, but he didn't strike me as the country living type despite his thick drawl. Everything else about him, from the perfectly sculpted hair to the manicured brows to his perpetually shiny shoes, screams high-rise apartment. Not that we have any of those in Loveless.

"Home sweet home, for now," he says by way of introduction to the space, holding the door open for me to pass through. There's a lamp illuminating the undecorated living room. My gaze scans the blank walls before falling onto a leather recliner facing a setup I recognize from hours spent watching my male cousins play at family gatherings. Kit's a gamer.

"Do you seriously only have a recliner for seating?"

"Any guests I bring over aren't really looking to spend time in the living room, Zoey." His voice has taken on a familiar rasp, one that sends a shiver running down my spine. When I turn to face him, he's dropping his keys onto a hook by the door and kicking off his loafers, but his gaze is trained on me with a heated intensity. "There's plenty of space on the bed, though."

I swallow back the sudden thickness in my throat. *This is what you wanted*, I tell myself. *Casual relationships lead to casual sex.*

"Show me," I tell him, sounding braver than I feel.

The corner of his lip twitches as he reaches for my hand, pulling me toward the hallway on the opposite side of the room. We pass a door swung open to reveal a bathroom and two more that are pulled closed before he stops at a threshold, guiding me into a room that barely has any walking space left to navigate around the king-size bed in its center.

He flops back onto the mattress, pulling me down with him. A lazy grin unfurls on his face, stretching his thin lips so taut they blend into his skin. "See, what did I tell you, plenty of space for activities."

He wiggles his eyebrows at me and I groan. Heat fills his eyes, and in an instant his fingers are laced in my hair and he's extinguishing that sound with a kiss.

His mouth is hard against mine just like the last time, but the alcohol in my system helps soften me to it. I loop one arm around his back, clutching at his shoulder blade. His tongue slips into my mouth, and all I can taste is beer.

He rolls himself on top of me with a grunt, and I can feel the thick ridge of him pressed against me. *It feels good to be wanted.* I grasp at the reminder, trying to lose myself in the feeling. In the weight of him, the heat, the way his mouth forges a lazy trail of kisses down my neck to that spot just above my collarbone where Topher always dug his teeth in when we fucked, like he was claiming me as his own, trying to mark me forever.

It didn't work, at least not physically. There is no scar in my skin to show that he was there. But the minute Kit's lips brush that tender skin, the ghost of the memory is all-consuming. I'm hurtled back through time, locked in the body of my seventeen-year-old self. Kit's weight is Topher's, pressing down on me until I'm desperately searching for air but unable to find it. I'm drowning in the fear, lost in the past, until Kit reaches for the button of my jeans and I'm catapulted back into the moment with a gasp of air.

"Idontwanttodothis," I murmur, the words slurring together.

Kit's fingers freeze on my zipper, and he looks up at me, the heat in his gaze dissipating like morning fog the moment the sun rises overhead. He shifts off me and sits up, showing me his hands so I know that he's removed all contact. "We don't have to do anything you don't want to do."

My teeth burrow into my lower lip, pulling at a piece of skin until the metallic taste of blood reaches my tongue. "I'm sorry."

"Don't be. Sex is kind of a bummer if both parties aren't into it." He studies my face, head tilted like that might help him understand what just happened. Whatever he sees draws a resigned sigh from his lips. "Would you like me to take you home?"

I nod gently, feeling rattled and—perhaps even more so—embarrassed. He acknowledges my request with a quick nod and rises to his feet, righting his shirt from where it became twisted. I stand up on two wobbly feet, the panic having replaced my alcohol-induced stupor with a shocked one. Looping my jean button back into place, I follow him out of the open doorway with my gaze trained on his back.

Before Aaron, I could lose myself in the nothingness, in the numbness of sex without feelings. But letting him in, letting him grow and spread like a vine of ivy within my heart until he cracked open the door keeping my past at bay, has proven detrimental. Because the numbness is no longer a balm but a blank slate, and my memories playing out across it are all I can see.

Chapter Twenty-One

When I wake the following morning, I attribute the pounding in my head to three-too-many shots of tequila and a whole lot of regret. But it doesn't fade with the handful of ibuprofen I swallow nor the cup of caffeine. Soon my body begins to ache like I've been passed through a wood chipper. Every nerve ending is screaming in pain, from my toes to the muscles in my legs to my fingertips. I begin to shiver and the realization hits me: I've got the damn flu.

Every year around this time, when the leaves begin to change and the days grow shorter, my immune system decides to take a vacation and some virus capitalizes on the absence. Strep throat, sinus infections, COVID when that became a thing; one way or another something finds me. Last fall, it was flu type A, and it felt exactly like this.

An hour later the urgent care confirms my suspicions and sends me home with a prescription for Tamiflu, lots of fluids, and rest. I call Eden to let her know I won't be in for a few days, sounding as horrible as I feel. She says she'll inform the team and asks if I need anything, but I'm drifting off to sleep even as we speak. I have just enough presence of mind to shoot a text over to Kit before I pass out, letting him know that I'm sick and he might be, too.

I drift in and out of restless sleep, feeling like my body is slowly becoming one with the couch. A *Schitt's Creek* marathon is running on the television, my go-to comfort show for sick days. Last year's bout with the flu was Aaron's first time watching the series, when he came over to take care of me and keep me company despite being slightly germaphobic. He wore a surgical mask but still insisted on kissing me through it. When he ended up coming down with the flu three days after me, he swore he didn't regret a thing.

I don't know if it's the muscle aches or the memory, but tears prick at my eyes and the resulting condensation is fogging up my glasses. I pull the frames off and deposit them on my coffee table, rolling over and resigning myself to just listening to the show rather than watching it.

Someone raps their fist against my front door to the tune of "Shave and a Haircut." I groan an unintelligible, "Come in," but I don't roll over.

Whoever it is understands me well enough to push open the door, and the smell of fresh pastries barely muddles its way through my stuffy nose. "I come bearing the fruits of the spirit: love, joy, sticky buns, croissants, cookies, goodness, muffins, gentleness, and... well, no self-control." Eden singsongs the words, dredging up a long-forgotten memory of a song we were forced to memorize when I'd accompany her to children's church after a Saturday night sleepover.

I grunt in response to the grating jingle but crane my neck to take in her hazy form. She holds out a white blob, so I reach for my glasses. They bring her into focus, alongside the box with 8th & Main's insignia on the front that she holds in her outstretched hands.

"Gimme, gimme, gimme." I thrust a hand out, palm up, waiting to be surprised.

She giggles, dropping the box on the smooth marble of the coffee table before venturing into the kitchen. I let out an involuntary whimper, and she clicks her tongue in response. "I'm just getting napkins, relax."

I force myself into a seated position, trying to ignore the way the world tilts on its axis when I do. My head feels like a clown car, except instead of red-nosed entertainers, it's full of congestion, pain, and a never-ending highlight reel of every mistake I made last night.

"I also brought you some DayQuil and kombucha, because I know you like to drown yourself in both when you're sick." Glass bottles clink against one another as she unloads the fermented beverage into my fridge.

"Have I told you lately how much I love you?"

She stands upright and closes the fridge, smiling at me. "Never hurts to hear it again."

"I love you."

"Love you, too, Gilly-Bean." She slips out of her shoes and pads across the room with a handful of napkins and an industrial-size bottle of DayQuil. Slipping into her college role of mom-friend, she presses the back of her hand against my forehead, letting out a shrill whistle and shaking her hand like it's just been burned. "Did they give you anything for the fever?"

A heavy sigh drifts over my lips. "Yeah, the Tamiflu. Should kick in soon."

Her lips flatten into a grim line, worry clouding her evergreen eyes. "Have you eaten anything today?"

I simply shake my head.

She pulls a ham and cheese biscuit from the box of Rose's goodies, setting it on a stack of napkins and handing it to me. "Here, eat this before any of the desserts. Rose made it fresh for you so it's still warm."

My stomach grumbles in response, and I devour it in the time it takes Eden to situate herself next to me on the couch. With a mouth full of the last bite, I say, "You might not want to sit that close. We can't leave Santi alone to run the place."

"Relax." She waves a hand to dismiss my worries. "I've had my flu shot."

"So have I." I practically growl the words. Every year I put aside my fear of needles and get every vaccine known to man, and still somehow get sick.

"Just imagine how much worse you'd feel if you hadn't," she says, patting my knee through the stack of blankets.

I've had my fill of sitting up, drowsiness pulling my head back down to my pillow. Eden's situated it into her lap, and as soon as my hair is splayed across it, she begins running her fingers through the tendrils, rubbing them away from my face the way my mother did when I was little. Even as sick as I am, I relish the sensation. It settles a peace in me that is hard to come by as an adult; the distinct feeling of setting down everything that I'm carrying and letting someone else bear the weight of it for a while.

"Thank you for coming here," I whisper, hoping if I say the words quietly, I won't cry. It's all too much suddenly, the sickness and things with Aaron and my date with Kit. And beneath it all is that foundation of anguish, the cemented sadness Topher filled me with all those years ago that I've unwittingly built my life upon.

"Of course, Zo. You know I'm always going to be here when you need me." She can feel the shift in my mood, just like I can sense it in hers. She knows that I'm grappling with something far worse than a virus and she's responding accordingly.

We sit like that for a while, her tender scratches on my scalp lulling me back to sleep. It's the first nap of the day that actually feels like rest, and when I wake, the pounding in my head has finally faded to a dull thud.

"Hey, sleepyhead. How was the nap?" She lifts her head from where she'd sunken into the couch cushions, peering down at me.

"Good," I croak, sitting up and reaching for my water glass. "How long was I out?"

She scans the television and scrunches her nose up the way she always does when doing mental math. "Um, long enough that Patrick and David are engaged now."

"Damn it, that's my favorite episode!"

She grabs the remote control and holds it up, finger poised over a button. "Want me to go back?"

I take another swig of water, relishing the cold against my sore throat. "It's fine, I'll live."

She chuckles, dropping the remote back onto the couch.

The blinds on my windows are cracked open, golden light drifting in through the slats. I know she'll have to go soon so she can be there to support the team, and I want her to the same way I'd want her to take care of my child if I were down for the count, but the thought of her leaving is like a vise around my lungs. I'm worse than a man when it comes to being sick.

As if she's read my mind, Eden pipes up. "So is Kit sick?"

I reach for my phone, clicking the lock button to light up the screen. No texts. From anyone. I realize it's not his name that I'm disappointed is missing. "No clue. He seemed fine last night." But then again, so did I.

Eden makes a humming sound at the back of her throat. "How'd that go, by the way?" She's watching me out of the corner of her eye, an unreadable expression on her face.

I shrug. "It was good, I guess."

She turns her head my way, and I can tell by the downturned corners of her mouth that my half-assed response isn't going to fly. I try to wade through the murky depths of my thoughts, past the veil that my conversation with Aaron laid over the whole night, to get to the truth of it. "He surprised me a little. I think I wrote him off as this hotshot who thought he could have any girl he wanted, and

165

while I do think that's some of the case, I could also see he carries around a lot of hurt from things that happened with his ex-wife."

"I overheard him say something about her at the bar to Tomas." She scowls, looking back at the television for a moment. "What kind of jerk cheats on their husband while he's gone away to war?"

I think about what Kit told me on the car ride over to Dooley's, about military wives and their more *unsavory* habits. "Apparently it's not unheard of."

"That sucks." She keeps her gaze trained on the TV, one finger picking at a loose thread in my blanket. I watch as she pulls at the string until it unravels enough to form a small hole, which she continues to dig at.

I reach over and settle my hand on top of hers. "Something on your mind?"

She studies our hands thoughtfully before lifting her gaze to meet mine, an apologetic frown framing her lips with parenthetical wrinkles. "I like Kit, I really do."

I hear the conjunction she fails to add out loud, so I say it for her. "But?"

"*But.*" She draws in a breath and lets it out, the sound shaky and uneven. "I just don't like him for you."

"Eden—"

"No, listen," she interjects, squeezing tightly onto my hand. "What Topher did to you? That was absolutely unforgivable. And if I ever see him in person again, which is unlikely since I'm never going back to that hellhole, but *if I did...*" A darkness I don't recognize on her hardens her gaze, her pupils constricting until they're nothing but a pinprick in a sea of green. "I'd kill him in an instant. There are not a lot of people in this world that I wish death upon, but for him, I'd deliver it myself."

Her admission takes my breath away. The fierceness in her tone, in her expression is like lightning. I'm standing so close I can feel the zing of it buzzing through her.

"What does that have to do with Kit?"

She worries at her lower lip, that crackling energy dissipating into the anxious tick. "Because, I see the way you are with Aaron. The way he is with you. I've felt it since the first time I saw you two together. What you and he have—it's beautiful, Zo. And I'd hate to see you let it pass you by just because you're scared. I almost did that, and that near-miss haunts me every day. Every time Chase looks at me, I think, *I almost gave this up*. And for what? For Mark? For Topher? They don't deserve one more piece of our happiness."

Now I'm the one fumbling with the blanket, trying to look anywhere but at her and the mirror she's holding up for me to stare into, to see the truth reflected back to me without any filters.

"Kit is great, but Kit doesn't make you a better person. Not like Chase makes me. Not like Aaron makes you. Relationships without growth are pointless. And you deserve better than pointlessness."

A fat, lonely tear spills out of my eye and forges a path over the swell of my cheek. I suck a shuddering breath into my constricted lungs. For once, my mind is empty of Topher's cruel, twisted face or Aaron's open, kind one. Even Kit, with his firm jawline and amused stare does not show up. In this moment, all I see is myself, my skin littered with every invisible scar left behind by a love that hurt instead of healed. I realize how desperately I want to let them go while simultaneously having no clue what that looks like.

"This is all I know how to be," I murmur, hoping desperately that she understands what I'm trying to say.

Empathy softens her features, because of course Eden understands. Those who have suffered recognize suffering in others. But they also recognize hope.

"I should've told you this that day behind the bar, but I didn't have the words until now." She leans her forehead into mine, the sweet scent of a sticky bun dancing on her breath. "It wasn't love that made my mom stay with Mark. Love doesn't do that, *wouldn't* do that. It was fear. And you, Zoey Allen, are not afraid."

Chapter Twenty-Two

Long after Eden has left to go shower off any possible germs she's obtained, I'm still sitting cross-legged on my couch, lost in thought. For the first time I feel like I might understand just a fraction of the pain she was going through when she first moved here, before she felt like she could talk about what had happened. Even being talked *to* about Topher was agonizing while it was happening, but afterward there's a measurable shift. My heart feels a little lighter in my chest, a fraction freer, like the cage isn't open but it has expanded.

Another dose of medicine takes me one step closer to feeling human again. I stagger into the bathroom and hunch over the pedestal sink, washing my face and trying not to picture Aaron a year prior, holding me in the shower and gently washing my hair for me when I was too weak to do it myself.

My reflection startles me when I finish drying my face and drop the towel. The bags under my eyes and my sickeningly pale skin leave me looking like death warmed over. I shudder, turning away so I don't have to see myself as I loop my curls back into a French braid, the only thing that'll keep them truly at bay.

I change into a fresh pair of pajamas and return to my station on the couch, reminding the television that yes, I am still watching. Sadly.

Another knock, this time with more force, rattles my door.

"Come in!" I croak, hating how pathetic it sounds.

Whoever it is struggles to turn the doorknob for several moments before it becomes clear they will not be getting through without assistance. I groan, untucking myself from my couch-bed and marching over to the door. When I glance through the peep-hole, I see a fish-eye lens view of Kit with his hands full.

"Took you long enough," he grunts when I swing open the door. He's carrying a pizza in one hand, the scent of garlic fighting its way into my clogged nostrils. His other arm is wrapped tightly around a Wii gaming console and two remote controls that are wired to tiny handles adorned with wobbling buttons. "I've brought food and entertainment. Don't breathe on me."

I step aside, making a big show of covering my mouth as he passes. He's halfway to the kitchen by the time I complete the absurdly hard eye roll his comment induces.

He settles the Rocky Mountain Pizza box onto my island, lifting the top to reveal a meat lovers that leaves my stomach in knots. The four pastries I already ate this morning from Rose's didn't digest well, and my gut is telling me this won't either. Still, on some level I know I need food. And my stomach must understand that, too, because it lets out a blush-inducing grumble.

Kit eyes my belly. "Jeez, someone's demanding."

I self-consciously wrap my arms around my center. No matter how many years, diets, and body-positivity movements pass me by, there is still a corner of my mind that resents that part of me. Some neuron deep in my brain that broadcasts replays of Topher's voice every time I see my soft middle in the mirror.

Kit doesn't seem to notice, or care, because he's already flipping open every cabinet I have in search of plates. He finally discovers them, leaving all the doors wide open in his wake as he grabs what he was looking for and returns to the countertop to load up two servings of pizza. I march behind him, shutting each door with as much force as is allowed by the soft-close hinges I installed myself, trying to make a point.

Kit peeks up at me with a mouthful of pizza, eyes blanker than a dog's. Point clearly not taken. I sigh and reach for a plate, resigning myself to the fact that he isn't mine to train.

"How're you feeling?" he mumbles around a particularly large glob of cheese and pepperoni. We're standing at opposite ends of the island, which feels a bit ridiculous, but any time I move closer, he steps away.

And I thought Aaron was germaphobic.

"Shitty," I reply honestly. I take mental stock of my subdued body aches as well as my congested sinuses. "Better than this morning, but still pretty awful."

He nods along with my answer, like it's what he suspected. "I'm just glad I don't seem to have it. I hate being sick."

"Who doesn't?" I'm not sure if it's just the fact that I'm ill or how on edge I've been, but his callousness is making me particularly prickly.

"You know what I mean."

"Do I?"

He stares at me for a moment, expression unreadable, before gesturing to the gaming console. "I brought Mario Kart. It's what my brother and I always did when we were home sick as kids. Thought you'd enjoy a distraction."

My iciness toward him melts ever so slightly. "That was very kind of you."

He shrugs. "Figured it was the least I could do after last night."

"About that, I'm so sorry—"

He holds up a hand to stop me. I bite down on my tongue in the process of halting my words, wincing at the hot flash of pain. "No need. All's forgotten, yeah?"

My tongue is still stinging, but I manage a nod. "Yeah."

"All right, then it's time for me to kick your ass in Mario Kart."

"How are you kicking my ass right now?"

I chuckle, watching as Princess Peach zooms across the finish line of Rainbow Road long before Luigi even has it in his sights. "My cousins played a lot of video games when we were kids. Occasionally they'd let me join."

"More than occasionally, it seems." He reaches for one of my kombuchas he snagged from the fridge, taking a sip and grimacing. "This is disgusting."

"No one told you to steal it."

He whips his head around to face me from his position on the other side of my sectional. "Hey, I brought you pizza! A drink is a fair exchange, in my opinion."

I'm toggling through map options for our next race, but I toss him a sidelong glance. "That's fine, but beggars can't be choosers. Which map do you want to do next?"

"You've beaten me at all of them." He scratches at the crown of his head. "Can we just watch a movie or something? Today was rough and I don't think I can take any more losses."

He sounds so suddenly exhausted that it draws my gaze to him. I study his not-so-perfectly gelled hair and disheveled appearance, noticing for the first time a small scratch on his left cheekbone. "What made today so bad? I thought I was winning at having the worst Saturday."

"Some guy started a bar fight that we had to break up over at Dooley's."

I glance at my watch, squinting to make sure I'm reading the time right. "It wasn't even five yet when you got here. Who starts a bar fight in broad daylight?"

171

"Some drunkard named Shawn Pinkerton. It's the fifth one I've booked him for since I moved here." He sighs heavily, his head lolling back into the cushions. He swallows, his Adam's apple bobbing along his outstretched throat. "He was especially riled up today, clipped me with a right hook before I could cuff him."

The name rings a bell, drawing up images of a perpetually sweaty man covered in blown-out tattoos. "He used to work with us. Well, not *with* us, but he delivered our kegs. He assaulted Eden last year and got fired for it."

Kit furrows his brow. "I didn't see an assault charge on his rap sheet."

"She didn't press charges," I say, shaking my head. A small frown tugs at my lips. "I wish I'd forced her to, but she was dealing with a lot and just couldn't have one more thing on her plate."

His eyes are distant, his jaw ticking as he mulls over something in his head. I study the cut, noting that it's shallow and will likely heal before the week is over. No scars will mar his pretty face, if that's what he's worried about. My gaze falls to his crooked nose, the one thing about his appearance that will never be perfect again.

"How'd you break your nose?"

The question jolts him, pulling him back from wherever his mind had wandered. A wry grin tugs at the corner of his mouth. "My wife had *forgotten*"—he puts air quotes around the word—"that I was coming home from my deployment that day. When she wasn't at the airport to pick me up, I grabbed a ride with a buddy back to our house. She was fucking some guy in our bed, with our wedding picture mounted on the wall behind her."

"Yikes." It's an insufficient response to what he's just told me, but it's the first word that comes to my mind. Now who's being callous?

He just nods, seemingly unbothered. "Yikes is right. I might have gotten a little carried away and ended up with my nose broken. But he fared far worse."

Listening to him talk about his past causes a strange sensation to wash over me. Suddenly I feel the urge to tell him about Topher, not because I'm particularly keen to bond with him, but because I envy the easy way he tells such an obviously painful story. The way the words roll off his tongue with no hint of regret or sadness, just mildly bitter amusement at how it all played out. I'd gotten the barest taste of it earlier, talking with Eden and feeling that weight lifting off me ever so slightly.

Before I can form the words, though, Kit is already changing the subject, and the moment passes so quickly it's almost as if it never happened at all.

"So there's this thing two weeks from now, it's the annual mayor's dinner or whatever. Have you heard of it?"

I've seen the invitations each fall when they arrive at Nomad's, the ones decorated in filigree too fancy for a town like ours and calling on every city official, business owner, and public servant alike to dress to the nines and attend a formal dinner at the courthouse. They always end up buried in the trash beneath food scraps and empty wine bottles. The idea of turning into Cinderella for an evening would be a lot more appealing if it didn't bring with it the requirement to brush elbows with every old, white man in our neighborhood who fancies himself a politician just for being on the city council.

I don't unleash my ramblings on Kit, though. Instead I mumble a quick, "Yeah, I think so."

He studies a hangnail on one of his fingers. "Tomas is making those of us who aren't on duty that night go, and we're supposed to bring a date."

"Oh yeah? You must be devastated." He strikes me as someone who'd be overjoyed to deck himself out in a suit and tie, reeking of hair gel and expensive cologne.

He rolls his eyes over to meet mine, shaking his head like, *What can you do?* "I was wondering if you'd come with me."

I balk at him, but he just matches my hard stare with one of his own, his eyes looking particularly murky this evening. Like a swamp.

"I don't know if that's such a good idea, Kit." I feel the shivering returning to my body, and I wonder if my fever is coming back. I reach for my medicine where it rests on the coffee table, knocking back another dose.

His face is blank, gaze holding steady. "Teachers aren't on the list, if that's what you're worried about."

Heat creeps up my neck, but I'm determined not to give him the satisfaction of affirming his guess at my concerns. I clear my throat with a cough so he knows the flush is from my illness, swiping the back of my hand across my forehead to check if my fever has returned. My skin is warm but not broiling like it was this morning.

If I double down on my refusal, it will only make him more smug. Something the world definitely doesn't need from Kit Llewellyn. "If I'm not needed at the bar, I'll come."

"Great. I promise date number three will be better than the last two." He settles back into the velvet-clad cushions.

"Number three?"

"Yup." His face screws into one of mock disappointment. "Zo, you wound me. Did you forget those beautiful moments we shared at the grocery store?"

I groan, throwing the remote at him and covering my ears with the blanket to avoid hearing him laugh. The grocery store, of course. How could I forget?

Chapter Twenty-Three

"**Y**our first problem is that your hand isn't wet enough!"

I let the door to the bar settle closed behind me, watching with amusement as Maddie catches the miniature can of ginger ale that drops out of Zander's grasp. She demonstrates a trick that I taught her, cupping her palm and twisting the bottom side of the can flush against it. When she flattens her hand out, the can is suctioned to her palm. She then picks open the tab with a satisfying hiss and pours the amber liquid into a waiting whiskey glass, the can seemingly defying gravity by sticking to her flat palm.

"I can assure you my hand is wet enough, if nothing more than from stress sweat," Zander grumbles, trying again to perfect the move. When he flips it over to pour, the can immediately detaches from his hand and ginger ale spills everywhere.

Maddie lets out a rare boisterous laugh before Zander clamps his hand over her mouth. "Is that wet enough for you?" he shouts.

She ducks, shoving his hand away with a resounding gag. "God, it was salty!"

"No one told you to lick it." He wipes his hand on his pants before retrieving a microfiber cloth to mop up the mess.

"You've got to make sure your hand stays flat when you flip it over. That's why you're losing suction," I say, taking a step in their direction.

"Freeze!" Maddie bends over to retrieve something from beneath the bar. A can of Lysol lands on the countertop with a metallic clank. "I have a midterm for Risk Management tomorrow, and I cannot get sick. I'm already in danger of failing."

"Sounds like you didn't manage your risk very well," Zander grumbles.

"Don't shoot, please!" I reply, hands up. My exclamation draws the concerned eye of a few patrons, and I shake my head at them to assure them I'm only joking. I turn back to Maddie, who has her finger poised on the trigger, ready to douse me. "The doctor cleared me to come back; I'm not contagious. Don't even have a residual sniffle."

Her dark gaze remains suspicious, but she places the Lysol back below the counter.

Zander retrieves a fresh can of ginger ale and follows my advice, keeping his palm flat as he flips the drink over. To our mutual admiration, it stays suctioned in place. Several gentlemen from the law firm down the street erupt in applause, and I join them, my chest swelling with pride.

"That is awesome!" One of the men, Jake Henderson of Henderson and Lowe Divorce Law, says excitedly before his eyes quickly go dull again and he presses his lips into a firm line. I guess dealing with arguing former couples all day doesn't leave room for a lot of joy. "Can I have my whiskey ginger ale now, please?"

"My bad, man," Zander replies. He finishes off the beverage with a lime-wedge garnish and places it in front of Jake. "Enjoy."

I smile and shake my head, walking past the row of stern-looking lawyers and pushing through the saloon doors into the bustle of the kitchen. Marcelin shouts a hello over the echoing sound of the tin baking sheet he's hosing down. The other guys grunt a similar greeting before returning to their respective tasks of prepping and plating, while Santi mans the grill.

A familiar messy top-bun of auburn hair is barely visible through a gap in supplies on our dry goods shelf. I join Eden on the other side of the supplies, finding her knee-deep in counting boxes of potatoes.

She glances over at me, an unknown smudge of something brown streaking across the bridge of her nose. A thin sheen of sweat glistens on her forehead. She hefts another fifty-pound box of potatoes back onto the rack, grunting with the effort, before relaxing into it with a heavy sigh. Her gaze scans my body, taking in my freshly washed hair and my clothes that are finally something other than pajamas. "You look so much better!"

I brush the top of my nose to show her where to wipe while a chuckle escapes me. "Wish I could say the same."

She smacks me, but a warm smile plays on her lips. "Well, I've been doing inventory by myself since *somebody* had to go and get the flu."

"Believe me, if I could've avoided it, I would've." I reach for the clipboard she's left sitting on a stack of unopened spices, and scan the pages. "Damn, girl, you've nearly finished."

"Just have the walk-in and the liquor left to do. Dry goods and freezer are done." She tucks a flyaway back behind her ear, the edge of her lemon tattoo peeking out from beneath her taupe-colored sweater sleeve.

"What can I do to help?"

She brushes her hands off on her leggings, leaving a dusting of dirt from the potatoes on the black fabric. "Let's knock out the liquor first. I've been waiting to place an order so I'd have less to count, and Maddie already took care of tallying up the bottles out front before we opened so we just have to do the back stock. Plus I'm still recovering from the freezer and not exactly keen to jump into the fridge just yet."

"Makes sense." I pull my work keys from where I keep them carabinered to my belt loop and open the door to the back storage room, unlocking the alcohol cage that's nestled inside.

She rattles off the different bottles to me, and I survey the spreadsheet she's created, marking a tally next to each unit that she names. We move in a mindless sync, the process as practiced and familiar as our friendship.

My mind begins to drift, leaving me wordlessly marking off vintage merlots and bottles of Smirnoff while I return over and over to our last conversation, wondering how on earth to ask what I have to when I know her opinion of Kit.

"Something on your mind, Zo?" She settles the box she's holding back onto the tile floor, the glass bottles rattling against one another in protest. One hand finds her hip while the other pokes me in the side. "You're being suspiciously quiet."

I chew on my words for a moment, preparing to spit them out like sunflower seeds. "Do you remember that mayor's dinner I get an invite to each year?"

"The one you throw away whilst grumbling about the patriarchy? Yes, I'm familiar." She laughs and resumes her counting, satisfied that she's kickstarted the conversation. "One case of that vanilla vodka you insisted would come in handy—untouched." She throws a pointed look over her shoulder. "And don't feel bad, Chase gets those invites too since he owns Taylor's Landing. They usually live on our fridge under an old brewery magnet for three months before I finally toss them out."

"In my defense, I really thought those alcoholic vanilla Cokes would sell better than they did." I scratch the nape of my neck. "So he doesn't plan on going?"

She stands up straight, hearing the tone in my voice shift even as I try to suppress it. "If it were up to him, we probably would. You know Chase; he'd talk to a wall and become its friend. But no, we don't plan on going because I detest small talk. Why, are you?"

"Kit asked me to come with him. I guess the sheriff and fire departments are also invited." I doodle a flower on the page to the right of my failed experiment with cocktail design, that full case of vanilla vodka a reminder to leave it to the professional who is, in this case, Eden.

"And you said you'd go?" she asks incredulously. "When that invite arrived, I had to listen to a fifteen-minute rant on how this city wants to pretend they support local businesses by inviting the owners to this 'hoity-toity'—your exact words—dinner every year but won't make changes that actually benefit them. Now you're saying you'd like to share a meal with those people?"

"In my defense, their refusal to pass my proposed open container ordinance was still very fresh." Having grown up taking annual beach trips with my family to Tybee Island, I know how a quaint downtown that allows patrons to wander from business to business with a plastic cup in hand can draw in tourists. I've seen it firsthand on Savannah's River Street district when my cousins and I were finally old enough to break away from family game nights and go barhopping on the mainland. Unfortunately Loveless City Council didn't see it the same way. Something about old family values or whatever.

She crosses her arms over her chest, that wrinkle between her eyebrows deepening into a canyon. "Does Kit really make you happy?"

The question throws me for a loop. I realize happiness isn't really what I've been seeking, just a distraction from the pain. I shake my head subtly in an attempt to distance myself from the unsettling thought. "It's not about that. He was kind enough to bring me dinner and keep me company when I was sick. I owe him one."

"By that logic, you also owe *me* one." Her tone is teasing, but she throws in a wink to drive her point home.

"The debts owed in our friendship run so deep God only knows who owes whom at this point." I hug the clipboard against my stomach, willing it to stop churning from her earlier question. "But it would be really nice if you'd come, too, so I have someone to complain to about the misogyny at hand. Kit's from Mississippi; he won't understand." Hell, he'd probably agree with the stiffs.

She watches me for a moment in that way she does that makes it feel like she's seeing right through my skull and into the inner workings of my brain. I squirm but hold her gaze. Finally she relents. "Okay, fine, I'll go. But only because I'll take any excuse to see Chase in a suit." She blows out a whistle to show her appreciation.

I laugh at how into him she is, even after a year and a half. "Thank you."

"You're welcome." She turns to the last box, counting each bottle with a phantom tap to the lid. "Jot down five bottles of Maker's Mark and we're done with the alcohol."

I scribble the tally and then turn the clipboard to show her. "Finished. Does that just leave the walk-in?"

She nods. "Back to the arctic we go."

I beat her to it, tugging at the metal latch until the suction relents and I'm able to pull the door open. My breath immediately forms a thick puff of fog flowing out from my lips. Santi's been running a thin inventory as well in anticipation of the month-end count, which I owe him a big hug for later. Any minutes saved in the giant refrigerator are worth their weight in gold.

Noting the two bags of Halloween candy left over from the past weekend, I write on the bottom corner of the inventory sheet to remind myself to check how many bags I ordered and document for next year, since we seem to have pretty much nailed it. I hate that the flu made me miss the annual costume contest, but the sexy cop outfit gathering dust in my closet would have been a bit in poor taste given the current state of my life.

I pop a mini Snickers into my mouth and delve deeper into the cooler, Eden trailing behind me, and mentally note the number of lettuce cases stacked on the shelves. A lump of fabric on the floor catches my eye, and I crouch to grab it, holding out the bulky jacket in front of me to examine. It's too large to be Eden's or Maddie's, and I'd recognize it if it belonged to either of them.

Wiggling past Eden, I step back into the kitchen. "Hey, guys!" I shout, drawing the crew's attention over the dull roar of meat sizzling and pots clanging against pans. "Someone left their jacket in the walk-in; whose is it?"

Four pairs of eyes stare back at me blankly, and I'm met with a ripple of shrugging shoulders. Just then, Zander pushes through the double doors to retrieve the meal Mateo has finished plating for a customer.

"Zander, is this yours?" I ask, my voice wavering slightly.

He glances over at the bulky Carhartt in my hands and shakes his head. "Nope, not my style."

Eden steps up beside me, reaching out to rub the fabric between two pinched fingers. Something passes over her face before she shakes her head to clear it. She turns to the team. "It has to be somebody's. It didn't wander in here by itself."

Eric has already resumed the task at hand, Mateo and Marcelin quickly following suit. Santi studies the jacket for another beat. "Maybe it's time to start thinking about security cameras."

The suggestion triggers the anxious voice in my head—the one that's partially convinced Santi and Kit might be right—and I find myself speaking louder to drown it out. "I will not be getting security cameras. Some delivery guy probably just forgot it. I'm not going to let some pathetic vandal make us all paranoid."

Santi shakes his head wordlessly and returns to the pot of chili he's stirring. Out of the corner of my eye, I can see Eden staring at the jacket, gnawing at her bottom lip. I toss the bulky thing onto an empty plastic crate, reassuring myself that I'm absolutely right. There's no need to assume anyone has been in the walk-in that didn't belong there. A few stupid pranks aren't going to make me spend thousands on a security system that we don't need.

I try to tell myself that I believe this with all my heart, but I can feel the anxiety rippling just underneath my skin as I return to the cooler, a shiver skirting down my spine that has nothing to do with the cold.

Chapter Twenty-Four

I hold up the thumbs-down side of my placard, frowning apologetically as I do it. "I'm sorry. You're gorgeous, but that thing swallows you up. I can't even see you through all the tulle."

Eden grimaces. At least I think she does. It's hard to see her under all the fabric. Gary flips his placard over as well, munching on one of the madeleine cookies Rose brought. Rose pretends to be distracted by something Cleo is babbling at her so she doesn't also have to give her disapproval.

The ever-positive attendant, Naomi, simply shrugs her shoulders and turns to Eden with a broad smile. "How do you feel about it?"

Eden worries at her lower lip, holding back everything I know she wants to say for fear of hurting Naomi's feelings.

"She didn't design the dress, Eden. It's okay to be honest," I say. Gary grumbles his agreement, spraying a few cookie crumbs onto his beard.

Naomi looks from me back to Eden, her face growing as serious as I imagine it's capable of with two round doe eyes opened wide and a pouty smile affixed on her expression. "Exactly. I can't find you the right dress unless I know what you're liking and not liking about each one you try."

"You're right, I'm sorry," Eden says. The break in her voice is so slight most people would never even notice. But I do. "I guess it's just too big? I don't really know. It's just not right."

She hefts the bulky skirt into her arms and ambles awkwardly back to the dressing room. Naomi starts to follow her, but I stand and put an arm out to stop her. "Can I talk to her for just a sec?"

There's a nod and another frown-smile. I offer her one of my own and then follow Eden's trail.

I knock lightly on the wall to the right of the dressing room curtain. I hear sniffling and then a wavering, "Just a minute."

"It's me, Eden."

There's the sound of too much fabric rustling and then the curtain pulls aside just wide enough for her head to fit through. Her face is mottled from freshly shed tears, eyes swimming with the dark depths of mourning when she meets my gaze. "Sorry, I don't know why I'm so emotional. It's just a stupid dress."

"It's not just a dress," I say softly. I point to the curtain. "Can I come in?"

She offers the ghost of a smile before stepping aside and pushing the curtain open wider. "Welcome to my crib."

It makes me chuckle, and when she joins me on the dressing room bench, I can see the faintest glimmer in her eyes beneath all the sadness. "Do you want to talk about it?"

She shakes her head rapidly at first, and then it slows to a steady metronome, her gaze falling to an indiscriminate point on the baseboard. I watch her lower lip tremble each time she releases it from the grasp of her teeth. One unsteady breath after another fills the air between us with the minty scent of the mouthwash she carries in a miniature bottle in her purse. My best friend, always prepared for everything. Except for this.

"I've been okay, you know? With the menu selection and

picking the colors and even the venue visits haven't been so terrible. I don't know why this feels so different." She laughs but it sounds more like she's choking. "I just always thought I'd share this moment with my mother."

With that, her tears begin to spill over. I reach for her, but she jumps to her feet, away from my grasp.

"Get this off me," she demands, giving me her back so I can fumble with the clips. When I hesitate, her voice grows louder. "*I want it off.*"

I stand, hot tears of my own streaming down my cheeks. I tug the clips away and loosen the corset back. After some finagling, it drops to her waist, held up by its own ginormous skirt. Eden turns to me and braces an arm on mine, stepping out of the abyss of fabric in just her underwear.

She's so frail looking, her normally muscular frame seeming smaller after emerging from that behemoth. Her arms cradle themselves, goose bumps prickling her flesh.

"Why didn't she choose me? I try and I try but I just can't wrap my head around it. Why wasn't I good enough?" She drops to her knees in front of me, and I join her on the ground without a moment's hesitation, wrapping my oversize cardigan around us both. She sobs into my shoulder, damp tears mingling with mine on their journey over my collarbone and beneath the neckline of my shirt.

"You have always been good enough," I manage to choke out. I squeeze her against me like my life depends on it, like if I just hold her close enough, none of the pain will be able to reach anymore. "None of her choices are a reflection of your worth, only of the way she perceives her own. You are so loved. So wanted. So cherished. I am the luckiest girl in the world to have you as a best friend, and I am so damn honored to be here today, to help you decide what you want to wear to marry the love of your life. Your mother is the one who is missing out, not you."

185

"I would also like to say that I'm a damn lucky man to have been asked to join today," Gary grumbles from the other side of the curtain, startling me. He pulls it just slightly to the side, hand covering his eyes tightly. "I know I'm not really your dad, Eden, but that doesn't stop me from thinking of you as my daughter. From loving you like one."

If I weren't still drenched in a combination of our tears, I'd be tempted to laugh. He looks so ridiculous surrounded by all this glamour while wearing his signature tucked-in flannel shirt, his bushy white beard bobbing as he speaks. The hand clamped over his face still sports the wedding ring his late wife placed on his finger, and he swears it'll stay there till the day he joins her in the ground. He reminds me of my father, with all his gentle ribbing and abounding love. I feel it now, buffeting out from him and wrapping Eden and me in its warmth.

Eden lifts her head from where it's nestled in the curve of my neck, wiping her snotty nose on the back of her hand. Her mascara has run in two stark rivulets down her flushed cheeks, but it's nothing a makeup wipe and her best friend can't fix.

She reaches for the silk dressing robe they left her to wear between changes, wrapping it around herself as she stands. One hand tugs Gary's away from his eyes as the other pulls him into an embrace, which he quickly takes charge of. He squeezes her tightly against him and twirls her around in a move I'm sure he'll pay for with back pain for the next few days, but I know he'd deal with it tenfold for Eden. For us.

"Come here, Zo. I need both my girls in on this." He gestures for me with one grabbing hand, which I take hold of, letting myself be tugged into the fray. We're wrapped in the embrace of a man who's barely taller than me but somehow feels like the safest haven I've ever found, second only to one I cannot bring myself to give a name to.

"Gary," Eden whimpers.

"Hmm?" he replies, tugging his sleeve down over his hand and using it to wipe away the remnants of her tears.

"Would you walk me down the aisle?"

I'm almost certain Gary's going to lose it too and then we'll be left in a heaping pile of tears once more, but he manages to hold himself together, save for one tear that slips out of a smoke-gray eye.

"It would be my honor." He tousles her hair, making a mess of the intricate updo her hairstylist tried out this morning. He clears his throat, brushing away the one tear he couldn't keep inside. "But we've gotta find you a dress first. I could escort you in this robe, but I think we'd get a few funny looks."

"Not from Chase, he'd be thrilled." I waggle my eyebrows at her suggestively. They both swat me, but it gets her laughing again, and Naomi takes that as her cue to resume control.

The petite woman steps into the alcove of the hallway, this time with a fit-and-flare gown draped over her shoulder. It's formed with simple fabric, no lace or frills or sparkles about it, and I know instantly that it's the one, but I bite my tongue so Eden can find out for herself.

I squeeze her elbow before looping my arm through Gary's and letting him escort me back to the sales floor, where I see that Chase's mom has arrived and taken her seat next to Rose.

Laura is dressed in a multicolored button-down and high-waisted pants in a complimentary navy blue. She's effervescent as always, a wide grin stretched across her face. "Zoey! Gary! So good to see you both. I'm so sorry I'm late; traffic was nuts. Why anyone would want to live in a town as big as this is beyond me."

I chuckle as I lower myself back into my seat. "This is hardly what I'd call a big city."

"Bigger than our town," she says matter-of-factly.

She's got me there. The way she calls Loveless *our* town causes my chest to swell with pride. Though I've only been living there for a few years, it feels like I've been a part of the community forever.

Eden steps out from behind the curtain to a shared gasp from all four of us, plus an awed, *"Wow,"* from Cleo, who is perched on her mother's lap and wearing a flower crown fit for her task in the ceremony.

The dress drapes along every curve of Eden's body, the ones she's always been convinced she doesn't have. Her collarbones peek out each side of a high-necked halter, but when she turns, I see that the back is completely open save for four strands of pearls that dangle from the nape of her neck to the waist of the gown. She looks delicate but also strong, simple yet so stunning. It's everything Eden is in a collection of fabric and thread. I snap a photo and send it off to Ella, knowing her big sister will want to be a part of this.

The moment Eden's eyes land on Laura, I see a fresh set of tears begin to form. She bends down to wrap her arms around her future mother-in-law before she even looks at herself in the mirror. In the gesture, I see the love she has for the woman. Not a replacement for her own mother, but a damn good bonus mom.

Finally she takes Naomi's outstretched hand and steps onto the pedestal, facing herself in three different mirrors. She gasps too, and suddenly she can't contain the tears anymore. It's the loudest, "Yes!" I've ever heard, earning an applause from the entire store.

Laura offers to take us all out to lunch after, but with a quick gaze shared among ourselves, we all decline so she can have some time alone with Eden. Gary and I load up in my car, watching Eden walk toward the main street with her soon-to-be mother-in-law, their heads tucked against one another while they speak.

I turn onto the highway back to Loveless, scanning the mountains on the horizon. The reds and yellows are fading and falling away, leaving brown in their wake. The snow caps are slowly lengthening, swallowing more and more of the mountaintops each day. It won't be long until the valley is blanketed in its first dusting of the season.

"She reminds me so much of Wendy," Gary murmurs, so quietly

I almost don't hear him. My gaze flickers over to the man, his own eyes aimed toward his window. "Such a gentle spirit. Sometimes I swear you two really could've been our daughters, with the way you take after us."

Emotion forms a thick knot in my throat. "I remind you of her, too?"

He barks a laugh. "Oh hell no, Zoey. Blonde hair, blue eyes, and a wild streak to boot? You are all me, sweetheart."

"Your eyes are gray, not blue," I say with a *harrumph*. Deep down though, I'm flattered. Gary's everything I want to be. He ran a successful bar for years; his name will go down in the history books of this town. He's beloved by all who know him. I can't think of higher praise.

"They were blue once, when I was younger." He turns to study my profile, watching me as I drive along the winding highway. "I was a lot of things you are, at one time in my life. Before Wendy came along, I was fresh out of the military and sewing my wild oats wherever I could plant them, if you know what I mean."

I block the mental image before it can take root. "Gross."

"Oh *waah*," he says, making the crying sound of an infant. "Don't mock too much, you'll be old as dirt one day, too."

"You're not old as dirt," I say, patting his leg. "Old as those trees maybe, but not the dirt."

He glances toward the giant Ponderosa pines I gesture toward, their size suggesting they're at least one-hundred years old, if not more. Then he flips me the bird.

I giggle, triggering the blinker to take my exit. "If you were so wild in your youth, hot stuff, what made you want to settle down with Wendy?"

He mulls over the question, rolling his jaw back and forth. "With the military moving me here and there, I always felt so unsettled. So on edge. I never knew where they'd send me next, and even after I got out and I was, erm, sampling"—he grimaces at his own

189

terminology, as do I—"I felt like I was adrift, if that makes sense. Which is freeing, until it's not. But then I met Wendy, and she filled me with this of calm I'd never felt before. A stillness. She was the only thing in the world that didn't wind me up. She was the safe place I always found myself running back to.

"I miss her so much. One lifetime just wasn't enough, especially since hers was cut so goddamn short." His voice grows husky. He coughs suddenly, sounding like he's drowning. "I don't know if that made any sense."

I nod without looking over at him, lost in thoughts of arms that feel like my own kind of safe harbor. Of a stillness I'd never known until Aaron. One I didn't think I'd miss until it was gone.

"It makes perfect sense to me."

Chapter Twenty-Five

> Me: I can't decide what to wear tonight.
>
> Me: Send me a picture of your outfit.
>
> Me: Eden??? Hello? I need your help here!

All three messages have gone unanswered, though her read receipts are on and betray the fact that she's ignoring me. I pull her contact information up and call her, but it rings through to her voice mail instantly.

"Hi, you've reached Eden. I'm unable to come to the phone right now, but if you'll leave your name and a brief message, I'll get back to you. Thanks."

"Hi, Eden, maybe you remember me? It's your best friend, Zoey. I'd really appreciate it if you'd stop ignoring me and help me figure this dress crisis out. If Chase is trying to squeeze in a quicky before the dinner, tell him I said it's nothing personal but to please keep it in his pants. Okay, love you. Bye."

I toss the phone back onto my bed with a groan, the lock screen lighting up to inform me that I have only fifteen minutes to make a decision before Kit arrives to pick me up. My gaze travels over the pile of discarded options that lay scattered across my floor. Too tight. Too short. Too matronly. Why do I even keep these in my closet?

Tugging the absurdly flashy piece I bought for a New Year's party over my head causes my hair to spring out in every direction. I run my hands through it, trying desperately to tame the frizz. If it's not the humidity in the summer, it's the static electricity in the winter. I cannot win.

I begrudgingly resort to the last option that seems remotely appropriate for the event, stepping into the strapless piece and pulling it upward over my breasts. The dress is burgundy with a pleated design across the chest made to look like one of those folding fans. It fits snug around my waist and down over my hips, flaring out just below my knees. Objectively I know that it is flattering, but there's still a nagging voice in the back of my head telling me I'm trying too hard to get attention. That the dress shows every bit of extra weight I carry.

"Why are you trying to show everyone else what you should only be giving to me?" Topher sneers in my memory. *"Nobody wants my sloppy seconds, Zoey."*

The doorbell rings, signaling that my time to get over my reservations has passed. My face has grown pale in the mirror, and I turn away, resigned to the fact that I will hate whatever I put on tonight.

Waiting on my doorstep is a dressed-to-the-nines Kit, just as picture-perfect as I suspected he would be, holding a bouquet of red roses in one hand. I try to contain my disappointment at the sight of the cut flowers, taking them with a smile that I hope doesn't appear as forced as it feels.

"Come in while I get these into some water." I turn and retreat to the kitchen. I don't keep vases in the house, but I have a tall water bottle that should do the trick. I'm filling it up when Kit leans against the counter to my right with a question in his quirked eyebrow.

"As many plants as you have and you don't own a vase?" He crosses his arms, an expensive-looking watch flashing on his wrist.

I finagle the bouquet into the water bottle and place it on the counter next to my little peperomia. "'If you love a flower, don't pick it up. Because if you pick it up it dies and it ceases to be what you love.' Osho said that."

Kit studies me carefully, as though he's searching for the hidden meaning in those words. "How does picking a flower stop it from being what you love? Those roses are still roses." He gestures to the bouquet.

I offer a ghost of a smile, remembering the first time I had this discussion with Aaron. How he'd immediately known what I meant when we passed by the selection of bouquets in the grocery store floral department, lamenting about their cut-short lives.

"Flowers—plants in general, really—are beautiful because they are living, breathing things just like people. They come in as many varieties, they can be as small as a blade of grass or as large as a redwood tree. They grow with reckless abandon when left to their own devices." My gaze flickers to the doorway into my bedroom, where the roots of my once-wild pothos are still struggling to recover. "When we cut them, we do it because we selfishly want to keep their beauty for ourselves. But it kills them, and that beauty is gone forever."

I can see that he's struggling to keep up, and I wave a hand through the air to disturb the feeling of melancholy that settled between us as I spoke. "Ignore me. I'm just a sentimental old plant lady. They're beautiful, thank you."

He makes a humming noise at the back of his throat and nods, happy to let the subject drop. I remind myself that this is the price paid for keeping people at a distance: the lack of true understanding.

Glancing at his watch, he says, "Well, we better get going if we don't want to disappoint the mayor. Are you ready?" His gaze roams briefly over my body, the flickering embers of desire warming his eyes, but he doesn't comment on my dress.

I realize I'm waiting for some type of affirmation that I've made the right choice, that Topher's voice in my head wasn't telling the truth about me after all. Not that it would've made much of a difference anyway. No matter how many times Aaron raved about my body, no matter how thoroughly he worshipped every inch of me in bed, there was still that hollow feeling in my chest when I found myself faced with my own reflection.

Perhaps it's not Kit's, or any other man's, job to speak loud enough to drown out that voice in my head. Maybe the responsibility of changing its tone is mine alone.

"Let me just grab my coat," I say, pressing a quick kiss to Kit's stubbled cheek that leaves a smudge of red lipstick on his skin.

He rolls his eyes and rubs at the mark, a smile stretching across his face. "Yeah, better hurry it up before I go make myself a bouquet from all the flowers in your garden."

Annoyance sizzles under my cheeks, but I swallow it and force a laugh. "Don't think for a second that Tomas wouldn't help me cover up your murder."

His grin falls flat at that, a brief flash of concern filling his features before his usual smugness returns.

I grab a leather jacket from my closet and slip into it, retrieving my phone from my bed along with my heels before returning to the living room. A heavy sigh escapes my lungs when I see there are no missed calls or texts from Eden.

"Everything okay?" Kit asks. He's looking at himself in the gold-framed mirror mounted on my wall, tugging at the collar of his navy-blue suit to make sure it's covering his crisp white undershirt. When he's satisfied with his efforts, he turns to face me.

I finish strapping on my heels and join him at the doorway, still dwarfed by him even with the added inches on my side. I reach up to fix a bit of the undershirt that's still peeking over, tugging his collar up to cover it. "Everything's fine. Eden's just not responding to texts or calls."

He holds the door open for me, an appreciative gaze landing on my ass as I pass him. "I'm sure she and Chase are already there, shaking babies and kissing hands."

I roll my eyes at his attempt at humor, locking the door before following him down the steps, careful not to land a heel in one of the cracks between the wooden planks that make up my porch. "I'm sure you're right."

As Kit slowly cruises down Main Street, force of habit draws my gaze over to the row of businesses where Nomad's sits snugly between Taylor's Landing and 8th & Main. The ugly sheet of plywood still mars the face of my bar. The window company Mitchell referred me to assures me I'll have a replacement by the end of the month, something about a custom order they had to place from a company in New York, but I'm not holding my breath. Still, it pains me to see it every day.

The road gives way to a roundabout that encircles the historic courthouse. The brick structure stands tall and proud in the center of the square, with wraparound columns and a clock tower adorning it like a royal crown. I've only ever been inside its echoing halls on unpleasant occasions, when paying my yearly property taxes or updating my car's registration. After we've parked and Kit bends his arm for me to grab on to, we make our way into the building, a weird sense of being overdressed for an occasion trickling down my spine when I pass the room where I go annually to renew the bar's liquor license.

At the back of the building, a grand marble staircase curves up to the second story. The click of my heels against the stone punctuates each step as we climb. A long hall mirroring the first floor stretches out before us, this one looking less dulled down by mundanity than the lower level. A red carpet embossed with golden flowers warms the hall, while white walls sporting blown-glass sconces and historical paintings of the town frame the path.

At the end of the hall, a pair of double doors that stretch all the way to the ceiling are propped open. There's a man acting as the greeter standing out front with a list that he checks before admitting each person into the room. He almost looks like a magician, wearing a black tux with coattails and a top hat to boot.

"Rabbit or dove?" Kit whispers, bending down to filter the words right into my ear.

"What?"

He raises his eyebrows and nudges his head in the general direction of the door checker's top hat.

I cover my mouth to quiet the sound of my resulting giggle. "Rabbit, no doubt."

When it's finally our turn to be checked, I say my name out of habit, though I'm technically here as Kit's plus-one. The magician checks his list, presumably finding my name because he scribbles something on the paper. His gaze travels up to Kit, who stands taller than him by almost six inches, even with the hat. "Are you Miss Allen's date then?"

I follow his gaze, catching sight of the flash of what appears to be annoyance crossing over Kit's face. He rights himself quickly, assuming a debonair expression that cools his features. "Actually, it's Christopher Llewellyn, and she's with me."

"Whatever." The man scribbles something else on his list. The casual word is so uncharacteristic of the way the man is dressed that I'm almost tempted to laugh, but I hold back for Kit's sake. A white-gloved hand beckons us forward, along with the parting words, "Have a lovely evening, Miss Allen. And Miss Allen's date."

A low grumble escapes Kit's parted lips, but no further

comment follows. Damn Southern men and their fragile masculinity.

The room reminds me of the library from *Beauty and the Beast*, sans books. The ceilings rise high above our heads, adorned with elaborate chandeliers that match the sconces on the walls. Luxurious, maroon-colored velvet drapes frame each window, the glittering lights of Main Street just visible through their glass.

I recognize a lot of the faces we pass on our way to the bar, people I've stuffed full of Santi's food and our signature drinks while they go on and on about how this tourist season will be their best one yet for equipment rentals or relaying the gossip told to them at the barber shop. A few of the stone-faced city council members who shot down my proposal eye me dispassionately, simply nodding in my direction before returning to the conversation at hand.

"What would you like to drink?" Kit asks, gaze dropping to my cleavage before settling on my face.

I smile at the bartender, a glinting metallic name tag telling me his name is Bryan and he's a hospitality student at the local college. "Tequila sunrise, please."

"And I'll have a scotch on the rocks."

Bryan nods and gets to work on our drinks. I fumble through my clutch for a few dollar bills and drop them into the tip jar, earning an extra-long pour of tequila and a smile from Bryan. Kit watches the interaction but doesn't comment, simply accepting his drink when it's ready and guiding me into the fray with a steady hand at my lower back.

"Llewellyn! You clean up good for a rookie." I've seen the man in the bar a few times here and there with groups of deputies when they come to blow off steam after work, but his name floats just beyond the grasp of my memory. His dark eyes are framed with the type of long, thick eyelashes that God only seemed kind enough to give to men. His gaze falls to me, an appreciative smile twisting his lips. "You weren't kidding; you did bring a hot date. Name's

Calvin." He offers a hand for me to shake, which I take begrudgingly.

Kit drags a finger across his throat in a threat I don't think I was meant to see. "You'll have to forgive him; he doesn't know how to act in social situations," Kit says, tossing a wink in my direction.

"If you didn't want it repeated, you definitely shouldn't have said it in front of Calvin," another deputy comments. He's older, with a cul-de-sac balding pattern and a bulging beer gut pushing the buttons of his dress shirt to their limits. The three of them get lost in a conversation about the week's events and their equal reluctance to be here in the first place, a sentiment I'd gladly join in on commenting about if my gaze wasn't locked on a pair of jade-colored eyes that have just found their way to me despite the bustling crowd.

I wander from Kit's side, bobbing and weaving through a sea of heady cologne and too many elbows, until at last a cluster of firefighters part and I'm able to jab my pointer finger into Chase's chest. "Where's Eden?"

"Nice to see you, too, Zo," Chase says, a broad smile taking over his face. He hooks an arm around Aaron's shoulders and squeezes him into a hug, their height difference leaving Aaron snuggling Chase's armpit. "Eden had too much to do at the bar, so I brought Aaron as my date instead."

"Besides, who supports this city more than teachers?" Aaron adds, pushing away from Chase. His classic black suit fits him so well it has to be custom. He's watching me, measuring my response to his presence.

Except I don't even know what my response is, exactly. All I know is that my heart is a fluttering bird in my chest, two manic wings battering my lungs until I struggle to draw in a breath. I'm frozen, my drink sweating against my palm as I struggle to remember words and how exactly I'm meant to speak them.

"Yeah, they are raising the next generation of Loveless idiots, after all," Chase inserts, trying to revive the lifeless conversation after I let one too many beats of silence fill our awkward circle.

"Nice to see you two," Kit says behind me, his arm looping around my waist and pulling me close until my back is flush against his chest. "Do you mind if I steal my date for a dance?"

Aaron's eyes harden as Chase's smile falters, but he recovers quicker than his friend. Chase offers a nod in Kit's direction and then raises his draft beer—a Coors Light if I know him at all— toward me. "Sure, we'll see you around, then?"

"Sure," I manage to croak, already being pulled toward the dance floor.

Kit removes my drink from my hand and sets it on a cocktail table before escorting me into the small cluster of dancers. The fumes of his hair cream leave me more intoxicated than the alcohol, or maybe it's just the aftereffects of seeing Aaron that have me feeling hazy. Either way, I follow his lead dizzily around the floor, desperately trying to lose myself in the nothingness of it all.

Chapter Twenty-Six

"Are you okay? You've been a bit distracted this evening." Kit pats his lips with a cloth napkin, blotting away his words as quickly as they're spoken. His gaze falls to my plate, where I'm still pushing around the same piece of salmon I've been toying with for the last five minutes. I drop the fork, the metal clanking as it hits the intricately painted fine china.

"We don't have to talk about it." He gives a dismissive shrug, following it up with a sip from his watered-down scotch. "I know sometimes it's just something you've gotta work through on your own, without outside commentary."

The words take me by surprise with their kindness. Not that Kit is unkind, per se, but he so commonly operates on an arsenal of surface-level flirtation and sarcasm that these little nuggets of depth always manage to hit me like an ice-cold splash of water to the face.

He must track at least some of my trail of thought because he adds, "I might be an asshole, but I'm not blind."

"If you were an asshole, by definition you'd be blind, since anuses don't have eyes."

His face falls flat. "Why are you like this?"

I try on one of his signature smirks for size. "Keeps things interesting." I remove the black cloth napkin from my lap as I stand, draping it over my hardly touched plate of food. "I'm going to run to the restroom. I'll be back."

"Don't fall in," Kit calls out, earning the stares of a few surrounding city officials.

I offer a waggle of fingers over my shoulder but don't turn around.

The magician informs me the bathrooms are located on the first floor, which seems incredibly impractical if you ask me. I make my way down the marble staircase, decidedly less steady on my feet after a few too many tequila sunrises. I round the corner into the designated hallway, slamming into a brick wall.

Only it's not a brick wall; it's a chest. A man's chest. And that chest is attached to Aaron's face and he's staring at me, eyes hazy in that familiar way they get after he's had a couple drinks. I stumble backward, and he grabs onto my biceps to steady me. The problem is that he keeps holding on long after I'm no longer wobbling on my feet. One thumb begins to stroke the delicate skin of my inner arm, that slight touch burning a trail of sparks into my flesh.

"Hey." It's all I can manage to say. He's close, so close I can feel his breath as it washes over my face. So close I can count the three fine lines that are beginning to form in his expression of utter relief at my proximity: one between the eyebrows, two to frame his gorgeous mouth.

He notices my gaze falling to his lips, and suddenly his hands release my biceps, leaving his arms free to wrap around me and pull me tightly against him. Whatever breath was left in my lungs vacates the space with a soft *whoosh*.

It feels effortless to be held by him. Tears of relief press at the backs of my eyes, like I've just come home after circumnavigating the globe. But no foreign food gracing my taste buds nor vibrant music of some far-off culture in my ears could compare to this sensation in my heart. It feels so dangerously like freedom that when he leans in to close the distance between our lips, I almost let him.

But it's not really freedom to belong to someone like this. Panic laces its way up my vertebrae, entangles itself with my veins. I jerk back, removing myself from his embrace. The resulting flash of abandonment in the shadows of his eyes is almost too much to bear.

He turns away from me, rapping two fists against the peeling floral wallpaper with a dull thud that shakes the unlit candles in their sconces. "God, Zo, what are we *doing*?"

"I...I'm sorry. I just have had some drinks and I wasn't expecting to see you and I shouldn't have—" Shouldn't have what? Let him hold me? Let him see the walls come down for just a moment when I was weak? I don't even know how to finish my own sentence, so I leave it dangling in the air between us.

He hangs his head, letting it join his fists against the wall. I watch his shoulders rise and fall with each labored breath, the fitted black suit pulled taut by his outstretched arms.

Finally he pushes away from the wall, facing me with a stricken expression tarnishing his beautiful features. Kind, gentle Aaron torn apart by my inability to let him in. "I want you to know that if I thought for one second that you really didn't want me, I'd walk away. But it's written so plainly on your gorgeous face." He reaches out, and I don't know why but I let him cup my jaw. I may even lean into his touch just a little. "You can't ask me to walk away from that."

My own face crumples as the tears finally spill over, but he doesn't let me go even when they puddle against his palm. He's watching me, wondering why the hell I won't take the lifeline he's offered. And I'm so tired of him not understanding, of no one understanding, that the exhaustion nearly brings me to my knees. I place my hand over his, cradling my own face. Getting my own self through it as best I know how.

"I've told you before about my ex, Topher. Do you remember me mentioning him at all?"

He nods his head slightly, just enough to urge me onward. Of course he remembers. Everything I've ever told him, every little thing that slightly annoys me or weird outlook on life that I have, he carries it with him inside, infuses it so effortlessly into the way he treats me that sometimes I miss it. But it's always there. It's that understanding that nearly convinces me it's worth the pain to stay.

"He hurt you, didn't he?" His words are laced with regret like he's begging me to tell him he's wrong while being almost certain that he's right.

I can't help the tremors that begin to rock through my body. Even though I opened the can, the sight of the worms is still a shock. I know Eden would never have told him, but the only other option seems just as unlikely. "Rose?"

He shakes his head. "She didn't say a word. But I see it in you, that guarded look in your eyes." He drops his hand away from my face, taking mine with it so our fingers can intertwine and dangle between us. "Dani had this boyfriend in high school. She'd come home with bruises she couldn't explain. Anytime I pressed, she'd beg me to just let it go. For the longest time her eyes looked like yours. She didn't even tell me the whole truth of what happened until two years after she married Jeremiah."

I picture Dani's vibrant face riddled with the unseen bruises I know too well. It breaks my heart all over again, to share this bond with his sister that neither of us would choose for ourselves but are stuck with, nonetheless.

"Zo, when are you going to stop punishing yourself for what he did to you?" His brow is knitted with concern and his thumb moves like a metronome over the back of my hand. "You deserve a healthy relationship, a real relationship. One with commitment and the promise of a future together. One where the person knows you, *really* knows you, and chooses you. Keeps you safe."

It's that last word that breaks me like no other ever could.

"Aaron, lov—" I stop myself as soon as I realize what's coming out of my mouth, but it's too late. A glimmer of hope flashes in his eyes. "*Caring* for you feels like I'm wearing a turtleneck that's too tight around my neck. It's a cage I'm trapped in, where even if you hurt me, I'd never be able to leave."

I sense that bullet hitting its mark in the way he recoils immediately. I can practically see the wound blooming on his chest.

"Do you honestly think I'd hurt you?"

"No," I manage to choke out. "But I've been wrong before." *And it almost cost me my life.*

That's the problem, after all. There was a time when I never would've believed Topher could hurt me. The playful, reserved boy that I fell in love with didn't seem to have an unkind bone in his body. Even after the hateful words came, and then the shoving here or there, I truly thought he would never go further. Each step he took pushed the line I'd drawn back, until there was no longer a line at all. Until I was lying in the dirt clutching a bruised rib, unable to breathe through the tears and the pain.

We stare at each other for a moment, both of us drowning in our own versions of the same sorrow. Our standoff finally ends when a heavy arm settles around my shoulders, causing me to flinch. I don't even have to look; I know who it is by the watch glinting on his wrist.

"Hey, Kit," Aaron bites out gruffly. He offers a hand for Kit to shake.

My gaze flits up to Kit's face, and I can practically see the gears turning in his head as he takes in our tense body language and the tears streaking across my cheeks. Unfortunately for all of us, he completely misreads the situation.

"My friends call me Kit." He takes Aaron's outstretched hand, squeezing so tightly his knuckles go white. "It's Christopher to you."

"Well, respectfully, *Kitty Cat*," Aaron says, the eye roll present in his voice if not on his face, "we're having a private conversation."

The tension is so thick in the air between them that it's almost physical. I'm suddenly reminded why I came down here in the first place, my screaming bladder begging for this to be over.

"You two broke up; let it go," Kit says, stepping aside to create an escape route between us for Aaron; one that he doesn't take.

Instead his eyes lock on mine and for a moment we're the only two people in this hallway. In this building. In this world. "I can't let it go. She's my soulmate. She knows it, too; she's just scared right now. But I'll be here when she's ready."

His soulmate.

My bladder—and my heart—have had enough. They can remain in this pissing match, but I won't stay here one second longer. I push past Aaron to the sounds of both men protesting, locking myself in the bathroom so I can pee—and cry—in peace.

Miraculously it takes at least ten minutes before another woman desperate for a toilet begins banging on the door of the restroom. I've been drawing in slow, measured breaths in an attempt to calm my nerves, taking advantage of the full mirror while I thumb through my clutch for anything that might save my tear-ravaged face. With the help of a makeup wipe and a tinted lip balm, I've managed to clear most of the wreckage by the time the knocking begins.

I draw in one last breath and hold it, steeling myself for what might await me on the other side of the door. When I turn the lock and pull it open, I'm surprised to find it's not a red-faced woman doing the potty dance. It's Kit, leaning an arm on the doorway that he's resting his forehead against.

Before I can shut the door in his weary-looking face, he stops it with an outstretched hand.

"Let's go home, yeah? This party sucks." His voice carries none of its usual sardonic spice. Instead he sounds utterly exhausted.

"Okay," is all I can manage to say. I peek under his arm into the hallway, searching for Aaron, but there's no one here aside from us.

Kit follows my gaze. "Chase came and got him; they already left. He would've kicked me out, too if I wasn't your ride home."

I nod, my lips pressed together in a thin line. When we step out of the hallway, there's a queue of women standing just around the corner. They each eye me with pity, save for one particularly desperate lady who glares at me while clutching her gut. One glance cast in Kit's direction reveals an amused smile tugging at his lips.

"I may have herded them out of the hallway by telling them you had explosive diarrhea and would need a minute to clean it all up." My jaw drops, heat flaming my cheeks. He simply shrugs his shoulders. "Aaron said you'd never come out of there if you saw ten pairs of eyes aimed at you the minute the door opened, knowing they heard you crying."

Though it seems impossible, my bruised and beaten heart swells even further. "Does that mean you all heard me crying?"

He holds the door open for me to step out into the brisk night. I suddenly remember my jacket is upstairs, wrapped around my abandoned chair, but there's no way I'm going back for it now and risking running into one of the women who thinks I just spent the last ten minutes shitting my brains out. I just wrap my arms tightly around myself as we hustle to the car.

"Oh yeah. Chase made Aaron leave before he busted the door down, and I just had to stand there listening. You make these pathetic blubbering sounds when you really get going. I almost thought I'd have to give you mouth-to-mouth." He adds the last part with an accompanying wink before ducking into his unlocked car and cranking up the engine.

His attempt at innuendo falls like razor blades across my already-tattered nerves. I take my place in the passenger seat, immediately turning the heat all the way up to thaw out my frozen bones.

Kit finally notices my chattering teeth, a flash of shame mottling his features. "Shit, sorry, I should've offered you my coat. Want me to go back in and get yours?"

I shake my head. "I'd really just like to leave."

"Understood." He puts the car in drive and pulls away from our parking spot as my gaze travels up to the second-floor windows of the courthouse and the shadowy figures that dance by without a care in the world.

Or perhaps they do have a million concerns, a million burdens they carry that are just as heavy as my own, and yet they're choosing to dance anyway.

When the shivering finally subsides, I let my gaze fall from the passing buildings over to Kit, who has one hand lazily draped on the steering wheel and the other resting on the gearshift. "I'm really sorry about all that."

"Don't be." He keeps his eyes trained on the road as he speaks. "Though, correct me if I'm wrong, I know you said things just didn't work out between you two because you didn't want something more serious, but from an outsider's point of view, things looked very serious to me."

I let out a heavy sigh, resigning myself to the fact that brushing it off at this point would classify me as certifiable. "You're not *entirely* wrong. It's just complicated, I guess."

He snorts, flipping the blinker on for my street. "What's so complicated?"

"You wouldn't get it."

"Try me." He casts a withering, sidelong glance my way.

I pause for a moment, considering my options. I either give him some sort of explanation now, or he'll nag me for one until I'm so annoyed that I spill, just like he did with the date. *Bet he's regretting that right about now.* The thought makes me smile ever so slightly.

We pull to a stop in my driveway, but neither of us make an attempt to get out. The idea of facing the cold without a jacket, even just for the twenty steps to my front porch, has me shivering preemptively.

"Come on, Zo, just spit it out."

I turn to glare at him, annoyed that he's proving me right. Annoyed at this night in general. Finally I decide to just give him what he's asking for. "You want the truth, Kit? I was in an abusive relationship in high school, and I've never gotten over it. I don't want to be tied down because I refuse to be trapped in another terrible relationship ever again. I let things go too far with Aaron, and that's my bad, but don't worry. I'm paying for it royally now."

He chews on the inside of his cheek, staring out the front window of the car. The silence stretches out so long that my patience begins to wear thin. I want to say something snarky to him like, *That's what you get for sticking your nose where it doesn't belong,* but instead I reach for the handle, ready to leave this night behind me.

A firm hand clamps down on my knee, stopping me in my tracks. His broad palm nearly encapsulates the knobby bone, the heat of his touch penetrating the fabric of my dress with ease. I try to grab on to that feeling, to draw a familiar comfort from the touch of another, but my heart resists. It's had a taste of being touched reverently, being known intimately, and now nothing else will ever compare.

"I'm sorry that happened to you." The gentleness in his voice surprises me, a raw edge to the sound that cuts at my agitation. I turn back to face him, trying and failing to read his clouded expression. "I can tell Aaron cares for you, almost as much as you care for him. My ex-wife and I never looked at each other the way you two did tonight. Even when I thought we were in love."

"I never said I didn't care for him. I do." I nearly choke on the words, a knot swelling in my throat that I struggle to breathe around. I've always felt out of my depth in the ocean of Aaron's love for me. That Kit of all people is suggesting my own feelings may even surpass that level lands like a red-lettered *A* at the top of the paper I've written on emotions. The one I'd thought I bombed. "That's what scares me the most. I've only felt like this once before, and now you know what happened there."

It's the first time I've admitted as much, and I can't believe I'm doing so to Kit Llewellyn of all people. But he just nods his head like he understands completely, his hand squeezing two rapid pulses on my knee.

"Do you think that jackass who hurt you stops himself from getting close to anyone, for fear of what he might do?"

"No, probably not." The words come out sharp and hateful. I try to rein in my tone, reminding myself that Kit is not the enemy here. "Why?"

"Just seems like you're missing out on an awful lot of life over some deadbeat who isn't missing out on any of his," he muses, his drawl making the words sound like they're dripping with honey despite being the opposite of sweet. He must catch the anger in my eyes, and perhaps some of the sadness too, because he releases my knee and locks both hands back onto the steering wheel.

"I'm not saying I don't get it; clearly I've got some fucked-up ways of approaching relationships myself. I just hate it for you. I don't know if I believe in soulmates or whatever Aaron called you two, but if the real deal does exist, just based on the way you look at him, the way you look right now listening to me talk about him... well, you two might be it."

His words crack and splinter the very foundation of my mind, the one Topher set in stone all those years ago, leaving me wondering why I let myself build on it in the first place. I got rid of everything else the man gave me; why hold on to the very worst part of it?

Why have I spent so long letting him take up any of the space in my head?

I know the reason almost before my internal monologue has

asked the question. Because it's hard. Because it takes waking up every day and rewriting the programming of my brain, so that the shortcuts and assumptions he created are no longer the paths my thoughts default to. It's daunting and terrifying to think of facing those demons, so instead I've walked on eggshells ever since, avoiding every place that held the possibility of containing a land mine.

Looking at Kit, at his smug face and perfectly coiffed hair, I could kiss him for being so blunt. But I don't, because for better or worse, my heart already belongs to someone else, and for the first time terror isn't the only feeling that accompanies that thought. There's a glimmer of hope, too, riding on its coattails.

Chapter Twenty-Seven

I f it weren't for the tequila still running through my veins, I doubt sleep would've been as easy to come by as it was last night. When I finally force my eyes open, they crack apart with extreme resistance, sticky sleep residue holding my lashes together like glue. My contact lenses burn from being in overnight, a sin I commit so often I'm halfway tempted to invest in Lasik.

I roll onto my side with a soft groan, reaching for the contact case on my bedside table and depositing the miserable things in their prisons. My glasses bring the world back into focus, and the first thing I see are two green stems poking hesitantly out of the soil where my maimed pothos has sat dormant for weeks.

Jumping out of bed, I lift the pot into the cradle of my arms, studying those baby branches up close. They are brand-new, but I can tell they are healthy. No trace of the poison that nearly claimed the plant's life remains. Relief bubbles up in me, starting in my toes and floating all the way to the crown of my head. I feel it vibrating underneath my skin, so strong I'm almost certain I can see the pale blonde hairs on my arms quiver.

The excitement makes me brave—or stupid, depending on how you look at it. Either way, I find myself pulling my laptop off the small L-shaped desk in the corner of the room and bringing it with me to the kitchen, where I load up the coffee maker while a long-untouched Facebook account fills the screen. The most recent photos were uploaded on my twenty-first birthday. I'd blocked Topher after the breakup, but for years he would still use fake accounts and those of mutual friends to send threatening messages to my inbox. By the time junior year of college rolled around, I quit social media altogether so he wouldn't be able to find me.

Call it paranoia, but I'm still not willing to risk it, so I log out of my account and create a fake profile with some throwaway email address I've been giving out to cashiers at every retail store I've entered in the last decade. I don't bother adding any details or photos. I go straight to the search bar and type in his name: Topher Nichols.

As the results begin loading on the page, I marvel at the way my hands don't tremble. My heartbeat stays slow and steady. What might seem miniscule to some is monumental to me. I can't remember the last time I could even *think* his name without terror coming right in alongside it.

The first few results are men living in California and Pennsylvania, respectively. Knowing Topher, there's no way he'd ever leave our hometown. I scroll past the two unfortunate souls that share his cursed name, before the third photo turns the blood in my veins to ice.

Time has not been particularly kind to him. His hairline is already receding, and I'd be lying if I said it didn't bring me some level of satisfaction to see that those years of loading up on steroids and pushing himself in the gym did not save him from the softening body that age delivers all of us. He's flexing toward the camera, his undefined bicep no longer sporting rippling muscle but a tattoo of an AR-15 along with the phrase *Come and Take 'Em.*

He's exactly who I always imagined he'd be, but that thought doesn't make me happy. It doesn't make me feel anything at all.

Before I can think better of it, I click on his profile. My lip curls at the sight of the Confederate flag he's using as his cover photo. His page is filled with ignorance and bitterness, that rotten core of him that I discovered long ago seemingly metastasizing all the way to the surface. I can't imagine any goodness in him could have survived it.

I don't know what I was hoping to find, or if it's just Kit's words circling in my head that made me come looking, but I've resigned myself to delete the fake account and go back to forgetting him when a post he's tagged in catches my eye.

I recognize the name of the girl who posted it; she was a few grades younger than us in school but made varsity volleyball as a freshman because of her talent. Chunky blonde highlights streak through her chestnut-colored hair, and she's wearing an Abercrombie V-neck I'd venture to guess she bought all the way back when I knew her. In some ways it's like time stopped in Ardmore, Alabama, and everyone's frozen exactly where I left them.

But it's not her highlights or her clothing choices or even the tense smile turning her cheeks into hard round apples that stops the air in my lungs. It's the glimmering diamond on her finger that she's holding up to the screen, along with Topher nuzzling his head into her shoulder from behind, his mouth spread in a tight-lipped smirk. It's the words *We're engaged!* typed out as the caption, and the well-wishes of everyone I went to high school with in the comments section.

Suddenly I'm filled with a seething anger. It crackles through me so violently it makes my teeth hurt. Anger for that girl, for the life she's probably living.

For the one that I am not.

Kit was right. While I've spent the last eleven years of my life holding myself back from anything real for fear of getting hurt, Topher has missed out on nothing. He hasn't punished himself at all.

Did I really expect him to? No, I guess not. But the fact that he's getting married makes me sick to my stomach. I can't bring myself to believe he's changed. Evil like that doesn't change. I look at her uneasy expression, and I'm overwhelmed with the urge to weep for both of us. Because if he hasn't hurt her yet, one day he will, and it'll be just as much my fault because I kept this to myself.

I click on her name and type a quick message. It's nothing profound, but it will let her know someone sees her. Someone cares. I pull up the contact I've kept in my phone ever since college—the number for a domestic violence hotline—and I add it to the end of my message, praying she never needs it. Worrying she already might.

I press send and then clamp my laptop shut, nearly pinching off my own fingers in the process. A million different sensations are flooding through me at once. Anger, hurt, relief, loneliness. And there, underneath it all, the most inexplicable, intense desire to fall into Aaron's arms and lose myself in the exact opposite of the emptiness I've made a home of for so long.

The line for Taylor's Landing rings twice before Chase's cheery voice comes through the receiver. I can't help the pang of disappointment that it isn't Aaron who answers, but I forge ahead before I lose my nerve.

"Hey, Chase, is Aaron there?"

"Zo?" His voice softens considerably. "How're you doing this morning?"

"I'm...better." It doesn't feel like a lie, I'm surprised to find. Despite the revelations of the last half hour, I feel free for the first time in so long. It's as though all along the suffocation I felt at even the hint of love was in fact a rope tethering me to Topher being pulled taut. But that rope has been severed. He has no hold over me anymore. "I need to talk to Aaron."

"You sound better. I heard the whale noises you were making in that bathroom last night. Not. Pretty." He chuckles at his own joke while my cheeks warm from embarrassment. "Aaron's not here

214

today. He pulled the short straw and had to host Saturday detention. He'll be at the school all morning."

"Thanks." I pause for a moment, and then I add, "For every-thing, Chase."

I hang up the phone before he can respond. Slipping into the nearest sweater and a pair of jeans, I grab my keys from their hook and make my way to the car.

Loveless Middle School is a squatty brick building surrounded on three sides by dense forest that doubles as a local park with walking paths that wind through the woods. Those trails are the closest I've been to the building, since it's a bit weirder to visit Aaron at a school than it is for him to come see me at the bar. At least, that's what I told myself until now. I'm surprised to find the words ringing a tad hollow as I pull off the main road and onto the winding driveway that stops directly in front of the main entrance.

There are signs directing me to the administrative office to check in for a visitor's pass, but when I approach it, the room is dark and the doors are locked. Of course they aren't here; it's the weekend. I make my way to the doors that lead into the main building, worrying that my plans are about to fall apart. Someone up above is on my side, though, because one of the double glass doors comes open in my hands, bringing with it the unmistakable scent of middle school: body odor and industrial chemicals.

Various shades of construction-paper cut into the shape of maple leaves are taped to the walls of the hallway, arranged haphazardly as if they are being blown by some imaginary breeze. I pass a door labeled *Teacher's Lounge*, noting the posterboard to the right of it with the staff's faces cut out and imposed upon turkey bodies. I giggle when I see Aaron's playful grin over an orange turkey, but it's the only sight of him near the room. The window shows nothing but the glow of a few soda machines in the darkness.

Farther down the main hall, various smaller arteries break off on either side. I scan the name placards hung from the ceiling outside each classroom to no avail. I've nearly given up when I make it to the last hallway and find *A. Moore* hanging above the farthest door.

It's slightly ajar, a familiar voice drifting through the gap as I make my way closer. Aaron stops talking and a younger voice begins to respond, the adolescent boy either upset or deep in the throes of puberty based on how badly his voice is cracking.

"It doesn't make any sense; I didn't do anything to make her mad."

"When did she start saying those things to you?"

The boy hesitates to respond, and I hold my breath, nervous for him even though I don't have a clue what's being discussed.

"Aiden told her friend Maya that I liked her. I didn't want her to know, but it was too late. She had written me a note that made it sound like she liked me, too, but ever since Maya told her, she won't even talk to me except to tell me my breath stinks or my clothes don't match." The words come out in a rush of air from the kid, and I feel a distinct urge to wrap him in a hug. Middle school sucks, and the convoluted grapevine of gossip doesn't sound like it's changed much over the years. "Why would you be mean like that to someone you like?"

Before Aaron can respond, I push open the door, surprising both him and the kid. The boy is maybe thirteen, though I'm terrible at gauging children's ages, and he's got the same swooping haircut as every boy band member from my youth. Acne sits in small clusters on his face, and he's wearing black-framed glasses similar to mine. They don't hide the fact that he has kind eyes, which I notice right away.

By bursting in the way I did, I've inadvertently put myself on a metaphorical stage, and they both watch me like they're waiting for my performance. I glance at Aaron, hoping he's listening closely, because I'm fairly certain I'll only get through this once before passing out. "She might just be scared, erm..."

"Joey," the kid says, pointing to himself.

"Joey," I confirm. "Sometimes we don't know how to handle our feelings, and so it comes out like we're just being mean. And that's no excuse, but it's the truth. People like you, with soft hearts, are so good, *too good*, and if she's smart, she'll do better so she can be what you deserve."

"O...kay?" Joey responds, earning a chuckle from Aaron, who's leaning against his desk with arms folded over his chest, watching the exchange with a raised eyebrow.

It isn't a Hallmark moment, I'll admit, but the words aren't really for Joey, and I can tell by the way Aaron's gaze travels over me now that he knows it, too. We watch each other, lost in the wide-open space my speech has left in the place where a wall once stood between us. I take one step toward him, and then another, until a shrill ringing interrupts the moment.

"Yeah, Mom?" Joey says into his phone. "Let me ask." He clamps a hand over the receiver. "Mr. Moore, my mom wants to know if she can pick me up early. Says my little sister's got a fever and she doesn't want me to get anyone sick."

I clamp a hand over my mouth and nose, giving the petri dish as wide a berth as possible until my back is against the dry erase board. No way am I getting sick again.

Aaron tosses an amused look over his shoulder at me before turning back to the expectant tween. "Yeah, that's fine. When will she be here?"

Joey relays the question to his mom, then listens for her answer. "She's out front."

"How convenient," Aaron replies. "Go ahead, just give some thought to what Miss Allen here said. I'm sure there are some nuggets of wisdom buried in that dirt."

"Hey!" I exclaim, the sound muffled against my hand.

Joey giggles, gathering his things into a gaping backpack and hosting it over his thin shoulders.

"And no matter how mean she is to you, that doesn't mean you can deface my desks with dirty words."

Joey's face falls, guilt coloring his features. "Sorry about that. Won't happen again."

"Good. Now I'd ruffle your hair or something, but you've got germs, so go home and try to stay well. Deal?"

"Deal." With that, Joey leaves the room, slamming the door shut behind him in a distinctly teenager way.

I let my hand fall to my waist, sucking in a breath of not-palm-scented air. Aaron rounds the corner of his desk, positioning himself so close in front of me that I have to remain pressed against the whiteboard to avoid touching him. His hands flex and close at his sides, as though he is struggling to avoid touching *me*.

"That was quite a speech."

My gaze roams over his face. I memorize each of his features—the curve of his jaw, the swell of his cheeks, the freckle hidden by the awning of his lower lashes—and I tuck them away in my mind to revisit on a rainy day. "It was long overdue."

"What are you saying, Zo?" That fine line between his eyebrows deepens, his teeth worrying at his lower lip.

I draw in a ragged breath, filling my lungs to capacity, knowing there isn't enough air in the world for all the apologies I owe him. But I'll start with this one. "I'm sorry I took so long to be honest with you about everything. I feel like I caused a lot of unnecessary heartache for both of us."

He shakes his head. "Nothing with you has ever been unnecessary. I just don't know why you never felt like you could tell me."

"It's not that." I find myself reaching for him, grabbing onto the seam of his shirt. I'm afraid if I'm not anchored to him, I'll float away. "It's more that I felt like if I told people, they'd see how weak I really am. They'd think I was a fool for staying."

He grabs onto the hand that's white-knuckling the edge of his shirt and uses it to pull me to him, burying his nose in my hair. "You are not a fool and you're not weak. The only weak person in this situation is that sick guy who thought it was okay to hurt someone smaller than him. Someone who trusted and cared for him."

"I've been so awful to you." I can see it so clearly now, how horribly I've treated him while trying to keep myself safe. I breathe in his scent, trying not to disintegrate beneath the weight of my shame. "I don't understand why you ever even liked me in the first place."

"Because, Zo." He tucks his other hand into my curls, scratching delicately at my scalp in a rhythmic motion. "There are moments when you slip up and I get to see you for who you are. Not who you think he made you, or who you have to be, but your true self. And it takes my breath away, every time. I'd sit through a thousand of your rightfully earned breakdowns for even a momentary glimpse of your beautiful soul."

I fall apart against his chest, amazed that I have any tears left to cry. But I do and they flow from my eyes with abandon, soaking the cotton Loveless Middle School long-sleeve tee that he's wearing. He makes no move to ease the crying, to get me to stop. He just rides the wave with me, holding me steady, keeping me afloat.

The next full breath I draw in scrapes against the raw edges of my throat. "What happened with Topher, it's not an excuse. I've just spent so long living in the shadow of what he did that he's managed to accomplish exactly what I didn't want him to: he's taken my life from me."

I feel Aaron's chin roll over the crown of my head as he shakes his vigorously. "No, he didn't take your life."

"But he did, didn't he? Look at how long I've spent avoiding everything that would anger him. Dieting to be the right size, refusing to get back on a horse because it reminds me of him and everything he cost me." I lift my head to face him, wrapping a hand around the back of his neck. "Not letting myself fall so far into love that it looks anything like it did with him."

"Love doesn't look like that," Aaron whispers, his breath minty as it flows over my face. I'm suddenly insecure, realizing I rushed out of the house before even brushing my teeth. I probably have the worst combination of morning and coffee breath.

"I'm tired of it, Aaron. I want to let you in, all the way in. I want to love you without barriers, without worrying that I have to turn myself into something that I'm not. I'm not perfect. I'm broken and I'm dealing with the damage one day at a time but I'm willing to try. Not just for you but for myself. I don't want to spend one more minute living my life in the cage he created for me."

"I never wanted you to be anything but yourself, Zo. The good, the bad, the ugly." He traces his thumb over the swell of my cheek, smiling. "Not that any part of you could ever be ugly. When you're hurting or something triggers you or you're just annoyed with me, I want you to tell me. I'm damn sure going to tell you, because I have problems, too. We all do. I want all of you, not just the parts you think are perfect. All of it's perfection to me."

I forget about my morning breath, tilting my head to capture his lips as they fall to meet mine. Suddenly every week, every day, every second I've spent not kissing him overwhelms me and I'm filled with a desire so strong I desperately need to be closer than I am. I want to crawl inside his heart and never leave, but I settle for a hand buried beneath his shirt, pressed against that thrumming beat, racing because of me. Because of us.

A deep moan rumbles in his chest, and his fingers lace into my hair so he can keep my lips pressed to his as we stumble backward toward his classroom door. I hear the lock click, and then he's lifting me, carrying me to his desk. He rests me on it and continues devouring me, his lips blazing a trail down my neck and across my collarbone, grazing that hollow Topher once tried to claim as his own. It never belonged to him, and it doesn't belong to Aaron now. It's mine, my body to give, and I give every inch of it over to Aaron, trusting him to take care of me always.

He pulls away from me, panting breaths falling from his swollen lips. I let my gaze travel over his brown skin, his breathtaking eyes, his glorious mouth. It feels like a miracle to be here with him, not completely rid of all the things that once weighed me down, but lighter than I've been in a long time.

"Okay, we're not fucking in my classroom," he groans, more to himself than to me. "Because I'm a professional. And your breath stinks. Seriously, did you get right out of bed and come here?"

We're both laughing, but I smack him once on the chest for good measure.

"But we are going to go back to my house, because it's closer, and I am going to make sweet, sweet love to you until I collapse with exhaustion to make up for all the time we've been apart. Deal?"

I giggle like a schoolgirl. Appropriate given the setting. "Deal."

"Great, let's go." He grabs my hand and pulls me toward the door, unlocking it and hauling me into the hallway. We're nearly to the entrance in the blink of an eye, walking so fast I narrowly avoid slamming into him when he comes to an abrupt stop, whirling around to face me. "Just one thing before we go."

"What?"

"Back there." He jabs a finger in the direction of his classroom. "You said you wanted to love me without barriers. You wanted to *love* me. And at the dinner last night, before you caught yourself, you were about to say *loving* me. Weren't you?"

He's rambling a mile a minute, and it's so adorable that even though I know exactly what it is he's asking me to do, I decide to make him work for it.

"What exactly would you like me to say, Mr. Moore?" I flick his faculty badge for emphasis.

He shakes his head, a low growl forming at the back of his throat. "You know what I want."

I decide to take mercy on him. After all, he's shown me more than my fair share lately. "I'm so in love with you. Your kindness and your strength. Your humor and your sense of adventure. You're so good, down to your very core. I'm crazy about you, Aaron. You have no idea."

Two eager arms encircle my waist, and suddenly I'm flying through the air, his lips pressed against mine. So much for my breath stinking.

When he settles me back on my own two feet, his eyes are practically sparkling. He frames my face with one hand and uses the other to hold me close, pressing it tightly to my lower back. His forehead rests against mine, that minty scent washing over my face when he parts his lips to say, "I love...how cool you are."

Chapter Twenty-Eight

Bagel regards me with an unamused stare from his place on the sofa when I step out of the bathroom, toothbrush dangling from my mouth. I don't know why, after all we've said to one another today, the sight of my toothbrush still in its spot next to Aaron's was the thing that broke me. He could've thrown it away or moved it out of sight to be rid of the reminder, but he didn't. He knew long before I did that this day would come.

"Excuse me, ma'am, I'm going to need you to hurry up," Aaron says, grabbing onto my hips and pulling me against him, sporting a devilish grin. "I've got plans for you."

I speed brush my tongue and then rinse my mouth and toothbrush out, barely having time to dry my face before a strong arm hooks around my waist from behind and drags me to the bedroom. Bagel doesn't even bother to watch the ordeal, instead deciding this is the perfect time to distract himself with some overdue grooming.

Aaron plops me onto the bed stomach first, not even giving me a chance to flip over before he drags my leggings and underwear off in one fell swoop. The cold air has goose bumps prickling along my skin, but there's a burning heat concentrated between my thighs, begging for him.

"God, you're beautiful," he moans, one hand clamped on the backs of each of my thighs, spreading me for him. "And you're mine."

"Always have been," I manage, that heat reaching a boil when his breath brushes over my sensitive skin.

"Always will be." Then his tongue presses into me, and I lose the ability to speak. The tight grip he keeps on my thighs holds me in place while his teeth graze against my clit, the sensation leaving me gasping for air. My toes curl tighter when his tongue delves inside of me, his fisted bedspread my only anchor. He devours me, and I'm helpless to do anything but let him.

Suddenly the desperate need to see him, to slip into the cool depth of his jade-colored eyes and feel him deep inside me is overwhelming. His grasp on my thighs loosens ever so slightly, and I crawl forward, giggling at his disappointed whimper. When I flip onto my back, the first thing I see are his lips, tucked into a pitiful pout at being denied his favorite pleasure: tasting my orgasm on his tongue.

"Take your clothes off," I demand, demonstrating my request by removing my own shirt and bra.

His gaze never leaves my own as he strips himself bare. I let my gaze roam, traveling over every ridge of his taut body and down the trail of short black hair that leads to the valley between his hips, where I can see just how much he missed me.

"You done staring?" He chuckles darkly.

I bite my lip and nod, not trusting myself to speak.

He leans onto the bed and stalks forward, settles himself between my thighs and takes one nipple between his teeth while his fingers pinch and roll the other. I cry out, that fire in my abdomen exploding into an inferno. I grasp at his back, my nails scratching harsh lines like wings out from his spine, but he refuses to be rushed. He worships each breast in turn, leaving me trembling beneath him.

"Please, Aaron. I need you *now*."

His name captures his attention, drawing two glazed-over eyes up to my face. Whatever he sees there must convince him, because he reaches down between us and guides himself to my entrance, pressing in slowly, so slowly, until all of him is inside me and I'm complete at last.

Whereas everything up until this moment has been heated and desperate, now he rocks his hips gently, reveling in the closeness we're sharing. How long has it been since we were joined together like this? Weeks? A month? It seems like an eternity now that he's here, and yet this feels completely brand-new, like everything before this moment was a shadow of the real thing and this is what we've been working toward all along.

His lips press against mine, communicating everything that words cannot. His fingers tangle in my hair, holding me as closely as our bodies will allow as he thrusts into me, driving us both to the edge. The muscles in my abdomen tighten, my thighs clenching around his narrow hips until I'm falling, and he's falling, too. But we find each other on the way down.

"Okay, I really have to go," I groan, trying to pull away for the umpteenth time. Aaron whimpers, locking his muscular arm around my waist so I'm pinned against him. I level a hard stare on his face, which he peeps one eye open to see before quickly snapping it shut again so he can pretend that he hasn't.

I tap a finger against his forehead. "Excuse me, sir? Our annual Friendsgiving Dinner at the bar is just over a week away, and I have got to get the order finalized today because nothing will be delivered after Wednesday. Do you want to be the reason this town misses out on such a beloved tradition?"

I'm not sure how many years something has to be done to count as tradition, but it'll be the third year we've put on the community event at Nomad's and it's been incredibly well-attended the past two times. Aaron sighs and loosens his grip, letting me unravel myself from our tangle of limbs. He does manage to grab one final squeeze of my left breast on the retreat, the corner of his lip pitching into a smile.

He props himself up on his elbows to watch me get dressed, not even bothering to cover his own nudity. Something I'm thankful for, because it means I get to admire every inch of his statuesque body while I begrudgingly get ready to leave.

"What are you doing for actual Thanksgiving?"

My head pops through the neck of my shirt. "I fly out on Wednesday night, back on Saturday morning. It's my mother's favorite holiday so I've been required to make a blood oath to return every year, no matter where in the world I am living. What about you?"

"My parents are actually going on a European cruise this year, so they have passed the hosting baton to Dani. Last I heard, Jeremiah was planning on going off script with something called a turkey roulade." His lip curls around the word like it tastes bad.

I look up from the shoe I'm lacing, my laughter falling away when our eyes meet. The mental image of him in my childhood home, laughing with my father over the slightly burned turkey and poking fun at my mother for the underdone corn casserole, plays like a movie in my mind's eye. The desire hits me out of nowhere, and suddenly I want nothing more in the world than to spend the holiday with him. To spend every holiday for the rest of my life with him.

Opening my mouth to speak, a swell of nausea begins in my gut and travels upward, constricting my airway. I've never brought a boyfriend home before, though that word feels inadequate for what Aaron is to me. The idea of introducing my mildly neurotic mother and boisterous father to any man has always brought with it sheer terror. But I realize the nausea I feel now is from fear of rejection, not fear of asking.

I swallow down the thick lump in my throat, suddenly fascinated by my own fingers. "Well, you could always come with me."

Silence settles between us, but it's not uncomfortable. It's sparkling and light, full of hope.

"I'd like that," Aaron answers quietly, his tone one of awe, like he's watching something brand new be born right in front of him.

"Yeah?" I'm standing now, shifting my weight. I really need to get to the bar before it opens, but part of me wants to stay in this moment forever.

He reaches for my dangling hands, capturing them and pulling me to him. "Absolutely." He presses his lips against mine, the faint scent of me lingering. It's almost enough to make me say to hell with the order and climb back into bed with him. But he releases me and smacks my ass firmly, winking when I yelp. "Now get to work so you can hurry back to me."

The morning is brighter than usual, or maybe it's just the way I'm looking at it, but the crisp air bites at my lungs with every breath I take, and the sky is so blue it nearly hurts, but it's a pleasant pain. The kind that reminds you you're alive. That you're still fighting.

I round the corner onto Main Street, glancing through the windows of 8th & Main to wave at Rose behind the counter. She returns the gesture, causing several people in line to turn and see who she's acknowledging. A few of them nod at me; the rest just return to the task at hand, desperate for a Saturday morning pick-me-up.

There's a bounce to my gait as I sidestep a dog walker on the sidewalk, her fluffy bichon frise straining to sniff me when I pass. I stuff my hands into my jacket pockets, smiling at a small family who walks by, but the expression stalls on my face when I turn to the bar door, noting the garish red spray paint adorning the plywood window covering.

Sorry yet? it reads in a font reminiscent of a serial killer.

Before I even know what's happening, my phone is in my hand and it's ringing. Aaron's melodic voice comes over the line, still husky with leftover desire when he says, "Don't tell me you've changed your mind already. No refunds, no exchanges."

His chuckle trails off when I don't respond at first, fear zapping down my spine.

"Zo? Are you there?" I hear him shuffle, presumably getting to his feet. In my mind I watch him don his jeans and tug on his long-sleeve shirt, the muffled rattling coming through the phone confirming my imagination. "What's wrong?"

"Can you come to the bar?" I manage to choke out. "Please?"

"I'll be right there."

And I know he means it, because he's always right there. I'm just glad I finally realized it.

<hr>

Aaron arrives at the same time Mitchell parks with fresh plywood strapped down in the bed of his truck. Aaron helps him unload it, gaze flickering between the vandalism and the small crowd that has gathered, before the two of them settle it against the wall and he's free to wrap his arms around me.

"What the hell is this? Why would someone do that?"

Mitchell removes the old wood while I quickly catch Aaron up on the things he's missed. Though he'd heard about the shattered window and Maddie's slashed tires, he assumed like everyone else that it was a group of dumb teenagers. When I add that my pothos was poisoned and we found a jacket in the walk-in that no delivery driver ever claimed, worry flashes in his eyes.

"Why on earth haven't you gotten security cameras put in?" He places his hands on his hips, expression riddled with disbelief. I don't miss the subtle shake of Mitch's head.

Indignance burns hot on my cheeks. "I don't want to be pushed into anything by a bully." It's the same defense I offered Kit, which he accepted no matter how stupid he may have secretly thought it was. But Aaron is not Kit, and he's much less apt to put up with my shit. The two of them start securing the new covering as the crowd disperses at last, but he pauses in the task and turns to roll his eyes at me.

"Zo, you're not somehow admitting defeat by making a smart decision to protect your business and your employees. How would you feel if things escalate? What if next time it's not a plant this guy hurts, but Maddie? Or *Eden?* How much will it matter that you didn't cow in fear then?"

My hackles lower, knowing that he's right. What if my pride had gotten someone I care about hurt? Or worse?

As if Aaron summoned her, Eden rounds the corner, taking in the scene. Her brow furrows as she approaches, eyes squinting to read the writing on the discarded plywood. I see the moment it registers, because her jaw drops open. "Oh fuck. Not again." She comes to a stop beside me, arms crossed over her chest. "Can we please get security cameras now?"

Aaron turns to me with a look in his eye that screams, *I told you so.*

Glancing back and forth between the both of them, I throw my hands up in the air, resigned to the fact that part of letting Aaron in is accepting when he's right. I've let go of so much in the last twenty-four hours; what's one more thing? "Fine, I'll call someone on Monday."

"Thank you," the three of them groan simultaneously.

"You're welcome," I grumble, but a smile tugs at my lips.

Chapter Twenty-Nine

With it being the Saturday before Thanksgiving, Nomad's lunch rush becomes more of a stampede. No one wants to cook today knowing what awaits them at the end of the week. By the time things begin to lull around three, my bladder is full and my brain is empty. Being this busy is good for more than just turning a profit; it also keeps my mind from spinning in circles over who could possibly have a bone to pick with my bar.

In fact, any thoughts that do manage to trickle in are centered around Aaron and his imminent introduction to my family. Now that the reality of the situation has had time to settle in, I wait for the anxiety to come, but it never does. I feel strangely at peace, like I'm finally standing still after a decade spent running. The temptation to constantly look over my shoulder is still there, but I choose to focus on what lies ahead rather than the things that trail behind me.

When I return to the dining room after a much needed bathroom break, Zander has already set to work refreshing the place for dinner. He smiles at me with his eyes wide, shaking his head in exasperation as he gestures around us. I can't even be overwhelmed by all the napkins littering the floor and the glasses spilling over on every table. I'm too busy feeling grateful that he and I are back on good terms.

"Come on, Zo. I've made a little afternoon pick-me-up for us all." Maddie lifts a tray onto the counter, four Apple Fizz cocktails arranged on the black surface. I pluck a slice of apple from the rim of one of them, munching on it to stave off my hunger.

Drinking on an empty stomach is probably not the best idea with a long dinner shift ahead of us, but I'm not exactly known for my stellar decision making. I've already downed half the bubbling gin drink by the time Eden pushes through the saloon doors carrying a large bowl of french fries smothered in Colorado green chili. Because what pairs better with a light buzz than heartburn?

"Courtesy of the chef." She grins, setting the bowl next to our cocktails.

Zander deposits the final dustpan full of food crumbs into the garbage and then reaches for a fry, only to have his hand slapped away by Maddie. "Gross, wash your hands first." He huffs but moves to the sink, leaving Maddie wide-open access to grab a handful of fries and drop them into her gaping mouth.

Eden takes a sip of her cocktail before smacking her lips in delight. "I think that's the most refreshing drink we've ever featured."

"Not to toot your own horn or anything." I laugh.

She shrugs. "If I don't toot it, who else is going to?"

"I'm sure Chase toots a lot of things for you, including your horn."

Now it's Zander's turn to say, "Gross." He shovels a few fries into his mouth, shaking his head at the two of us with mock disdain.

I roll my eyes at him. "Oh, come on, I know you guys are just as bad as us girls about discussing your sex lives with each other."

He grimaces and Maddie gags. "I have absolutely zero desire to hear about my boss and my best friend's...*escapades*." He leans forward to grab the remaining Apple Fizz, the curtain of his blond hair falling against his cheek. "Not that that stops Aaron from sharing about what *you two* do." He shudders at the thought. "Speaking of which, I heard he's coming home with you for Thanksgiving."

Heat creeps up my neck as Maddie and Eden turn to me with twin expressions of shock. No wonder I'm suddenly in his good graces again. "That literally happened this morning. How did you already hear about it?"

He pulls his cell phone from his back pocket—likely the oldest model of iPhone still functioning—and toggles through a few screens before shoving it in my face. At the top of the chain of texts is a random collection of emojis standing in as the title for the group chat. They include a tent, a mountain, and two men holding hands. There's a message from Aaron sharing the good news of our reunion and subsequent plans, along with a flood of clapping emojis from Chase and Zander.

"If you three are secretly in love with each other"—I tap an orange-painted fingernail against his screen—"I think I speak for both myself and Eden when I say we'd rather you tell us *before* they exchange vows."

Maddie snickers, taking a sip of her drink. Zander frowns at me, but there's a glint of amusement in his eyes.

"Well, I for one am so happy for you, Zo. That's a big step and I'm proud of you for taking it," Eden offers, patting my knee.

Maddie and Zander murmur their agreement, lifting their half-empty glasses in a toast. "To Zoey, for finally growing a pair," Maddie salutes. The sound of our glasses clinking against one another joins the clambering of pots and pans drifting out from the kitchen.

"Sucks you'll be missing out on our amazing group Thanksgiving though. Gary is going to fry a turkey," Maddie says.

"He's going to *attempt* to fry a turkey," Eden clarifies, worry knitting her brow.

"You and Camille aren't spending the holiday with one of your families?" I realize in all the time I've known Maddie, she's rarely commented on her home life. She has the faintest Midwestern accent, but beyond that not much to indicate where she's from. When she requests off, it's usually for a music festival or a vacation to some exotic location that they can drive their van to. I can think of exactly one time when she mentioned going home, but she gave no details.

She shakes her head, the many hoops dangling from her earlobes swaying with the movement. "Camille's family is super religious, so they haven't exactly come to terms with the whole having-a-gay-daughter thing, yet. And my family's in Wisconsin." Her nose wrinkles like she's smelled something foul. There's a lull as we wait for her to elaborate, but she just takes another sip of her drink and lets out a conclusive sigh.

I think of Camille's gentle personality and the adoring way she always watches Maddie, seeing beneath the rough exterior down to the molten core of her fiery spirit. She's quiet and kind, creative and affectionate. Why any parent would choose to give up a relationship with their child over something so trivial as who they love will never make sense to me.

Eden's eyes crinkle at the edges, her gaze trained on the mercury glass mirror hung behind the liquor display. She grinds her molars together, and I'm reminded how intimately familiar she is with shitty parents and all the ways their terrible decisions can weigh a person down.

"How are you doing?" I ask her, my tone growing serious. The holidays have been especially hard on her, though she pours herself into making them special for others so she can't spend time dwelling on what she lacks. Her gaze flickers to Zander and Maddie, who both smile at her gently.

It's taken time, but since she moved here, I've watched Eden's circle of trust grow exponentially, to include more than just Chase and me. Over the past year she has shared the truth of her reasons for coming here with each of our friends when the time felt right. Even Maddie with her prickly personality cried when Eden told her, wrapping her in the only hug I've ever seen her willingly give anyone besides Camille. I wasn't there when she told Zander, but from what Chase has said, he twirled his mustache in silence for so long they thought he'd never respond, before he finally turned to Penny and stroked her chin, whispering, "You have the bravest mom in the world, you know that?"

Eden clears her throat, eyes sparkling with unshed tears. She drags her finger along the rim of her empty glass, a faint ringing sound filling the heavy silence. "I'm okay." Her voice is faint but strong, like it may not be the truth yet, but it will be one day. "It never gets easier. I think that's something so many shows and stuff get wrong, you know? The pain and the memories come up less frequently, but when they do, it's still as fresh as the day it happened."

I nod, grabbing tightly to her hand where it rests on the counter. Her words echo in my head, striking a chord I didn't know I'd buried within myself. It's the aspect of everything with Topher that I've never been able to put words to; the way time passes and fills the empty spaces on my carousel of memories, making the ones involving him come around less frequently. But time does nothing to dull the pain when they finally arrive.

Maddie settles her delicate hand on top of mine, a gold ring glinting on her middle finger that depicts two snakes intertwined with one another. Zander's broad hand follows, the weight of it pressing down on mine even beneath the shelter of Maddie's. I marvel at the stack of hands, all connected to different bodies and stories and lives, but joined by the choice to love and support one another. No amount of shared DNA could be stronger than that.

The corner of Eden's mouth twitches, and then Zander's mustache quivers, and then Maddie's purple-painted lips spread into an all-out smile. Before I know it, we're grinning at each other like idiots, which is the sight Santi finds when he pushes through the saloon doors. At the same time, Gary steps through the entrance to the bar, tugging his jacket off and hooking it onto the antique coatrack I repurposed last year.

Choosing to ignore us, Santi nods in Gary's direction. "The usual?"

Gary's gray eyes lift from us to Santi, but before he can respond, we all chime in. "The usual, Santi."

Chapter Thirty

"So your mom's name is...?"

"Lynn." The rental car's tires shriek as I press a firm foot down onto the brake pedal, always forgetting how quickly the exit for Ardmore comes up and how short it is when it arrives. The steep landing strip of pavement comes to an abrupt stop where it intersects with the winding country road that eventually becomes Main Street.

Aaron grits his teeth, bracing himself with a hand on what my grandfather always called the *Lord Have Mercy* bar, because that's what he would yell when my mom slammed on the breaks while learning to drive. "And your dad's name?"

"Dennis."

There's a pause as I turn left onto the overpass that will lead us into my hometown, followed by a quiet chuckle. I shoot a look his way, and the laughter stalls on his tightly pressed lips. He sees the question in my raised eyebrows, and he mutters his response. "Lynnie and Denny?"

"Oh yeah, they love being called that."

"Really?"

"No," I deadpan.

My nerves are lodged high up in my throat, and I'm fairly certain I'm going to shit myself. I blindly navigate the roads I know by heart, mentally steeling myself to jump off this precipice. Aaron grabs hold of my hand, and though I know it must be unpleasantly clammy, he doesn't let go until I pull to a stop in front of the faded white farmhouse that three generations of my family have grown up in.

I know if I look over my shoulder, across the single-lane gravel road and beyond the pasture riddled with scum-covered ponds, there will be a red brick home just barely visible through the trees. It's the house where Topher lived with his grandparents. There were many summer days where I'd run through the pasture, dodging cow patties and tall grass that was no doubt full of ticks, making my way over to him. I start to wonder if the walls are still pocked with holes in the shape of his fists. Then I remind myself that what's behind me no longer matters, and I shift my focus to what's right in front of me.

I try to look at the farmhouse from Aaron's perspective. Two windows like eyes sit atop a sprawling front porch lined with orange mums that still thrive thanks to the warmer weather and my father's green thumb. The roof is green tin; when it rains the sound is both soothing and deafening. There's a single crooked shutter that's hanging awkwardly from the first-floor window that leads to my old bedroom. I sneaked out in high school once and used it to climb down, accidentally knocking it loose. Luckily a storm blew through before anyone noticed and it was easy to pass the blame. Apparently neither of my parents have given up on the pissing match they've had going since then over who will have to fix it.

Aaron's gaze falls from my childhood home to me, a smile playing on his lips. "I love it."

"Really?" I squeak.

"Yeah." He looks forward again, searching for the words to describe what he's feeling. "It's like it completes the picture I have of you, you know? Not just who you've made yourself into, but the building blocks you started with in the first place." He shakes his head gently. "I don't know if that makes any sense."

"It does." The breath I'd been holding finally releases, warmth climbing up to the tips of my ears. From the things Aaron's told me about his childhood, his father's job as a pilot afforded them a lot of luxuries. While my family had more than enough, we certainly led a simpler life than most. My great grandfather built the humble house before us by hand, and though I've never been ashamed of growing up here, I feel a newfound appreciation swelling in my chest as Aaron admires it beside me. I'm suddenly so grateful that this house, and the family it contains within its walls, allowed me to grow up to be the woman that he loves.

The screen door flies open, slapping against the wooden siding. My mother steps out onto the weathered porch wearing a sweater printed with turkeys and hams and high-waisted jeans despite the weather being in the upper seventies. A gingham apron around her waist is dusted with cocoa powder and flour, even more so after she wipes her hands off on it. Her cat-eye glasses sit low on the bridge of her nose, and the curly blonde hair we share is now streaked with gray and set high atop her head, held in place by the claw clip I got her for her birthday last June.

"Now or never." I smile over at Aaron, and he mirrors the expression, no sign of nerves on his beautiful face.

My dad steps out behind my mother just as I'm opening the car door, his thin frame draped in flannel and the same worn Levi jeans he's been wearing since I was little, complete with the faded outline of his folded leather wallet impressed upon the left back pocket. He cheers when my head pops over the car roof, and Mom joins in when Aaron's does the same.

"Lynnie! Denny!" Aaron shouts, running toward them with

open arms like they're old friends. I cringe, waiting for my dad to admonish him for using the detested nickname, but it never comes. They just wrap him up in a bear hug, and my heart explodes like a confetti gun inside my rib cage.

"I never thought I'd see the day!" Mom drawls, framing Aaron's face in her plump hands. She's curvy and short like I am, with bangles jingling on both of her wrists. I wonder if, when Aaron looks at her, he realizes he's seeing me thirty years from now.

He places a kiss on both of her cheeks. "You and me both."

My mother, usually uptight and somewhat stringent to make up for my father's happy-go-lucky approach to life, becomes a whole new creature when it comes to holidays. And apparently when it comes to Aaron.

"Nice to finally meet you, son." Dad squeezes Aaron's shoulders, both him and Mom seemingly having forgotten to greet their only child now that there's fresh meat to devour. They act like they didn't just learn of his existence when I called last week to inform them a guest would be accompanying me. Though the moment they learned it was a guest of the male variety, they grilled me with questions until they got the whole story. Now they're all up-to-date and as in love with the idea of Aaron as I am with the real thing.

"Um, hello, are you guys just going to leave your daughter hanging?" I throw my arms up in the air.

"Sorry, honey, he's just so cute I could hardly look away." She pinches Aaron's cheek, and he winks at her, soaking up every bit of attention he's getting.

"Hey now, don't go making moves on my wife." Dad loops an arm around Mom's waist, planting a firm kiss on her bright pink lips. "Stick to the younger model." He juts his chin in my direction just as Mom slaps his hip affectionately.

"Wouldn't dream of it," Aaron replies, smiling past them at me. "You three catch up; I'll grab the bags from the car."

He skips down the steps as I follow my parents inside, the

familiar smells of fudge pie and something distinctly tied to the old farmhouse tickling my nose. Not a thing has changed in the living room since the last time I came home to visit, or the twenty times before that. An old, knitted afghan my grandmother made is draped across the floral-printed couch, with three more like it hanging from a blanket ladder my dad made in his woodworking shop out back. My appearance may be a direct copy of my mother, but my green thumb and craftiness are all Dennis Allen.

Mom loops her arm through mine and guides me toward the kitchen, leaning in close to whisper-giggle, "He's very handsome, Zoey-Bear. You should be proud."

The nickname, a by-product of her calling herself Mama-Bear when I was little, never fails to melt me. I relax into her, relishing the contact. It's so good to be home.

"What do your parents usually make for Thanksgiving, Aaron?" Mom asks around a full bite of pizza. It's family tradition, the night before Thanksgiving, to buy out the local Dominos and save her the effort of cooking. A long string of cheese ties the piece of supreme I'm lifting from the box to the rest of the pizza. Aaron reaches over and severs the connection, popping the glob of cheese into his mouth with a satisfied grin.

"Hey, that was my cheese chunk, you thief."

He pinches my puffed-out lower lip, giving it a gentle tug. "Tough."

Mom watches the interaction with what can only be described as barely contained glee.

Aaron turns back to her, grabbing another slice for himself in the process. "My mother is Puerto Rican, so we always incorporate a few of her favorites into the traditional turkey and stuffing my dad prefers. There's usually *pernil*, a pork shoulder dish, and *arroz con gandules*. That's rice and pigeon peas."

My dad's focus shifts abruptly from the football game on the flat-screen—the fanciest thing in this house—to Aaron. "Did you say rice and pigeon meat?"

"Pigeon *peas*," Aaron emphasizes. "They're legumes."

"Le-*what*?"

Mom groans, interrupting their exchange. "A *legume*, sweetie. Try not to sound so dense. He'll think we're some dumb country people." We all laugh at that, except my dad, who turns back to the television with a *pffft*.

The oven lets out a shrill *beep*, and my mom pats me on the shoulder. "Tag, you're it. Can you go get the pecan pie out of the oven? It's the last one, I promise."

"Jeez, Mom, how many pies did you make?" I push back from the table and stand, feeling an uncomfortable pressure in my stomach from all the pizza I've eaten. "You act like we're feeding an army."

She shrugs innocently. "Just five. I didn't know what kind he'd like." I stare at her, my eyes round with shock. She balks. "What? I bake when I'm nervous!"

I make a *tsk* sound at her just as Aaron replies, "Don't worry, I'll eat enough you'll feel like you're feeding an army."

I eye the loose-hanging T-shirt he changed into after we arrived in the warmer climate, knowing there are abs underneath that fabric. "Doubtful, but okay."

"Oh hush." Mom swats at me, her bangles adding music to the movement. "Just do as I ask without all the lip."

"Sir, yes, sir." I give her my best salute, earning a chuckle from my father and a glare from her.

The conversation shifts as I leave the room, something about the teams that are playing and how well they're doing this year. I grab one of the worn-thin oven mitts that Mom left sitting on the counter, the padding no longer thick enough to save me from the heat of the pie pan when I remove it from the oven. I wince, dropping the pie onto the counter with a clattering sound, ripping the mitt off and drawing my mottled thumb into my mouth.

The pain finally subsides, and I bump the oven shut with my hip, turning it off for the night. "Rest well, buddy. You've got your work cut out for you tomorrow."

When I return to the dining-slash-living room, Mom and Aaron are in deep conversation about perhaps the most embarrassing subject they could be discussing: *me*. He's telling the story of our first date, exaggerating the severity of my two left feet and bragging about how leading me was like guiding a stubborn horse. Mom and Dad let out two earth-shattering laughs before my mother assures him that I didn't inherit that from her. "Is that so?" Aaron teases, and he offers her his hand, which she gladly takes.

The two of them begin a beautiful dance around the room, and soon it is apparent that I did in fact inherit my lack of skills from her. But Aaron doesn't seem to mind as he hums a tune for them to dance to, my dad clapping offbeat in a way that he thinks is helping.

It's everything I never knew I wanted, and still somehow more. Despite knowing him for nearly two years, I feel like I'm seeing Aaron for the very first time. Watching him blend so seamlessly into my family, seeing the adoration on my mother's face and the amusement on my father's, I feel a familiar pinprick of heat pressing behind my eyes. This time, when the tears fall, I don't resent them like all the others I've shed this month. They're the happiest thing I've felt in my whole life.

I fully understand now what Gary meant about how he felt with Wendy. There's a peace filling me like molten honey, all sweet and warm and golden. It starts in my fingertips and toes, tingling its way up my spine. My heart stills the way it always does the moment before something big happens, like when Gary slid the papers across the table for me to sign my way into ownership of the bar. It's the distinct sensation of checking something off my bucket list, though this is unlike any dream I ever allowed myself to have.

It's so much better.

Chapter Thirty-One

The next morning, I'm warming my hands on a full cup of Folgers, blinking myself slowly into awareness. It feels distinctly like déjà vu to be sitting at my kitchen counter, feet dangling against the lower cabinets while Mom bustles about the room. She'll only let me avoid helping for so long before I get roped into chopping carrots, celery, and onions until my hands cramp. I'd probably already be doing so if she weren't taking pity on me.

Loveless is an hour behind Ardmore as far as time zones are concerned, so Aaron's five a.m. alarm felt especially offensive this morning. His footsteps reach my ears a beat before he steps into the kitchen, dressed in neon-green running shorts and a tank top. I wait for my mother to make a snarky comment about the outfit, because she definitely would if I were wearing it, but instead she looks up from the potatoes she's peeling and smiles ear to ear at her new favorite person.

"I suppose I have you to thank for this one getting up to help me?" She gestures toward me with the paring knife.

He grins, taking the cup from my hand and swallowing a sip with the mildest of grimaces. We've both become spoiled by Rose's coffee, so this is a bit of a comedown. I mentally add three bags of her medium roast to my Christmas gift list for my parents.

"Are you disappointed that we're not a run-a-5k-on-Thanksgiving-morning type of family?" I ask, poking him in the belly button.

"People do that?" Mom exclaims, lip curled in disgust.

"My family does," he clarifies.

The sound of my father's snores drifting down from upstairs fills the awkward silence that ensues. Mom grits her teeth, her cheeks filling with a rosy tint. "Well, that's nice," she says in a way that implies she doesn't really think so, but she's determined to be polite.

Aaron barks out a laugh, which releases some of the embarrassed tension in her shoulders. "I should only be gone for about thirty minutes. If I'm not back in forty-five, send reinforcements. I've likely gotten a cramp from overindulging on all that pizza." He winks at my mom, which only makes her blush harder, and then plants a firm kiss on my lips.

The front door rattles as it shuts behind him, his footsteps fading once he hits the dirt of our driveway. I tilt my head back and open my mouth wide to capture the last drop of coffee before hoisting myself off the counter and padding over to the sink, washing it off and depositing it in the drying rack to avoid my mother's wrath.

I retrieve the necessary vegetables from the fridge and get to work alongside her, moving in sync as we perform the repetitive motions of chopping and peeling. Out of the corner of my eye, I see her gaze flicker to my hands, the corner of her mouth twitching with the effort she's putting in to suppress a smile.

"What?" I ask. This time it's my turn to point at her with my decidedly bigger knife.

"Nothing." She chuckles, shaking her head. She's wearing dangly, beaded earrings made to look like cornucopias. They match her sweater, another version of the one she wore yesterday, this time with the horn-shaped baskets scattered all over, overflowing with various foods. This seasonal version of my cardigan-and-pearls-wearing mother always comes with a bit of whiplash. "It's just been a really long time since I've seen you this genuinely happy."

The comment unravels a knot tied deep within my soul, the one I constructed a long time ago to rope off this part of my life from my parents. I wonder what it must have been like for them to have a wall come down between them and their only child, seemingly overnight. They did the best they could to protect me from what they thought was the enemy; withdrawing me from horseback riding lessons when the injuries got too severe, forcing me to quit the after-school gardening club when my grades started slipping. I spent so long being angry at them for taking away the things I loved, all the while forgetting that I'd never really given them a chance to protect me from the real threat.

Because while I was sneaking over to Topher's house under the guise of spending time with Eden, they were blindly trusting me to tell them the truth.

I glance over at my mom, feeling the twist of my gut. It turns out men weren't the only ones I kept at arm's length all these years. She senses me staring, and before she can see the relieved sadness filling my face, I reach for her. Her arms loop around my waist, and we both let out a shaky sigh. No matter how old I get, I realize, there will never be a comfort like that of being held by my mother.

She gives my back two quick pats before pulling away, using her apron to pat at her eyes. For as long as I've been alive, there's never been a day where she hasn't painted an elegant smoky eye on, and today is no different. The dark shadows make her blue eyes pop in contrast, and it's not lost on me that they're swimming with tears.

"Okay, we've gotta quit this now before we get behind schedule. Grab the noodles for the mac-n-cheese and set 'em to a boil while I wake your father up. He needs to get to work on the turkey."

The familiar staccato of her footsteps pounding up the staircase provides background music to my search of the pantry. Five minutes later, when she makes her way back downstairs with my groggy father traipsing behind her, I've still not located the elusive noodles.

"Mom, are you sure you got the noodles? I don't see them in here."

"'Are you sure you got the noodles?' Yes! I got the noodles!" She huffs in the way only mothers who think you aren't using your eyes properly do.

I step aside to give her access, and she leans forward to scan the shelves with her hands on her hips. Dad and I lock eyes the moment she realizes I'm right, the wrinkles around his eyes deepening with amusement just before she jerks upright with an exasperated, "Well shit!"

I don't hold my breath for her apology over not believing me. Instead I grab the rental car keys off the counter and make my way to the door, yelling, "Tell Aaron I ran to the store—metaphorically, of course. I don't run."

———

There's only one grocery store in Ardmore; an old Piggly Wiggly in a flat, tan-colored building where neither the *P* nor the *W* have lit up since I was a child. At night, it simply reads *iggly iggly*.

The store is nearly empty save for a few other stragglers picking up last-minute items that they too forgot. One lone cashier who looks to be in his late eighties stands hunched over the only open lane, happy to chat with the people that pass through his line. He's wearing one of those hats that's made to look like a turkey with the flaps dangling by his ears to represent the legs. They sway as he reaches for each new item to scan, slapping his scraggly white beard.

I pass by him and head deeper into the store, the layout of which luckily hasn't changed since I lived here. The spot on the shelf where elbow macaroni should be is empty save for one already-open box. I grab four packages of bowtie pasta and hope for the best.

Just as I'm rounding the corner to leave the aisle, a cart turns, coming to an abrupt stop just short of leveling me.

"*Zoey?*"

One of my hands is braced on the front of the cart, the other gripping tightly to the noodles, but they both begin to tremble when I look up.

"Julie, how are you?"

It's only been about a year since I've seen Eden's mom, but she looks at least a decade older than I remember. She's smaller now, both physically and in the personality that she carries with her. Used to, you could feel her coming a mile away if you hadn't already heard her boisterous laugh ahead of time. She had a colorful countenance, the kind that made you feel brighter just for having shared the same space as her. Now she's unassuming and almost delicate, like one strong breeze could break her—body and spirit.

"I'm doing all right; how've you been? When did you get to town?" She's got just a few items in her cart. There's a small, precooked turkey breast, a package of brown-and-serve rolls, and a refrigerated container of mashed potatoes. It's a dinner for two lonely people who have no one to cook for but themselves.

For a moment I'm filled to the brim with pity for her. I've loved Julie like a bonus mother for most of my life. Seeing her like this is heartbreaking. Except it can't be, because she chose this. If she'd chosen Eden and Ella over Mark, she'd be gathered around a table with one or both of her daughters right now, eating a warm meal prepared by loving hands.

"We got in last night." I choke on the words.

Her cloudy green eyes brighten. "'We'?"

At first happiness and pride blooms in my chest, but it's quickly snuffed out by the realization of what she's assuming. "My, erm, boyfriend and me."

She deflates with a soft, "Oh."

The silence stretches out between us, thick with all the

unspoken tragedy that I'll never be able to forget, even if she's convinced herself she can.

Her gaze lifts from where she's been studying the gold wedding band she twists around her ring finger, apprehension riddling her features. She opens her mouth several times like she's going to speak before clamping it shut. I read her question, even if she's unable to speak it.

"She's doing really well." My voice cracks and I have to clear it several times before I can continue. "She's getting married."

Julie's eyes light up ever so slightly, her mouth forming a small O before the cloud of sadness moves back into place. "Is he...?"

I study her for a moment, trying to ascertain what it is she's wondering, before her fidgeting with that wedding band registers in my brain. I nod quickly. "He's a good man. The best, actually." Aaron's face flickers in my mind before I add, "One of them, at least."

A heavy sigh passes over her quivering lips, the edges of which curve infinitesimally upward. "She's stronger than I ever was." The words are a whisper, a ghost. As soon as she stops speaking, I'm not certain I heard them correctly, if at all. She reaches up to tug at each of her earlobes, and just when I think she's developed a new nervous tick, she drops an earring from one palm to join its twin in another, extending her closed fist to me. "Give these to her for me, would you? They were her grandma's. Something old. Something blue."

I open my hand, examining the sapphire studs she's placed there. The memory of Eden, heartbroken and sobbing as she tried to find a wedding dress without her mother, comes rushing in. The tightness in my chest becomes nearly unbearable, but I use what little air I have left to say, "I will."

"Thank you, baby." She seems to consider her options for a moment before stepping forward and wrapping her arm around my neck so quickly I don't even have time to react. She squeezes me three times before drawing in a ragged breath and pulling away, pressing her lips together in a grim line. "For what it's worth, I'm so very sorry."

I stare at her familiar features, now weathered by time and grief, and try to imagine how it would feel to hear those words from Topher. Because despite the fact that I was hurt by her decision to stay with Mark, the true victim in the situation was Eden. And I realize if Topher ever said those words to me, my gut reaction would be that it's not worth very much at all.

Julie nods, as if she too knows this, and walks away without waiting for my response.

Chapter Thirty-Two

"I expect you to send me a Christmas list, too, Aaron," my mother warns, pinching his cheek and jostling his face the tiniest bit. "And you'll join us for the annual beach trip in the summer?"

I send a silent thanks to my past self for never bringing a man home until now. Part of me knew my parents would be a bit much, but I never suspected they'd be marrying me off after the first introduction. If it were anyone other than Aaron, at any time other than now, I'd have died from embarrassment two nights ago.

Aaron peeks at me over the top of Mom's head, her frizzy curls blocking my view of his face from the nose down. Her hair is stuck in the eighties, teased so high it's as if she thinks her ancient can of Aqua Net is a new and exciting product rather than a relic she should donate to a museum.

He's studying my face with a guarded expression like he's waiting for permission before he gives in to Mom's plans. I drop our suitcases at my side and reach around her from behind, sandwiching her in a group hug between us. "Yes to both, Mom."

She does a giddy happy dance, the bells on her Christmas sweater tinkling. It's the day after Thanksgiving, which officially marks the beginning of the Christmas season in the Allen household. I toss Dad a pitying gaze. His life will be nothing but carols and fruitcake until December 31st.

"Love you, kiddo." He pulls me away from Mom and into his own embrace, pressing his lips to my forehead. "Don't be a stranger, Aaron."

"Yes, sir." Aaron offers him an easy smile.

"Are you sure you two can't stay another night?" Mom worries at her lower lip, her plum-colored lipstick staining her teeth. She's wringing a kitchen towel covered in poinsettias, her bangles jingling in harmony with the bells on her sweater. My mother is music incarnate; there's no better way to describe her.

"Yeah, our flight's early so we got a hotel near the airport in Nashville. Plus, Aaron's never been. I've gotta give him the ole Tennessee welcome." I wink at her, and she giggles, the majority of her sadness forgotten.

"You two have fun. I'll take care of this one," Dad says, grinning. He wraps his arms around Mom from behind and pulls her against his chest, her long red skirt swaying with the movement. Her eccentric outfit looks comical against Dad's camouflage ensemble, but I stifle the laugh trying to escape my lungs.

She swats his arm but nuzzles into his neck. "He won't take care of me. He'll watch football all day and only speak to me on commercial breaks about nonsense!"

"This is the trade-off we agreed to: I listen to you read my horoscope each morning; you have to sit through my game commentary." He purses his lips thoughtfully like he sees a way out. "Are you saying you'd like to renegotiate our terms?"

She frantically shakes her head. "How else are we going to know when you'll be in one of your moods." Her gaze falls on Aaron, and she gives him an exasperated sigh. "Damn Scorpios."

"Don't I know it," Aaron commiserates, though he's got the same glazed-over look in his eyes as my dad.

"Hate to interrupt"—I flatten my palm against Aaron's chest and push him toward the car— "but we better get going. I've got a hot date with the microphone at WannaBe's."

Mom and Dad shout their goodbyes as we skip down the steps, the house's own version of a farewell being the chorus of groaning boards underfoot. We toss our bags into the back seat of the compact rental car, locking eyes over the roof for a brief moment. Just long enough for the corner of Aaron's mouth to twitch as he shakes his head. "What the hell is WannaBe's?"

"*This* is WannaBe's!"

An assortment of neon lights advertising various beers reflect in Aaron's eyes as he scans the bar on the far-right wall of the room. The dark space is packed with people pressed shoulder to shoulder closer to the stage but disperses to a more manageable closeness toward the emcee's booth at the back. We push our way through the crowd, striking gold when a couple relinquishes control of one of the coveted high-tops in the middle of the room.

I throw my arms over top of it, grinning at Aaron even as I feel the grimy surface sticking to my skin. "You're my lucky charm! I never get a table here."

"Happy to be of service." He offers a firm salute.

"Will you stand guard while I grab our drinks and put my name in to sing?"

"Sure." His eyes glitter with amusement as he takes in the stage, where a homeless man is currently singing a surprisingly soulful rendition of "Baby" by Justin Bieber. One of my favorite parts about the classic karaoke bar situated in a prime location on Broadway Street is that everyone who wanders in seems to have at least a little talent. This man is no exception, belting out the chorus while he swipes his greasy hair back with a hand covered in dirt. Aaron glances at me out of the corner of his eye, one elbow leaning on the cocktail table. "What are you going to sing?"

"It's a surprise." I wink, earning one of his easy smiles before I make my way past him toward the bar. I sashay my hips a little extra, knowing he's watching me walk away.

Weaseling my way in between two larger men dominating the counter, I pop my head through the gap in their shoulders just as the bartender passes. I recognize the girl almost instantly; she's been working here since Eden and I would come in college, taking advantage of the slower foot traffic on weeknights. Her black hair is streaked with purple instead of green now, but she still wears it in a thick French braid that reaches midway down her back.

She catches a glimpse of me between the two brutish men who are jostling me each way as they vie for her attention, less interested in the drinks she offers than they are in something a little more personal. She ignores them, reaching for my outstretched ID and cocking her ear toward me as she reads my date of birth.

"Two whiskey ginger ales." I hold up two fingers in case she doesn't hear me over the blaring *Grease* track that's currently being butchered by a bachelorette party. Okay, so I was wrong about everyone having talent.

She gives a quick nod and then sets to work prepping our drinks. The two men grumble at her aloofness. In an efficient minute I have two cocktails and she has my money plus a healthy tip for dealing with every asshole she'll inevitably encounter tonight. It earns me an appreciative smile before I retreat and testosterone swallows up the hole I leave behind.

Skirting the perimeter of the room, I make my way to the emcee booth where a Black gentleman with a graying Afro wearing a bowling shirt is bobbing his head along with the beat. When the music fades out, he scans the playlist and calls the next singer. I set my drinks down on the table in front of him and wait for his attention to come my way. Finally he gets an Avril Lavigne classic going and turns to me.

"Need a song book, honey?" he drawls, his Southern accent drawing his words out long and slow, which is perfect when trying to hear him over the dull roar of conversation and music.

I shake my head at him with a smile. "I'll do 'Man! I Feel Like a Woman' by Shania Twain."

"A woman who knows what she wants." He gives me an appreciative top-to-bottom appraisal. "I like it. Song's up in twenty."

"Thank you!" I singsong, dropping a few crumpled dollar bills in his tip jar before turning.

And my heart soars into my throat.

The crowd has parted, giving me a direct line of sight to our table. Aaron's brows are drawn together, casting a shadow over his eyes. His jaw is set, the twitch of the muscle there just visible in the light show that the emcee is controlling. Across from Aaron, a man barely older than me stands with an anger lacing his features that I'd recognize in a heartbeat, even if I hadn't just looked him up on the Internet last week.

"Hon, you forgot your drinks!" the emcee calls after me, but I'm already crossing the room, moving as if through water. Each step is met with resistance, my body determined not to go through with what my brain is commanding.

When I finally make it to the table, I'm fairly certain my legs are going to give out beneath me. I brace myself against the wooden surface, gripping the edge so tightly my knuckles turn a sickening white. Aaron glances over at me, and in that moment everything he needs to know is conveyed by what I can only imagine is sheer terror displayed on my face.

"Zoey Allen, as I live and breathe." Topher's voice is all rasp and bite, another part of him that time has been unkind to. He sneers, eyeing me up and down with derision. "I was just telling your boyfriend here how *well* we know each other."

Aaron leans in, placing a firm hand around my bicep to keep me steady. His lips brush my ear as he whispers, "Let's go."

I want to, but I can't make my legs cooperate. Whereas before I was walking through water, now I'm knee-deep in quicksand. I'll starve to death here, unable to escape. That is, if a predator doesn't find me first. I eye Topher warily, realizing one already has.

In person his features are even harsher. He's slicked back his hair, giving an unencumbered sightline through the thinning strands straight to his scalp. His eyes are dark and beady like those of a raven, only not nearly as intelligent. His face is a mask of hatred, though I realize for the first time in my life that it's not aimed at me. Not really, anyway. It's directed at the entire world, something I just happen to be a part of.

Aaron tugs at my arm again, but I brace myself for it, resisting. My spine straightens out, shoulders squaring off. When I first started hiking with Chase and the crew, they told me if I ever found myself face-to-face with a bear, to make myself as big and loud as possible. Bears don't like to pick on anything bigger than them. Topher's like that, too.

"What do you want, Topher?" Each word is clipped, and I bite the end off, nearly spitting his name out in the process. The sound of my teeth clicking together reverberates in my ears, somehow cutting through the bass that's been rattling my senses since we arrived.

After a beat, Aaron relaxes his grip on my bicep. He sees the resignation, or he senses it, but either way he realizes we're doing this. *I can't believe I'm doing this.* I watch him turn toward Topher as he does what he always has: he stands beside me.

Even as dark as they are, I can see that Topher's eyes are glazed with an alcohol-induced film. He sways on his feet, upper lip curled so high I'm almost certain it's going to merge with his nostril into a permanent expression of disgust. "I'm getting married, Zo."

I swallow down the bile that rises in my throat when he uses my nickname. Correcting him will only egg him on, so I choose to let it pass. Not for him, but for me. He studies my reaction for a moment, not waiting for me to respond before he adds, "Though I guess you already knew that, seein' as how you felt the need to fill her head with a bunch of nonsense. I'd recognize your bullshit in a heartbeat, even if you hadn't included that little bit about the *horse* kicking your rib." He tilts his forehead toward me, pausing to see if I'll bother correcting him. When I don't, he continues, looking even more annoyed if that's possible. "She's run off somewhere, won't answer my phone calls or texts."

The relief that washes over me is golden and light, filling every corner of my soul with warmth. Aaron reaches for my hand where it rests on the table and gives it a squeeze, meeting my gaze with a question in his own. *I'll tell you later*, I mouth.

Topher watches this interaction, not missing a beat. "I wouldn't go feeling all self-righteous just yet. She'll come back to me, just you wait and see. I've gotten a lot better at choosing the right whore since wasting my time on you."

The responding rage that flows through Aaron crackles like lightning, and I see his face grow hot with it. He surges forward, bumping the table, but I hook my arm around his waist before he can go any farther. Topher staggers backward, fear flashing in his eyes before he quickly recovers, a bark of laughter accompanying a sniffle as he wipes his nose and steps forward once more.

"It's not worth it." I press my lips against Aaron's cheek, breath tickling the short brunette curls by his ears. I swallow back the hot rush of tears Topher's words brought forth. I tell myself I'm fine, that he doesn't have that kind of control over me or my emotions anymore. I will it to be true. "Don't waste your energy on him. You're better than that."

Aaron's chin juts out as he gives a tight nod, placing an arm on my back to turn me toward the exit. As we do, one song slows to an end, the room filling with a brief moment of blessed silence before the next loads up. In that quiet, Topher's voice carries farther and wider than it normally would, so that all our ears are hit at once with his searing words. "Have fun fucking my sloppy seconds. Hope what's left of her is at least entertaining."

The crowd gasps and Aaron's hand fists against my spine. Without hesitation, I pivot on my heel and rush toward Topher, alcohol slowing his reaction time so that he can't even pull his arms up to shield himself before my fist lands with a resounding crunch against the bridge of his already crooked nose.

"What's left of me is *everything*," I growl. "You took nothing from me. You're pathetic, and you know what I regret even more than loving you in the first place? I regret not reporting you to the police so you could rot in jail like you deserve. So you could finally find out what it's like to be on the receiving end of the abuse you dole out."

Two security guards push through the crowd that surrounds us, eyes dancing between the three of us while their mouths hang agape. I expect a brutish arm to hoist me into the air and drag me toward the front door, tossing me out onto the street like they did when I got too drunk once in college and picked a fight with some man who insulted Eden in front of me.

But instead, that arm extends toward Topher and grasps the center of his T-shirt in a clenched fist, yanking him toward the door. I don't even look at him; I can't look at him. I'm trembling and tears are clouding my vision and I think I see the bartender offer me a proud smile as the crowd erupts into cheers but all I can focus on is the feeling of Aaron's arms enveloping me and the broad expanse of his chest against my cheek as I cry and cry and cry, cradling my bruised knuckles against my stomach.

The music finally resumes, and the crowd awkwardly disperses, slowly converging on the wide berth they initially gave us as the drama is forgotten. But I cannot forget. It's written in the blood blooming across my still-clenched fist, the same blood that began pouring over Topher's lips before he was dragged away.

Aaron's lips press against each of my cheeks in turn, and I wonder if he can feel the heat of my embarrassment under the wetness of my tears. I glance up at him, worried he will be ashamed that I lowered myself to Topher's level. That I went against my own advice. Instead he smiles down at me, stroking my temple in a soothing motion. He grabs a condensation-soaked napkin from under the drink on the table to our right, wiping it against my knuckles. It comes away bloody but leaves my skin clean.

He presses a kiss against my injured hand, holding my gaze the entire time.

"I'm so sorry," I whisper, doubting he can hear it over all the noise.

He shakes his head at me, the corner of his lip curving upward. "Don't be. Zo, you are a force to be reckoned with. It's a privilege to watch you up close."

Chapter Thirty-Three

I've just broken the news to Marcelin, Eric, and Mateo, and they're each taking it a little bit differently. Mateo has an appreciative smirk permanently carved into his tan face, similar to the one Santi had when I told him this morning. Eric is smiling wider than I realized he was capable of doing, and Marcelin has tears forming in his eyes. He removes his black ball cap and swipes a hand over his head, and I swear I see his bottom lip quiver.

The crew currently dicing, prepping, and cooking the entire menu Santi designed for Friendsgiving normally work for my friend's catering company, but for today they are my temporary kitchen staff.

"You guys don't have to ogle them," I tease. "Consider this an early Christmas gift from us to you. Go home, get yourselves and your families ready, then come back tonight and enjoy the dinner as guests."

"With free drink tickets," Eden adds, passing a red envelope to each of them in turn. When she finally gets to Marcelin, he wraps both arms tightly around her and squeezes three times for good measure.

None of them even had a chance to shed their belongings in

their lockers, so they turn and file one by one out the delivery exit toward the parking lot. Only Santi lingers, wordlessly wringing his chef coat between his fists while he watches the crew move about his kitchen with quiet confidence.

I sidle up to him, locking my hands onto each of his tense shoulders and squeezing. "Relax, they've got this under control, and I'm here to supervise. You deserve a night to be served instead of serving, Santi."

He eyes me warily but finally relents, his shoulders slumping beneath my touch. "I don't know if bringing my wife and children here is more or less work, but thank you nonetheless." With that and a subtle smile that crinkles the corners of his eyes, he turns to follow his crew out the door.

"That went better than I'd hoped," Eden remarks, watching his back disappear through the doorway before turning to me with her eyes wide. "I thought for sure he'd put up more of a fight."

"You must've run him ragged while I was away."

She doesn't honor that with a response, instead turning on her heel with a huff and grabbing the case of glasses from a rack nearby. "Come on, we've got lots of prep work to do."

"It's like the good ole days all over again." I load my arms with several bottles of mixers and follow her through the saloon doors, each of us depositing our bounty on the counters.

"Oh sorry, sir, we're closed for lunch today," Eden calls out. "You're welcome to come back for our Friendsgiving event this evening at five, though!"

I glance up at a man standing just inside the door who looks at her questioningly and then refers back to the clipboard in his hands. He's wearing a puffy coat that hangs open, revealing a blue quarter-zip underneath bearing a label I can just barely make out.

"You're here to install the security system!" I wipe my hands on the towel hanging from Eden's back pocket before rounding the counter and offering my outstretched hand to him. "I'm Zoey, the owner. Thanks for coming so soon after the holiday."

"No problem." The man smiles, revealing a front tooth that's chipped in half. He offers the clipboard to me and rests his pen on top, inscribed with the logo for the company. "Just review this and sign, and I'll get everything going."

I scrawl my name nearly illegibly across the bottom and pass it back to him. "You really should stick around for the dinner; I hear the bartenders are the best in town."

Eden and the guy, whose name tag reads *Payton*, share a chuckle as I return to my station and begin laying out garnishes in various containers for ease of use. Payton scans the room with watchful eyes —a hazard of the trade, I'd bet—before returning to the van he has parked outside, which I catch a glimpse of through the closing door.

"Thank you for finally doing this." Eden expertly slices lime after lime before moving on to shaving off spirals of lemon peel for gin and tonics. "Not that I really understood why you were so reluctant in the first place, but you've certainly let plenty of my eccentricities pass so who am I to judge?" She nudges me with her elbow, offering a knowing smile.

The sound of a drill on the other side of the boarded-up window interrupts the silence that ensues. I set the strainer down in the sink basin, still full of cherries, and rest my hands on the edge of the counter. "That's the crazy thing, I think. It seemed logical to me, at the time. Now I look back and I just feel stupid."

She drops the peeler, fisting the lemon she was working on while reaching for me with her now free hand. "You're not stupid. Trauma makes us do crazy things, and no matter what you've tried to convince yourself all this time, what you went through was definitely traumatic." Her lips press together tightly as her gaze travels over my face. "All we can do is the best we know how to in order to get by, and then when we know better, we do better. Give yourself a little grace, Zo."

I suddenly become fascinated with my boots, studying the smattering of salt I collected from where they prepped the roads for snow. "I punched Topher in the face."

"You did *what*?" She bends at the waist so that her eyes are level with mine. "When did this happen? And why am I just now hearing about it?"

"Friday night. I took Aaron to WannaBe's—"

"Love WannaBe's."

"And Topher was there. He walked up to Aaron while I was getting drinks and said all these awful things. He blames me for breaking him and his fiancée up."

"How could that possibly be your fault?" Her lip curls. "And who on earth would agree to marry him in the first place."

"I might've sent her an anonymous message on Facebook with resources for abused women."

Eden's eyes grow round while her features simultaneously soften. Before I know it, her arms are locked around my neck so tightly I'm afraid I've lost all access to oxygen, but it doesn't matter anyway because the tears that begin to fall clog my airways.

"I am so unbelievably proud of you, Zo. You did an amazing thing for that woman." She smooths a soothing hand over my hair, again and again, while I just let myself be held. When it finally subsides, she pulls back, holding on to each of my elbows. "Where did the punching come into play?"

I choke on a sound that is equal parts laugh and sob before my lips firm into a tight line and I shake my head. "He said something disgusting to Aaron about enjoying his sloppy seconds, and I couldn't help it. I might've broken his nose just a little bit."

"Of course you couldn't." Heat floods her cheeks, one of which I can see she's chewing on from the inside. "He's lucky that's all you did. He's not worth the air he wastes by breathing." The last words are a harsh whisper as Payton reenters the room.

"Got the front and back entrances done. I'll finish up here and be out of your hair," he says, dragging a ladder to the corner of the room where we discussed placing another camera.

I grab the rag out of Eden's back pocket and wipe away the tears from my eyes, cursing myself for not bringing my makeup bag with me. I'm not used to being this person who lives with her emotions so close to the surface, especially after spending so long shoving them down where no light can reach them.

Eden grits her teeth. "Is now a bad time to tell you I used that rag to wipe up a spill on the floor earlier?"

"Oh God, why'd you let me do that!" I toss the towel to the floor, my laughter coming out more like a snort due to the phlegm in my throat. Eden bends over laughing, clutching her stomach as she gasps for air between guffaws. Payton, to his credit, ignores the fiasco completely.

"So sorry," Eden says, her voice coming out winded. "By the time I remembered, it was too late." She scrunches her nose up at me, reaching out to tug at a strand of my hair. "The germs are good for you. They build up your immune system."

I roll my eyes at her, but I'm smiling, too. A final, stubborn tear trails down my face, and she catches it, this time with a clean paper napkin. There's a mascara stain on the napkin as she pulls it away. I force myself to draw in a breath, letting it out slowly between clenched teeth. "Maybe I need to talk with Stephen after all."

She holds up a finger and half jogs to the office while Payton begins drilling into the ceiling. When she returns with a business card pinched between two fingers, he's got the camera hung securely and aimed straight at me. "I'm sure he'd be thrilled to talk to you."

I jerk my head back toward her. "I'm sure; more money lining his pockets is always a good thing." I chuckle at my own joke and slip the card into my back pocket.

She shakes her head. "I think he'd probably like to thank you."

"Thank me? For what?"

"For saving my life."

She says it so matter-of-factly that it nearly knocks me unsteady. I place a hand on top of hers. "I didn't save your life, Eden. You did. But thanks for giving me a front-row seat to the whole thing."

Maybe that's all friendship is, at the end of the day. Supporting each other through those inevitably tough moments that life throws your way. She ducks her head, and I suddenly remember what the shock of seeing Topher nearly buried in my subconscious.

"I, erm, actually have something for you." Now it's my turn to step past her into the office, pulling my purse off the hook by the desk and opening the zippered side pocket where two sapphire studs wink up at me. She studies my closed fist curiously as I return, reaching for her hand and nestling the earrings there. I don't immediately withdraw my hand, keeping them covered so I can explain.

"I ran into someone else while I was home. Your mom, actually." Her eyes lift from our hands to my face, a glassy sheen covering the forest of her irises with a dense fog. "I told her you were getting married, and she asked me to give you these." I pull my hand back, revealing the earrings. Eden's mouth opens with a soft *pop*. "She said they were your grandma's, so they're old."

"And they're blue," she whispers, turning them over with a finger. She seems to consider them for a moment, measuring their presence against the boundaries she's built around her heart. After drawing in a shuddering breath and swallowing hard, she places them one by one into her earlobes before tucking her auburn hair back and smiling sadly at me. "How do they look?"

"Beautiful." And it's more than just the earrings. It's the way she faces each of these moments with more and more bravery, growing in her strength as time continues to pass. I send a silent wish up to the universe that maybe now that I've finally faced what happened all those years ago, I can start moving forward, till one day I'm as brave as she is.

"Sorry to interrupt," Payton says, gaze trained on the clipboard in front of him to give us some privacy. "Everything's installed, just wanted to give you a quick tutorial before I go. Do you have a second?" He gestures toward the office where my laptop sits open on the desk.

I nod, indicating for him to lead the way; then I grab Eden and hug her as hard as my arms will allow until she and my muscles are both screaming. "Happy Friendsgiving."

"Every day is Friendsgiving with us." She smirks, returning to her lemons.

Chapter Thirty-Four

Aaron drops onto the bed beside me with a moan, clutching his bloated belly and wincing. "Between you and your mom's cooking, I think I've gained ten pounds."

I poke his stomach, resulting in another grunt. "Want some laxatives?"

"No, I do not want to take a laxative at my *girlfriend's* house." He shoots me a glare. "Though it would serve you right for doing this to me."

"Hey, no one told you to go back for seconds." I bite my lower lip to contain the smile trying to bloom on my face in response to being called his girlfriend. *What am I, twelve?* "And the thirds were really unnecessary."

He rolls away from me with a huff, pulling the blanket up over his head. His mock anger is betrayed almost immediately by the hand that reaches behind him and affectionately pats my thigh beneath the covers.

I pinch his butt in return, earning a growl.

Giggling, I retrieve my laptop from my bedside table, noting with a swell of pride that my pothos is beginning to grow the first leaf since its rebirth. I feel like I'm looking at myself, poking my head up through the soil of my past after so long being buried beneath it, finally blooming again. "We can do this," I whisper, stroking the leaf gingerly.

"Who are you talking to?" Aaron mumbles, flipping back over as I crack open my laptop.

"No one." He gives me a hard stare, letting silence fill the space between us until it makes my skin itch and I relent. "The plant."

He grins at me, his bright white teeth blinding in their beauty. "That's my girl."

I shake my head at him, returning to the task at hand. There's a neon-green sticky note on my screen with the step-by-step instructions Payton gave me for logging into the system. I go through all the necessary security pages, putting in passwords and multifactor authentications and signing over my firstborn child before finally the grid of camera angles opens before me.

Aaron sits up with only a minor wince crumpling his face. He props himself on the edge of my pillow and leans over to watch me navigate between each viewpoint. There are three cameras total—one at each entrance and one in the main dining room—but each of the outdoor mounts have two lenses to give a 180-degree view.

"Look, it's Chase!" Aaron points at the corner of the screen, where Chase appears with an overly eager Penny dragging him down the sidewalk. Her leash is taut as she bobs and weaves along the path, determined to smell every possible scent she can. Aaron snaps a photo of the two of them on his cell, texting it over to Chase presumably. They disappear into the darkness of the night as Chase breaks out into a jog. "Eden told me that if they don't take turns running her a few miles each morning and night, she wreaks havoc on their apartment."

"I believe it." Thoughts of the craters she has dug in my yard fill my mind. I toggle to the indoor view. It's a wide lens so I can see all the seating as well as the office door in the corner. The room is dark save for the backlighting I leave on behind the liquor bottles. If nothing else, this one will be good for when the local couponing group comes for their monthly lunch meeting and insists they didn't drink as much as is listed on their tab.

The back door has similarly poor lighting, with only a distant parking lot floodlight casting shadows of the metal staircases onto the brick. Stacks of wooden pallets from our recent food delivery sit by the base of Gary's staircase, awaiting pickup on Monday. I've checked one angle and I'm about to shut it down when a flicker of movement catches my eye in the other.

"What was that?" I expand it to full screen, my eyes straining to see details in the dark. Reaching over to my bedside table, I click off the lamp, leaving the laptop screen as our only light. Both Aaron and I lean in, as if getting closer to it will somehow make it make sense.

I've nearly convinced myself I imagined it when a figure moves again in the dark, snatching the breath out of my lungs. The person is portly, made bulkier by a thick coat that they haven't bothered to use the hood from. It's a man, I can tell from his profile, but he isn't turned toward the camera enough for me to make out his face. He's fidgeting with something, pacing back and forth along the brick wall and around the pile of pallets. A flash of red catches my eye, and I realize what it is I'm seeing.

It's a gas can.

"Fuck." I jump out of bed, grabbing my cell and dialing the police station. I'm rattling off the details while simultaneously trying to clothe myself one-handed when Aaron's head snaps up from the computer.

"Do you remember that guy who used to deliver your kegs? The one who got fired for grabbing Eden?" He flips the laptop around so the screen is facing me, and I see the man is picking at the lock of our back door. Aaron has grabbed a screenshot of the moment he made the mistake of looking up, and his face is filling my screen.

"Oh my God." I drop the phone. "It's Shawn."

269

Two cruisers jump the curb from the opposite direction just as Aaron turns onto the street. Their lights and sirens are blaring when they come to an abrupt stop in the parking lot and one door swings open. I see Kit come out with his gun drawn, quickly followed by Tomas. We stop short of the parking lot to avoid pulling in between them and Shawn, who staggers back with one arm drawn up over his eyes to shield them from the blinding lights. He falls to his knees beside the discarded gas can, but my heart doesn't resume beating. Even from here, I can see that he's got a lighter held up in his other hand, which he flickers to life with a disparaging smile on his face.

I grab for the door, and Aaron grabs for me, just barely catching my shirt hem as I slip out into the frigid night and rush toward the parking lot. Kit sees me coming out of the corner of his eye and shouts for me to stop, all the while keeping his gun trained on Shawn.

"Zo, it's a bar; it's not worth risking your life!" he shouts.

"I don't give a damn about the bar!" Aaron's arms come around my waist, holding me back while Shawn's eyes dart over to me. "Eden and Gary live upstairs!"

Kit's gaze jumps to the apartment windows on the second story. Gary's is dark, which means he's likely asleep, but there's a golden light flooding through Eden's kitchen window. All my calls to warn her went unanswered, but the commotion must have grabbed her attention. She steps out onto the landing, barefoot and wrapping her peacoat tightly around her middle. Her pale legs are visible and she's already shaking. "What the—"

"Go back inside!" Tomas shouts. His face is the most stern I've ever seen it, steadily calculating all the moving parts in this situation.

"No!" Shawn slurs. "I want her here. She's the reason for all this. The bitch cost me my job." Eden staggers backward, clutching the railing. Shawn sneers up at her, enjoying her fear. "You ruined my name in this town. I haven't been able to get work since. The damn cops won't leave me alone."

"Drop the lighter, Shawn," Tomas directs. "No one cost you that job but yourself."

"And you wouldn't keep getting arrested if you'd stop picking fights every time you have a drink," Kit adds, sounding exasperated. I remember him mentioning Shawn had been a thorn in his side since starting at the sheriff's department, and suddenly the concerned look on his face when I mentioned the assault brings a wave of nausea through my stomach.

"I didn't do anything wrong. It's not my fault she can't take a joke." Shawn continues to close and reopen the lighter, taunting us with a dare in his eyes.

I cling to Aaron, my lungs feeling like they're going to explode in my chest. I'm utterly powerless, and it's the worst feeling in the world. Eden remains frozen on her landing—in this weather, both figuratively and literally—eyes trained not on any of us but on the corner of the building, and I realize she's worried for Chase and Penny, hoping they stay far away.

"This is the last time I'm telling you, Shawn, turn off the lighter and toss it here. You're not walking away from this." Tomas and Kit move in some predetermined synchronous formation, fanning out on either side of Shawn, guns never leaving their target.

"You're not gonna shoot me," Shawn teases, words thick with the influence of alcohol. "If you do, this all goes up in flames. Got plenty of kindling." He gestures to the pallets, and my gaze zeroes in on the path of shimmering liquid stretching from there to the back door of Taylor's Landing, where discarded clothing boxes await their pickup on trash day.

Just then, so silent at first that I almost don't notice it happening, Gary's door begins to open. He hasn't turned a single light on so as not to give away his position. For a moment, watching the careful way he moves, I'm reminded that this jovial man once served in the military. He knows how to approach an enemy.

My gaze flickers to Tomas and Kit, neither of whom seem to have caught wind of it. Aaron tugs at my sleeve, and I look back, only to see Gary gingerly stepping out onto his balcony directly above where Shawn is kneeling. In his hands is a five-gallon bucket, which he hoists onto the railing with a grimace and the faintest grunt.

Every particle of air stalls in my lungs when Shawn hears the noise and jerks his head upward at the same time Kit and Tomas notice Gary. Shawn opens his mouth to speak, but the words are drowned out by the downpour of water released when Gary tips the bucket over, extinguishing the lighter and drenching Shawn in the process.

Tomas and Kit don't waste any time, converging on him before he can find his lighter in the puddle he's now sitting in. Eden drops to her knees in relief as Tomas locks a pair of handcuffs around Shawn's meaty wrists, earning a slew of curse words from the man.

Chase comes around the corner then, Penny lagging behind with her tongue lolling to the side while she pants with exhaustion. His eyes go wide as he takes in the scene, immediately searching for the person he cares most for in the world. "Oh my God, Eden." He sprints past Shawn and up their steps, Penny right on his heels with newfound energy.

I stagger forward to join them on that platform, preparing for my best friend to be leveled by all the memories this will inevitably bring up, but I pause when I see her step away from Chase with a pat on his chest and a reassuring glance. She makes her way down the steps to stand before the grunting, sweaty man Tomas is kneeling on. I doubt he has to do that since Shawn doesn't strike me as the running type, but I'm grateful he is, nonetheless.

Slipping out of my shoes, I nudge them toward her, and she steps into them with a wavering smile.

"What is wrong with you, Shawn?" Tomas says, jerking the man to his feet, which is a struggle because Shawn is not exactly built for languid movement.

"I told you, she cost me my job." He juts his chin toward Eden, sweat pouring off his temples and glistening on his forehead.

She shakes her head firmly, confidently, and her voice doesn't falter when she speaks. "You're lucky it was only that. I should've had you arrested for assault then and there. I realize that now."

Gary jogs down the steps to join us, discarding the bucket in front of Shawn. "Would've dropped the bucket on you, too, but the cops move too fast."

"I would've just killed you, personally," I mutter, earning a proud smirk from Aaron and a high-five from Gary.

"You hear that, Officer? She threatened me!" Shawn growls, his face turning beet red.

"Nope, didn't hear a thing," Kit says, offering me a wink.

Aaron comes up behind me, resting a hand against my lower back to steady me, and he and Kit share a respectful nod. After depositing Penny inside, Chase joins Eden, wrapping a blanket around her shoulders.

"I assume you want to press charges?" Tomas asks, though it's not much of a question.

"Yes," we all reply in unison.

Tomas nods as if he suspected as much. "I'll need a statement from Maddie for her tires as well. I assume that was you?" He pokes Shawn in the shoulder with his pen, clicking it open.

Shawn's brow furrows in confusion. "That bartender girl? I thought those were your tires." He glares at Eden. "I've seen you getting in that van!"

Kit and Tomas exchange looks of puzzlement before Chase tugs on a strand of Eden's hair, reminding us all that Maddie dyed hers a similar color this fall.

I shake my head in shock and disbelief at this entire evening.

"I'll give her a call tomorrow and have her go down to the sheriff's department to give you a statement."

"No need." Tomas shrugs. "I'll get it over my weekly beers. We still on for that, Gary?"

"Yessir."

"All right then, Rookie, let's load him up."

The two of them drag Shawn toward the flashing lights of the cruisers, depositing him in the back of one of the vehicles before shutting it all off and leaving us in blinding darkness, save for that one streetlamp at the end of the lot.

"I don't know if it's too soon to point this out," Aaron says. "But those security cameras did their job in less than twenty-four hours."

Everyone but me bursts into adrenaline-fueled laughter, taking turns poking at me before Eden breaks through them all and wraps me in a hug. Soon everyone's arms are looping around us and I'm squished in the center of it all, surrounded by the people who love me most.

No wall I could ever build would've kept them out.

Chapter Thirty-Five

A pair of kind eyes framed in a thick fray of blonde lashes find my face, gauging the type of person I am. Whatever her requirements are, I must pass the test, because Daisy takes a small step forward, just enough to close the distance between us. She brushes her muzzle against my cheek, the tickling sensation causing a giggle to bubble up in my chest. She whinnies at me, letting me know she's happy too.

The guide brushes a hand over her golden-colored fur, causing the gorgeous palomino to shake her head in delight. "I'd say she's a fan!" he comments with a smile.

"Hard not to be," Aaron says. He flashes a grin my way, the sparkling amusement in his eyes reminding me of dappled sunlight on an alpine lake.

I give her chin an affectionate scratch, her upper lip flapping in return. "I'm a fan of you, too," I whisper, pressing my forehead to hers.

"I take it you two are experienced riders, then?"

Aaron simply nods, but he glances at me, awaiting my response. When I asked him to bring me here, I finally told him all the horrible details of that final night with Topher, explaining that for me, horseback riding was just another reminder of what he'd taken from me.

For so long I've avoided anything that reminded me of that time in my life, nearly as much as I've avoided binding relationships. But I'm beginning to realize that it's not me who should avoid those memories. The feelings I've carried all these years of shame and embarrassment were not mine to carry, they were Topher's and Topher's alone. At the urging of Stephen, I remind myself daily that when those memories crop up, they are actually evidence of all that I have overcome. Of how much stronger I am than Topher ever led me to believe. Of the goodness all around and still to come.

I realize now that having been a victim is not a reflection of my weakness, but of Topher's, something I hope—in some secret corner of my heart kept tucked away from the light—that he's reminded of every time he looks in a mirror and sees the crooked bridge of his nose.

Aaron's features soften with relief as he reads whatever is written on my face. I turn to the guide and answer truthfully. "It's been a long time, but I think I've still got it in me."

"Well okay then." He nods, passing Daisy's reins to me. "The trail is all easy terrain, and the horses know it by heart. It'll take you down to the lake and then circle back around to spit you out here. Since you're both experienced riders, you don't need me to babysit, but the office number is sewn into their saddle blankets if you run into any problems."

We both nod, Aaron turning to mount his chestnut-colored horse named Ezekiel. He looks like a regular cowboy straddling the saddle, clad in jeans and a plaid button-down that he's covered with a thick winter coat. He's even wearing the Stetson hat that I got him in Nashville, its broad rim shielding his face from the glaring sun. There's a fresh dusting of snow underfoot—or underhoof, rather—and it reflects the sunlight in a dazzling display.

If I didn't have a thing for cowboys before, I certainly do now.

The guide offers his folded hands to help hoist me onto Daisy's back. I slip easily into the correct riding posture, my body remembering even before my mind. With the nudge of a heel and a slight tug of her reins, we are turning toward the trailhead and leading Ezekiel and Aaron in that direction.

"You're a natural," Aaron calls after me appreciatively, though I imagine the appreciation is less for my riding skills and more for the view he has of my ass in the tan jodhpurs I bought in anticipation of doing this more often. "And I'm a big fan of the view."

Bingo.

I toss a wicked smile over my shoulder. "I'll be sure to wear these around the house, just for you."

"You're too kind."

We ride to the lake in comfortable silence, the snow crunching under the weight of the horses as they trot along. Evergreens are interspersed with barren trees, a thin layer of snow covering their branches. The frigid air pricks at my cheeks and causes my eyes to water, but I keep them wide open, trying not to miss a moment of this day. A day I never thought would come for me.

The tree line thins out ahead, giving way to the shore of the lake. In the distance I can just make out the cottage where we stayed with Dani and Jeremiah, a plume of smoke rising from the chimney into the stark blue sky. I make a mental note to book that same cabin for us again in the spring.

Daisy eases to a halt when I tug back on her reins. "Do you think your parents and sister would want to spend a weekend with us here when it's warmer?"

Aaron sidles up beside me, Ezekiel bending forward to munch at a patch of grass peeking up through the snow. He follows my gaze to the cabin, a cluster of wrinkles forming around his eyes. "I think they'd love that."

Warmth blooms in my chest despite the cold. I pinch my lower lip between my teeth, taming my smile before it gets too big. "I can't promise I'll be perfect and get everything right with them, but I really want to try. I want to be a part of your family just like I want you to be a part of mine."

He reaches for me, holding out his hand for me to take it. I do. "You don't have to be anything other than yourself, Zo. That's all I've ever wanted. And that's all they expect."

I know my nose is turning red as tears press at the backs of my eyes, but I'm hoping he writes it off as a side effect of the cold. I suck in a shuddering breath, filling my lungs with the biting air. Shoving my free hand into my jacket pocket, I feel the smooth box I tucked away secretly this morning. Daisy shifts her weight, bringing me closer to Aaron so she can nuzzle Ezekiel. Taking advantage of the proximity, I lean over, and Aaron comes toward me a little more than halfway to close the distance. That no longer feels like a burden but a gift, because I know there will come a time where he needs me to lean in for him, and I'll be more than happy to oblige.

Tugging the black, square box from my pocket with one hand, I use the other to flatten his palm so I can deposit it there. His brow furrows as he studies it, before a hesitant realization starts to dawn on him.

"Zo, is this—"

"Relax." A peal of laughter rips out of me. "I'm not proposing to you, idiot. Just open it."

"Good, because I was gonna say, I have that all planned out and I'd be pissed if you ruined it for me." His words lodge my heart in my throat, sending my head spinning so hard I nearly miss his eyes widening and a smile spreading across his face that's so broad it has to hurt his cheeks.

With two gentle fingers, he plucks the object from its nest of crumpled tissue paper, holding it up between us. The sun glints on the metal surface of the key, highlighting the fact that I didn't wash it before placing it in the small box.

"Why is there dirt on it?" He quirks an eyebrow as his voice breaks, and his lips press together in a firm line, trying to contain his emotion.

I decide to spare him the story of my crazy, desperate self-depositing of it in one of Penny's many holes in the far end of my backyard. Instead I poke his side and with a teasing smile I reply, "It's covered in compost. You know, because it's our love language."

He rolls his eyes at me but pockets the key, leaning over to kiss me once more. His soft, warm lips are a reprieve from the winter air, thawing my skin with the gentlest touch. I slip into the goodness of this moment, let myself bathe in its glorious light. It fills every inch of my body, of my soul, until there's no room left for anything but this. These mountains, Aaron, and the feeling of coming back to myself at last.

———

Thank you so much for taking the time to read Zoey's story. If you liked WHAT'S LEFT OF ME, please leave a review at your favorite retailer and tell a friend!

Acknowledgments

As always, I owe a tremendous amount of thanks to my lovely fiancé, Andrew. Thank you for supporting me through the long writing days and cheering for me with every success. Sometimes it takes someone else believing in you before you can truly believe in yourself. Thank you for always believing in me.

To my wonderful team of beta and sensitivity readers. Quierra, Jennalee, Stephanie, Margaret, Lauren, Alex, and Sarah. This story was made better by each of you in turn, allowing these characters to shine brighter than I ever could've done on my own. Your unique perspectives, loving critiques, and enthusiastic cheerleading have challenged me to be a stronger writer. I'm so grateful for each and every one of you. Some of you were Team Zoey, and some were die-hard Team Aaron (looking at you, Stephanie) and I'm glad in the end we created a perfect Team Both-of-Them.

To my lovely editor, Lea Ann. This year has been filled with hurtles for you to jump over, and you've done so with more grace and bravery than anyone else could in your situation. The fact that you can still create works of art in the midst of it all (and help me perfect my own) speaks volumes to the type of person you are. I'm so honored to be your little sister, and to share this author journey with an expert in the field.

A special shout out to some amazing women (a few of which were already mentioned above, but I love them so much I have to talk about them twice) who make up what I have lovingly dubbed the Graduating Class of 2023. Ashley, Sarah, Margaret, Alexis, and Alex. We all brought our book babies into the world this year. WE

DID IT. Each of us write slightly different genres, with varying styles, and yet the talent each of you display absolutely blows me away. Thank you for letting me read your stories early. It's a privilege to cheer you all on.

I'd also like to thank each and every member of my ARC team from *The End and Then*. For taking a chance on a debut author and then absolutely running with the book. Every ounce of success I have seen is owed in part to your love for Chase and Eden. I hope you love Zoey and Aaron just as much, if not more, and that this conclusion to such a tender piece of my heart does justice to your love for the Loveless community.

Finally, while Zoey's story is not my own, it reflects the reality of so many women throughout history. Women who are very dear to me, and to you, dear Reader. It is my hope for every person that finds a piece of themselves in this book that they will look within their own hearts and realize that there is an immeasurable strength nestled there, one that no one will ever be able to take away. You are loved, you are cherished, and you are worthy of goodness and light. May an abundance of it find you and surround you all the days of your life.

There is help available with the National Domestic Violence Hotline at 1-800-799-SAFE (7233). They also have a live chat and therapy resources online at thehotline.org

About Hannah Bird

Hannah's accolades include a second grade teacher who said her story about bats had "very good potential" and enough accelerated reading medals to sink a body at sea. Her goals in life are to write Contemporary Women's and New Adult Fiction novels that will make you cry, and to check everything off the bucket list she wrote at seventeen.

Hannah resides among the rolling hills of Tennessee with her other half and their clingy golden retriever. When she is not writing, she is trying to outrun her sweet tooth in the gym.

You can travel along with Hannah on her writing journey at her website, hannahbirdauthor.com, and at all the bookish destinations below:

facebook.com/hannahbirdauthor

instagram.com/hannahbirdauthor

amazon.com/author/hannahbird

goodreads.com/hannahbird

tiktok.com/@hannahbirdauthor

9 798987 266625